W9-BYH-076

COLD CASE COLTON

Addison Fox

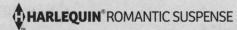
HARLEQUIN®ROMANTIC SUSPENSE

Special thanks and acknowledgment are given
to Addison Fox for her contribution to
The Coltons of Shadow Creek miniseries.

ISBN-13: 978-0-373-40214-4

Cold Case Colton

Copyright © 2017 by Harlequin Books S.A.

Recycling programs
for this product may
not exist in your area.

Printed in U.S.A.

Addison Fox is a lifelong romance reader, addicted to happy-ever-afters. After discovering she found as much joy writing about romance as she did reading it, she's never looked back. Addison lives in New York with an apartment full of books, a laptop that's rarely out of sight and a wily beagle who keeps her running. You can find her at her home on the web at www.addisonfox.com or on Facebook (Facebook.com/addisonfoxauthor) and Twitter (@addisonfox).

Books by Addison Fox

Harlequin Romantic Suspense

The Coltons of Shadow Creek
Cold Case Colton

The Coltons of Texas
Colton's Surprise Heir

Dangerous in Dallas
Silken Threats
Tempting Target
The Professional
The Royal Spy's Redemption

House of Steele
The Paris Assignment
The London Deception
The Rome Affair
The Manhattan Encounter

The Adair Affairs
Secret Agent Boyfriend

Visit the Author Profile page at Harlequin.com.

For Maddie and Vivian

Two of the most wonderful young women I know.
You both own Texas-sized pieces of my heart.

Chapter 1

The random bark of a dog and a puttering truck with a rusted out muffler battled each other for prominence in the early morning air. Claudia Colton juggled a to-go cup of coffee in one hand and her keys in the other as she fumbled with the door of her boutique, Honeysuckle Road. Dog and truck faded away as she closed the door, satisfied to simply stop and stare for a moment.

On a soft sigh, she smiled at the racks that spread out before her in welcoming arcs. Bright, vivid silks and bold prints swirled among the racks, offsetting more timeless pieces in soft pastels and classic solids. Her racks spanned all sizes, hidden among them a match for every woman in Shadow Creek, from the petite to the curvaceous and every iteration in between.

"It may be a long way from Fifth Avenue, but it's mine."

Shadow Creek, Texas, was a far cry from New York City, but she was determined to make it feel like home.

Bound and determined.

All the work that had gone into renovating the store and the grand opening preparations had diverted her mind for the past few months, and there was something deeply gratifying to see the fruits of her hard work.

Fruits that bore sashes, sequins and the occasional well-placed bow.

And if the life she'd attempted to divert herself from was still a raging mess, well, at least she had a few pretty things to look at while she dealt with it all.

She flipped the lock behind her back and headed for her workroom. Many of the designs at Honeysuckle Road were her own and she'd taken great joy in bringing her visions to life, but no vision quite compared with the wedding dress that had come to life on her dressmakers' form over the past few weeks.

Claudia had been equally touched and excited when her brother Thorne's fiancée, Maggie, asked her to make her wedding dress. And she was fast becoming a nervous wreck that the small details she'd envisioned for the dress wouldn't be completed in time for the wedding.

Wasn't that a twist?

Maggie was an easygoing bride with an exacting, seamstress-zilla.

Which meant Claudia's days were filled with quite a few early hours as she worked to finish up the dress.

That also gave her a chance to collect her thoughts. While getting Honeysuckle Road up and running had been a pleasant diversion, it couldn't change the realities of what she'd run from in New York, or her current situation here in Shadow Creek.

An ex-boyfriend who'd increasingly made the city she loved a nightmare of dark streets, threatening messages and late-night harassments.

And the small town she'd grown up in that seemed to exist in a perpetual state of fear of her mother. Livia's recent escape, ten years after being put away for multiple lifetimes, had once again gripped the town in her thrall.

Neither situation was tenable.

But what to do about it?

Claudia had innately understood her mother was different. It wasn't just the unique characteristics that made up her family, from a series of relationships that had produced Livia Colton's six children. Nor was it simply the large estate that had provided the backdrop to her childhood. No, it was the odd, nearly reverent way the entire town of Shadow Creek treated her mother.

Livia Colton was the town's patron saint and their resident demon, and everyone treated her with the softest of kid gloves. Livia could do no wrong, even when others suspected her of the worst sorts of crimes.

Theft. Human trafficking. Murder.

Which had left her children to puzzle through the realities of their mother. Was Livia Colton some misunderstood, benevolent benefactor or some demon temptress who used kindness as one more tool in her psychopathic arsenal?

Claudia had spent much of her childhood wondering, only to have the truth finally come out the year she turned sixteen. Her mother's crimes—all she'd been suspected of and more—had been exposed and she'd been soundly convicted by the State of Texas, sentenced to spend the rest of her life—as well as four more—in prison.

At the time and in all the years since, Claudia had tried desperately to feel some sense of sadness, or remorse or even relief that she and her siblings finally had some answers.

But none came.

Instead, she continued to struggle with this odd sense of indifference that kept her mother at an emotional distance. Separate, somehow, as if they'd never really had a mother-daughter bond at all. Claudia lived with the shame of that—that strange, unapologetic apathy—and used the guilt as a way to push herself forward.

She didn't feel it for her siblings. Nor did she feel it for Mac, the man who'd practically raised her. So maybe there was hope for her, after all.

Claudia ran a hand over the slender, gathered shoulder strap of the dress. Her brother would marry the woman who wore this dress. The wedding would be hosted on Mac's ranch. In addition to Thorne, the groom, all her siblings would be there.

Joy filled her at the thought of them all being together and in that, Claudia knew there was strength. Bonds that were forged in truth and honesty and love.

And in that joy, she felt no guilt. No empty ties. Not even a trace of sadness. Instead, she knew she was home.

It couldn't come at a better time, she thought as she fiddled with the ruching on the shoulder strap, seeking to match its folds to its twin. After nearly ten years in a Texas prison, Livia had found a way to escape.

Her mother's extensive network of contacts had helped engineer the escape, but it was the events that came after—including the kidnappings of Claudia's nephew and then Mac just last month—that had proven just what sort of people her mother had surrounded herself with.

Her brother Knox had spent a tense time in an emotional standoff that started with Cody's kidnapping and ended in the death of one of Livia's minions. Although her nephew was back, safe and unharmed, neither Claudia nor her siblings had fully rested easy since. The fact that the kidnapping had been the byproduct of an old enemy of her mother's, using the boy as a pawn to get money Livia would never have paid, had only added to the horror of the situation.

And Mac. Her heart still leaped into her throat at the thought they'd nearly lost him. Livia's cruelty—and the pain she'd exacted on her third husband—had contributed to the man's plot against Mac. Thank God they had him back, safe and sound. And through it all, Maggie and Thorne had found each other, as well. A challenging way to begin any relationship, but one that was firm and solid all the same.

One that had also reinforced another truth. Her family needed her and she needed them. And with her mother's disappearance going on nearly four months, she couldn't deny her fervent hope the woman would never come back. Livia's disappearance would finally give them all much-needed peace.

The prison break had proven her mother had established her influence far and wide. But the one thing, if she knew her mother at all, was that there was little Livia Colton wouldn't do to avoid going back to prison.

Life was calmer without her mother's presence. That had been as true ten years ago as it was now. And in the months she'd been back in Shadow Creek, she'd had the opportunity to reforge bonds with her siblings. To build an even closer one with Mac. He was still the most wonderful father figure and her time away hadn't changed their relationship.

Claudia ran a hand down the pale silk of Maggie's gown, the subtle fall of material plunging from the bodice in a dramatic, almost Grecian sweep. The suggestion of a goddess fit Maggie to a T and her future sister-in-law had been in love with the design from the start.

Now to stop woolgathering and finish it.

She settled her coffee on the edge of her station, far away from any material, and focused on today's work.

The bustle.

Claudia ran her fingertips over the silk, gathering large folds and pinning them to the areas she'd pre-marked with small pins. Fold by fold, the bustle came together, the elegant weight forming and reshaping the gown in her hands.

What felt like only moments later Claudia heard a different sort of bustling behind her. "Oh. Oh, wow."

She turned to find Evelyn Reed, employee number two of Honeysuckle Road and the woman Claudia fondly thought of as her partner in crime.

"What do you think?" She took a few steps back and reached for her coffee, frowning when she realized it had gone cold.

Evelyn already had a fresh cup out of a holder, extended in Claudia's direction. "I think Thorne's eyes are going to pop out of his head. We haven't had a bride this bedecked in Shadow Creek since the Thompson wedding of 2001."

"Sugar Thompson?"

"One and the same." Evelyn nodded, walking around the dress, her gaze sharp as she took in the gown from head to toe.

As Claudia recalled, Sugar Thompson's marriage hadn't lasted long, nor had union two and three. Last she'd heard the woman was off to California to make her name in Hollywood and Claudia hoped Sugar found what she was looking for.

Shadow Creek wasn't for everyone. Hell, she'd believed herself well and gone, so it was a surprise to realize how the town was growing on her as an adult.

"Claudia?"

"Hmm?" Claudia looked up from her musings, unwilling to even mention Sugar's failed marriages in front of the dress. "You see anything I missed, Eagle Eye?"

"Not a single thing. This dress is amazing. The only worry is that Thorne's not going to make it through the ceremony once he sees his bride coming toward him in this. Between the wedding and Maggie's pregnancy, Thorne has been floating about five feet off the ground."

"I could say the same about his daddy and the dress you're going to wear."

Evelyn's dark skin flashed with a decided blush as she busied herself once again around the dressmaker form. Claudia had recently settled in on the idea that Evelyn needed to make a move on Mac—or at least show her interest—but Evelyn had remained steadfast in her reticence.

"My dress is age and station appropriate." Evelyn's voice was muffled behind the dress, where she bent over to inspect the bustle.

"What station is that?"

"A widow in her fifties with two grown children, two grandchildren and one more on the way."

Claudia tapped her friend on the shoulder and waited until Evelyn stood, her petite frame still only reaching Claudia's shoulder. Waited another moment until Evelyn looked her in the eye.

"You're a beautiful, vibrant woman who deserves to be happy. Joseph Mackenzie is an amazing man. He practically raised me."

Evelyn rested a gentle hand against Claudia's cheek. "A ringing testament to just how amazing he is."

"Amazing." Claudia laid her hand over Evelyn's before going in for the kill. "And as stubborn and shy as you. I swear, the sparks practically erupt when you two get within ten feet of each other."

Evelyn dropped her hand and busied herself with putting her keys into her purse. "We saw each other once."

"Twice, including the day Mac stopped in here to drop off lunch." Claudia popped the lid on the fresh cup of coffee. "There were sparks, I tell you."

"Old people don't shoot off anything but gas." Evelyn wagged a finger as if to emphasize her point before she beelined toward the front counter. "Sparks are for the young."

Claudia wasn't so sure about that but she was a woman who knew when and how to pick her battles. Even better, she knew how to bide her time.

She might be stuck in the middle of her own personal dry spell, but there was no way she was giving up on making Evelyn and Mac see just how perfect they were for each other.

Hawk Huntley tossed a six-dollar tip down on his nine-dollar breakfast at the Cozy Diner and figured he'd still gotten a damn fine deal. The hearty steak and eggs would hold him nearly all day, but it was the side of gossip that had proven even more filling than the prime Texas beef.

He'd arrived in Shadow Creek the night before last and was surprised by how quickly the town gossips were willing to bend his ear. In his experience, most small towns protected their own, but one mention of the Colton family and he got an earful.

He had to play things carefully, but a well-placed question about how he was looking for an old military buddy, River Colton, had done the trick. Hawk knew he needed to work fast because if word found its way back to River that a man he didn't know was using him to pump the local gossip mill, he'd have hell to pay.

But he needed a sense of things before he could put his plan into motion.

He needed all the information he could find on Livia Colton and her children.

"Now, don't you go forgetting about our meatloaf special tonight." The waitress who'd proven so attentive throughout breakfast winked at him from the other side of the counter. "I'll see to it you get an extra slice."

"That's awfully kind of you."

Based out of Houston, Hawk wasn't a native Texan but he'd learned early how to adopt the local lingo and attitude. He was a chameleon, his wife had always told him. A man who could fit in and adapt to any situation.

All but one situation, Hawk knew. Losing her wasn't something a man adapted to. And widower was a suit that even after four years refused to fit.

His waitress picked up the check. "I'll get you some change."

"None needed."

The woman's eyes lit up at that, brighter than when she was flirting, and Hawk figured he'd best get to his plans for the day. There was no way Patty Sue was keeping her morning conversation with the stranger who'd rolled into Shadow Creek quiet for long.

He headed out of the diner and walked down Main Street. His B&B was at one end of town but it hadn't taken him more than a few minutes to traverse the town square to reach the diner and, by his calculations, it would be about two more minutes to arrive at his final destination. The Honeysuckle Road boutique.

All the work of the past few months led straight to that front door.

Although he prided himself on being a good PI, Hawk had found his calling working cold cases. To give a family closure—something he'd never been fortunate enough to receive—had gone a long way toward making Jennifer's death a situation he could live with.

Nothing could erase her memory and no case could bring her back, but if he could give other families the blessed relief that came from knowledge, he could take some solace from the endless questions that still filled his own mind.

"Honeysuckle Road." He whispered the words as he walked toward the small storefront. Two large windows flanked the front door, but unlike the other businesses that lined Main Street, from the diner, to the drugstore, to a feed store that looked to do a brisk business, these windows were full of vibrant jewel tones and items that screamed "haven for women."

He might have only been married for three years, but he'd dated Jennifer for two before that and had grown up with two sisters. Women loved color and shape and texture and design and if he wasn't mistaken, Honeysuckle Road offered all those things and a little something else.

A big, warm welcome that said everyone belonged.

While Patty Sue might have been a bit hesitant to speak about Livia Colton in anything but a hushed whisper, she'd been practically gleeful as she described the new boutique opened by Livia's daughter Claudia.

A bona fide New Yorker, Patty Sue had said reverently as she described Claudia, who'd left Shadow Creek to go to fashion school in Manhattan. The woman knew how to design clothes, match accessories and put together an outfit any woman would be proud to wear. But the clincher, to Hawk's mind, was Patty Sue's description of Claudia's designs. Claudia Colton made clothes for *real women*.

Hawk had no idea at the time what that could possibly mean, but now as he looked at the clothing in the window, he suspected it had something to do with a palette of designs that fit women of all shapes and sizes.

And as a man who appreciated women in all shapes and sizes, Hawk decided to like Claudia Colton on the spot.

Pushing through the door, he let his eyes accustom

to the darker interior, lit by a wall of soft lights that gave the boutique a warm glow.

He should feel awkward. Or at least ready to turn in his man card, but somehow he felt neither of those things. Instead, all he had was a deep-seated curiosity of how a person could make a room feel so simple yet so rich at the same time.

Since taking this case and narrowing in on the daughter of Livia Colton, Hawk had imagined a cold, calculating woman, much in the same vein as her mother. But the deep colors and rich fabrics and warm, welcoming environment flew in the face of all that.

A pretty, petite woman came out from behind the counter. He got a sense of competence and feminine grace, along with a subtle curiosity as to what he was doing in a fashion boutique at ten in the morning. "You look lost."

Funny words since he'd felt lost for the past four years. Lost until this case involving Claudia Colton had fallen right into his lap.

The mystery—a child stolen from her birth mother over a quarter century ago—had gripped him for some reason. Those icy fingers of awareness that always ran up and down his spine when he caught a case that moved him had been in full evidence with this one, yet there'd been something more.

Maybe it was the awareness he and Jennifer had been cheated out of their own family and happy-ever-after. Or maybe it was the feeling that she was pushing him toward this case.

He'd always loved the mystery of a cold case, but mystery had turned to mission when he lost his wife. If he was able to help others find answers, in some small way he believed it helped find one for Jennifer, too.

"Sir?" The woman came out from behind the main counter, her smile gentle. "Can I help you?"

"I'm sorry. Good morning, ma'am. And yes, I think you just might be able to."

"What can I do, then?"

"I'd like to speak with Claudia Colton."

Raw curiosity replaced the gentle smile, but she asked no further questions. Instead, she simply nodded. "I'll just go get her."

Claudia reached for the cup of coffee Evelyn had brought in earlier, surprised to realize it had gone cold as she'd once again wrapped herself up in Maggie's dress. The bustle was coming along nicely, the hidden hooks she'd begun to sew in matching to the precise places she'd pinned up earlier.

Standing, Claudia scrutinized the lines of the dress and the way the gathered material arced into precise folds, neatly pulled up in those small hooks. She hadn't designed many wedding gowns all the way to completion, but had always loved the process of sketching out all the different ways a woman could attire herself to walk down the aisle. Maggie's trust in her was both humbling and satisfying, but it was actually seeing the design come to life before her eyes that gave her a strong sense of pride.

Mac had been the one to suggest New York first. He knew her love of fashion and had freely indulged her madness for magazine subscriptions and sketch pads. But it had been the sewing machine he'd bought her shortly after she'd moved into his home that had clinched it.

A fashion mind needs to go where the fashion-minded are, he'd said to her. Just before he pulled one of the thick warm blankets that perpetually lay over the family room couch off the large box that housed her Singer Studio model. The machine had brought endless hours of bliss and madness, frustration and a special sort of creative delight that nothing else in life could quite compare to. She and her Singer were one, the machine an extension of her vision and her dreams.

And Mac had understood that, better than anyone else she'd ever met.

She tossed a fond glance toward the machine's place of honor in her workroom, right near the window that flooded her studio with light. The best gift she'd ever received.

The knock had her glancing up, breaking through the weight of memories that had seemed to haunt her all morning.

"Yes?"

Evelyn's breath caught as she took in the dress. "You've been busy. And it looks even more amazing than it did a few hours ago."

"It's not done yet."

"Maybe not, but you're well on your way." Evelyn waved her hand in a forward motion. "Which means it's a good time for a quick break and a moment with the gorgeous man standing out front."

The smile suffusing Evelyn's face faded almost instantly, a match for the immediate sinkhole that opened in Claudia's stomach. "Who's here?"

"A man's here. What's wrong?"

He found me. He found me. He found me. The words beat a rapid tattoo in her brain, freezing her breath in her throat.

"Claudia?"

She forced herself to take a breath, her words a whisper when she finally spoke. "What does he look like?"

Even as she asked the question, all she could picture in her mind's eye was the suave cut of a suit jacket, the artful wave of mahogany hair and dark brown eyes that could go nearly black in anger. Manicured hands and Italian loafers were simply fashionable window dressing when the package underneath was jealous, vengeful and, as of the past six months, increasingly dangerous.

"Tall. Dark blond hair that was likely all-the-way-blond when he was a boy. Sexy blue eyes."

It was the blond and blue reference that finally penetrated, tugging at the twisted knots of her stomach. "Blue eyes?"

"Blue eyes like a Texas sky, I might add." Evelyn's own eyes narrowed. "But that has no bearing on the ghost that just walked over your grave. Are you okay?"

"I'm fine." Claudia willed her galloping pulse to calm, breathing in and out of her nose. She'd seen Mac gentle his horses with the soft tones of his voice, never sure if they could understand him yet always fascinated when they seemed to. She willed that soft voice into her own mind, trying desperately to find the equilibrium that had just been snatched away.

Trying even more desperately to erase the haunting image of Ben Witherspoon from her mind.

Chapter 2

Hawk knew precious little about the world at large. He wasn't a fashionable man, nor was he particularly concerned with fancy cars or big houses. He cared little for power and cared even less for the trappings of wealth.

But he knew people.

And the woman who stepped out of the back of the Honeysuckle Road boutique wore a haunted look that had no place on a random Thursday morning.

"Miss Colton?"

She gathered herself quickly, that troubled look fading as if it had never been, but Hawk made note of it, regardless. "Yes, how can I help you?"

"My name's Hawk Huntley. I'd like a word with you, if I may."

"About?"

Hawk glanced at Evelyn, hovering in the back of the

shop. Although her gaze was averted, he had no doubt the woman was on high alert. "It's a private matter."

Claudia Colton followed his gaze before hers hardened. "Have we met before?"

"No, ma'am."

"Well, then, whatever it is, we can discuss it here."

She had a spine, he'd give her that. And from the photos of her that he'd reviewed online, he'd admittedly expected a bit more spunk and fire. All the more reason the frightened look she'd worn when she'd entered the shop had been a surprise.

"Your call." It was her call, but Hawk couldn't help thinking that she'd be sorry the moment he told her his reasons for being there.

What surprised him even more was how sorry he was to be the bearer of bad news. He'd taken the case to help the Krupid family find answers. Although it had taken him a while to work backward through a quarter century of empty threads and the sheer passage of time, it hadn't changed his willingness to work their case or try to help them.

Bit by bit, he'd combed through the leads that had brought him to Claudia Colton's door, each one a deliberate step forward.

How humbling, then, to realize the journey might only be beginning.

"How well do you know your mother?"

Her big gray eyes widened before narrowing quickly. "You're here about my mother?"

"In part."

"Why don't we start from the beginning, then. Who are you?"

Hawk produced a card and handed it over. "I'm a

private investigator. I have an office in Houston and I've been working on a case for the Krupid family for the past few months."

He deliberately tossed out the Krupid name, curious to see if it registered, but Claudia remained unaffected as she glanced up from the card.

When she said nothing, he continued on. "They lost a daughter many years ago."

Although confusion stamped her features, the wariness that had ridden her gaze at his arrival had faded in full. "I'm sorry for their loss, Mr. Huntley, but how does that have anything to do with me or my mother?"

"You're aware of your mother's ties to the skin trade?"

A flicker of something crossed her face, then vanished nearly as fast as it arrived. "Yes."

"The Krupids believe their daughter was a part of your mother's business, enslaved into prostitution."

He'd expected anger. Perhaps even a bit of denial. What he never expected were the clear signs of remorse and sadness. They filled her face in sympathetic lines and spilled over in the gentling of her voice. "I wish I could say I'm surprised, but my mother ruined many lives. More than I'm sure we can ever fully fathom."

"You're aware of your mother's crimes?"

"Of course. I was a teenager when she went to jail, but I'm well aware of what she's capable of. Worse, I'm aware of what she's done."

From her ties to sex trafficking, to the politicians she'd kept in her pocket, to the tight rein she had over most everything illegal in central Texas, Livia Colton had done enough damage for five lives. Even today, there were rumors she'd only been convicted for about a third of what she was actually responsible for, including several murders that remained unsolved.

Yet even with that knowledge, Hawk was surprised by Claudia's quiet acceptance.

The still figure captivated him and he paused a moment to simply observe her. She was a beautiful woman. Tall and voluptuous, she had blond hair that cascaded down over her shoulders in a golden glow, matched to gray eyes that could knock a man to his knees. She had a sophistication and grace about her—a refinement, really—that carried her beyond the simplicity of her current situation.

She was a diamond in a town that had very little polish on it. And if he weren't mistaken, Claudia Colton's shine came from who she was and the life she'd built for herself, not the life she was born into.

How did someone like this come from a woman like Livia Colton? Although he was still in college when the infamous woman's crimes had come to light, Hawk could remember the trial. The hunt for answers. And the relatively few details that had ultimately come to light for a woman purported to have such deep roots in criminal activity.

Those details had remained equally sketchy as he began investigating the Krupids' case. The only reason he'd even connected the Krupid family and the death of their daughter to Livia Colton had been almost a sheer accident. But once he'd made the connection, every line he'd tugged started in the same spot.

Shadow Creek.

The small town nestled in the Texas Hill Country boasted acres of farmland and some of the prettiest land in the entire state. It was also where Livia

Colton's six children had been raised and often made their home.

He'd done his research on all of them. Six siblings, all seemingly fathered by different men. Children who'd grown up in the shadow of a powerful mother and her shady life. Heirs who'd been abandoned by the town, left to fend for themselves when the truth of their mother's crimes came to light.

Claudia was a product of that. And, Hawk pulled her details from memory, she'd hightailed it out of Shadow Creek at the first opportunity. The moment she turned eighteen, Claudia headed for New York City, earning her degree before starting work in the fashion industry. Her return to Texas was recent and, from what he could see, something she'd embraced.

Yet something didn't add up.

Why was she back? The young woman's return to Shadow Creek coincided with her mother's prison break earlier in the year. And her reunion with her family seemed to have a permanence, especially since she'd become the newest proprietor on the busiest street in Shadow Creek.

"I'm afraid I still don't know how to help you, Mr. Huntley. Those crimes of my mother's were put to bed over a decade ago."

"Do you honestly think the police uncovered everything there was to find?"

"Maybe not, but I hardly have the answers on where they should look."

"Maybe you do."

"Why do you think that?"

"I've been working this case for the Krupid family for several months now. They want to find answers.

They want closure and the chance to still provide for their daughter, Annalise."

That gray gaze had shuttered, her voice brisk and businesslike. "But I still don't see how that affects me. Nor, I'm afraid to say, do I understand how her parents can possibly provide for a woman who passed many years ago."

"By taking care of her child."

Claudia shook her head. "Now you're talking in riddles. Whatever my mother was, she wasn't someone who killed innocent babies, Mr. Huntley. I'm afraid your leads have gone cold."

He moved in, just a few steps but it was enough to have her eyes going wide, her mouth dropping in a small O. He lowered his voice, unwilling to share every private detail in earshot of her employee.

"If I'm right, and I believe I am, Livia Colton didn't kill the baby. She took her and told everyone she was hers."

"I think we'd have known if my mother stole a baby."

The words were pointed fact, but Hawk didn't miss the thread of understanding beneath them. Nor did he miss the light quaver in her voice that ensured whatever he said next wasn't going to be a complete surprise.

"You're the baby, Ms. Colton. Your mother is Annalise Krupid."

"I'm what?"

Claudia had seen her mother pull a fainting spell several times throughout her life. Always dramatic, it was an act sure to bring several people running toward the delicate-boned woman with the features of an angel. She'd marveled at each occurrence, always surprised by the effectiveness of her mother's show.

And up until now, she'd never had the urge to do the same.

But if there was ever a time to get a case of the vapors, this would have to be it.

"If my suspicions are correct, you're Annalise Krupid's daughter, Ms. Colton."

"That's impossible."

Was it impossible? The question whispered over her senses, even as she caught sight of herself in the framed mirror that took up space behind the checkout counter. She was a big woman—her five-foot-ten frame and solid bone structure at decided odds with the delicate frame of her mother.

Claudia loved her body, but that hadn't come easy. She'd spent far too many of her teenage years comparing herself to her mother's small, willowy frame. A frame that good, old-fashioned biology had embedded in the genes of her sisters, Leonor and Jade. Claudia had always been the outlier. And it hadn't been until she'd discovered fashion, and all the ways to find clothes and makeup, shoes and accessories to highlight every body type, that she'd come to love who she was.

No, she'd never be a waif like her sisters. But she could strut herself with the best of them and she had come to adore the way clothing clung to her hips and rear like a lover's caress.

It had been at the heart of her focus for Honeysuckle Road and the core sensibility of her designs while living in New York. Every woman was beautiful. True fashion and all its artistry was about making every woman shine.

"Is it really impossible, Ms. Colton?"

The tantalizing belief that she might be someone else—that all the times growing up she'd questioned if she fit into her family might have been for a reason—were thoughts she needed to shut down.

She was a Colton. She'd been one for twenty-six years and in a matter of moments she was ready to throw that all away?

"Of course it is. I've lived here my whole life. I have a family—brothers and sisters—and—" She broke off, suddenly aware those things had very little bearing on how she came to actually *be* a Colton.

"Look, Mr. Huntley, it's just not possible. For all my mother was, or is," she quickly corrected herself, "she's not a kidnapper of infants. Besides, why kidnap one to then raise it on your own? My mother had four children before me and never had a problem carrying a baby to term."

"Maybe she saw something in you?"

"Another mouth to feed?"

"She's a wealthy woman," Hawk shot back, smooth and easy. "I hardly think that would have been a deterrent, do you?"

Nothing was a deterrent to Livia Colton when the woman set her mind on something. Claudia had seen that enough times in her life to know it as fact. More the point, she'd always sensed her mother had led multiple lives, anyway. There was the mother who raised them all, rarely present. On the occasions when she had been around, she'd exhibited a showy, over-the-top affection for her children.

Then there was the Livia Colton who'd contributed so much to Shadow Creek, from building a hospital to running the annual Christmas benefit for the widows and orphans fund, to even ensuring they had top-notch Little League ball fields. She'd set herself up well with the town leaders, and whether it was from a sense of benevolence or an attempt to buy off everyone in close proximity, it hadn't changed the outcome.

Her mother had made the town a better place.

And then there was the third Livia. The one who'd helped run an enormous crime ring, who managed several nodes on the central Texas drug trade and who had no compunction about killing to get what she wanted.

Her brother Knox had already lived with that reality earlier this year when an *associate* of her mother's kidnapped his son. Livia had returned from hiding to kill the man, saving her grandson. While Claudia had wanted to ascribe pure motives to Livia's actions, Knox had sworn saving his son was a side benefit to killing the man.

Was it possible that Livia—the one who took whatever she wanted without remorse—had stolen a baby, too?

Claudia cast a glance toward the back of the store. While she trusted Evelyn implicitly and knew she'd tell her most everything later, it felt wrong, somehow, to be discussing this there, with an audience. Huntley's accusations against her mother had far-reaching implications and at the end of the day, this was a family matter.

"Perhaps we can take this up somewhere else over a cup of coffee? You seem well-intentioned, but I hardly think this the right venue for a serious conversation. Especially when foot traffic picks up later this morning."

She'd gotten a new shipment in the day before and

she and Evelyn had spent several hours the prior evening setting up the new stock. They'd already braced themselves for a busy day when the suddenly hungry-for-fashion women of Shadow Creek wended their way into Honeysuckle Road.

A hot man with electric-blue eyes would only add to the excitement. It would also earn her a spot on the week's hottest gossip list.

"I'm happy to discuss this somewhere else."

"Let's go, then. I have an errand I need to run a few towns over in Whisperwood. There's a coffeehouse on their main street that makes a mean latte."

"Let's go."

He nodded, his smile easy and simple. The small dents of his dimples were contagious and Claudia found herself smiling back before she could check herself. How she'd missed this. That simple connection with a man, fraught with nothing more than basic appreciation and a subtle sense of flirtation.

Ben had taken that from her. He'd second-guessed every kind word she said to someone of the opposite sex, whether it was a waiter, the postman or the old gentleman who'd lived in the apartment two floors above her. No one had been off-limits and over time she'd lost that sense of basic kindness and easy conversation with others.

He'd taken it all away and replaced it with fear and domination and she was so grateful she'd gotten away.

"Let me just tell Evelyn I'm running out."

"I'll wait by the door."

Claudia hesitated a moment as Hawk drifted through the store, his hands by his sides as he navigated through the circular racks of clothing. A lean man, he was still big and there were several places where he turned sideways to avoid brushing along the clothes.

That simple show of respect—for her work and her store—went a long way toward calming the nerves that leaped in her stomach.

But it did nothing to drown out the dread of having one more mess, courtesy of Livia Colton, land on her front doorstep.

The SUV rumbled to life beneath them, the gentle purr of its engine humming as Claudia settled herself in the driver's seat. Hawk had quickly acquiesced to her desire to drive and had held the door for her before moving around to the passenger side.

Evelyn had been concerned when Claudia had let her know she was making a quick trip to Whisperwood but hadn't tried to stop her. Claudia suspected the fact Evelyn had all of the Colton men on speed dial, in addition to Mac, was what kept her from making too big a fuss. Claudia also made a point of leaving Hawk's card behind so Evelyn had a record of who she'd gone off with.

Even as she questioned herself, Claudia couldn't deny just how safe she felt in his presence. But it had been impulse that had her offering to drive when he'd headed out of Honeysuckle Road and beelined for his car to follow behind her. She knew she needed to be careful, but nothing about Hawk set off alarms.

Besides, she was curious about him. And while he'd had the element of surprise on his side, she gained significant home court advantage being in her car with her as driver. So she'd offered to drive, pleased when he'd accepted.

The man was a mystery—tall and lean, stoic and enigmatic—yet for all that he wasn't threatening. She suspected he could be if he tried hard enough, but so far nothing had set off her flight response. In fact, if she were honest, all that enigmatic masculinity had her the tiniest bit captivated.

Okay, a lot captivated.

The ordeal with Ben, followed by the move, had made her swear off men for the better part of the past year. When she then added on the additional year they'd been dating, she hadn't been actively on the market for quite a while. It was heady to feel that small spark of awareness; to look over and see a man filling her passenger seat, his long, strong fingers working the buckle of his seat belt.

Claudia waved at Evelyn where she stood inside the back doorway of the shop, her lips set in a firm line.

"She seems to have lost her fondness for me."

"Excuse me?" Claudia put the car into gear, navigating the small lot behind the store she and Evelyn used for parking and where her deliveries came in.

"Evelyn liked me when I walked in. I think she's changed her mind."

"The jury's still out on you, but I'm not worried you're going to hurt me." She decided to push a bit. "I'm not wrong about that, am I?"

"Of course not!" The answer flew back across the car with all the force of a rocket. "I may not be in law enforcement, but I collaborate in tandem with them for my work. I'm one of the good guys."

She couldn't hold back the small smile. "We'll see about that. In the meantime, let's hear more about my supposed past. While I'll admit it's an enticing thought to imagine myself not actually Livia's daughter, I left those fantasies behind when I grew up. The imagined princess just waiting until the time is right to receive her title or the Little Orphan Annie, hanging on until her real parents can come back to find her. Both were a kid's fantasy, nothing more."

"You're awfully easy about this." His voice was low, whispering between them like smoke.

Was that a small shot of remorse in his tone?

Or was it what she wanted to hear as she tried to process the feminine awareness of him that wasn't fading? She wanted to ignore the sensual tug but couldn't quite hold back the subtle awareness that had her nerves on edge.

Delicious nerves, she admitted to herself before coming to a stop at the four-way that led out of town. Willing away the quick flash of desire, she turned fully to face him. "I've had a lot of years to come to terms with my mother and her behavior. It's a hard thing, to think so ill of the woman who raised you, but it doesn't make the feelings any less true. My mother hurt a lot of people."

"It's different, Claudia, when the person she hurt was you."

"That's assuming you're right about all this."

"I am right."

His words hung there, stubborn and considerably more solid than whispers of smoke. Hawk Huntley wasn't a man who liked to be wrong. Most men didn't, and she had three brothers and a surrogate father who proved that fact each and every day.

But she sensed Hawk's determination came from

somewhere else. That it ran far deeper than stubborn male pride or a desire to be right.

"Okay, then. Convince me. Give me all your reasons why."

"It all started with your mother's recent escape from prison."

The welcome sign for Shadow Creek faded from her rearview mirror as Claudia fought the grimace that threatened at Hawk's comment. "As good a place to start as any, I suppose."

"It's put her back in the spotlight. I remember her case a decade ago—few who lived in Texas at the time have forgotten it—but like anything else in the 24/7 news cycle, life moves on."

It had moved on. Wasn't that why she'd gone to New York in the first place? To follow a dream, yes, but it had been something more.

It was a chance to start fresh. New. Unnoticed. An opportunity to start out as a nobody. In the competitive world of fashion, no one cared who you were, they just cared where you were going.

And she'd been going places.

Places that were hell and gone away from Shadow Creek, Texas.

Funny how she'd found her way back anyway.

The thought had dogged her for the past few months. She knew why she was there. Her family needed her. More, she belonged there. But she still hadn't figured out how the one place on earth she'd believed she'd never return to had been the first place she'd run.

Home?

Or was it something more?

Her entire life people had whispered secrets about

her mother. For a long time she'd managed to shut them out, simply pretending they didn't exist. Then her world had crumbled with Ben's increasingly menacing behavior and her brother Knox had dealt with the kidnapping of his son.

All of it had combined to pull her home.

"Your mother's always been big news in Texas—the entire Colton family is—but it was when I saw the blog article about her that I sensed a connection."

"What blog article? What connection?"

"The *Everything's Blogger in Texas* article that came out a few months ago."

Claudia's mouth soured at the mention. That article had nearly destroyed her sister Leonor. The betrayal— at the hands of her ex-boyfriend, who'd run to the press with every detail she'd ever shared—had made its way on to one of the biggest gossip blogs in Texas. Although the pain of the blog had oddly been the pathway for Leonor to find her fiancé, Joshua, the article had done sufficient damage to their family.

Worse, it had destroyed Leonor's self-confidence and sense of security.

"You mean the website that took private information obtained from my sister and broadcast it like it was some sort of fluffy infusion of cotton candy."

Hawk nodded. "That's the one."

"Just wanted to make sure."

"Even if their ethics should be questioned to the hills and back, it didn't diminish the information. Or the connection to the Krupid family."

Claudia came to another four-way stop. The sign for Whisperwood indicated downtown was two miles away. "And this family thinks my mother is involved?"

"The Krupids think nothing other than the fact that their pregnant daughter went missing nearly twenty-seven years ago. I've not yet shared this lead as I don't want to get their hopes up."

There it was again. That subtle thread of remorse that was layered beneath his words. She genuinely believed he didn't want to hurt that family.

And why did that streak of compassion strike her as so important? Deeply important, somehow.

"So walk me through this connection."

"The Krupids tried to leave Russia for many years. During that process, their teenage daughter, Annalise, became familiar with a shady group who'd offered to spirit them out through less legal means, pretending she was a mail-order bride. She'd encouraged her parents to consider the offer, but they were wise to the scam and told her to ignore the vague promises."

"So how did she end up here?"

"Based on the timing it looks like she got pregnant during that same time and the opportunity to come to the US through shady means suddenly seemed like a way out."

Despite her skepticism, Claudia could see it. A young woman scared at being discovered, desperate to take the promise of a new life far away. Hadn't she sought out the same by going to New York? Sure, her reasons were different, but she understood the desire to leave.

To escape.

"Did her parents know she was pregnant?"

"Her mother suspected, but it wasn't until the days after Annalise vanished that her boyfriend came around looking for her. He shared the news of her pregnancy."

"It's a sad story, but I still don't see what it has to do with my mother. Or me, for that matter."

"The trail for Annalise goes cold after she was spirited out of Russia and into Mexico. She was one of your mother's."

"How's that even possible?" Although she had no doubt he believed what he said, Claudia knew there were holes in Hawk's timeline. "My mother was convicted of prostitution here in the States."

"But she had to have a pipeline of women."

"A pipeline?" The tantalizing whisper that she might not actually be Livia Colton's daughter faded at the reality of what Hawk suggested.

"One of your mother's lines of business was human trafficking. It provided her ready supply of prostitutes. And her ring is known to have associated with the mail-order bride scammers, among others."

"And you think this girl was one of hers?"

"Yes."

"And you think she was in the early stages of pregnancy when she was enslaved into service to my mother?"

"Yes."

"Even if I can wrap my head around all of this, how would my mother steal her baby? Why would she even bother?"

"That's for your mother to know."

Claudia pulled into the parking lot of the small coffee shop that was their destination. While she couldn't deny the sincerity of his story, or even the possibility that this young woman had come into her mother's orbit, the leap to actually being this woman's child was still shockingly large.

"Annalise gave birth twenty-six years ago. You're twenty-six, aren't you?"

"Along with a lot of other people. Yes, it's a coincidence, but it still doesn't mean anything." She cut the ignition and turned to face Hawk. He'd kept that stoic calm throughout their discussion, but there was something in the depths of his vivid blue eyes that captured her. "What is it?"

"There's one other thing you should know."

Hawk reached into his pocket and pulled out his wallet. He'd carefully placed an old, faded photograph in the folds of the leather. Her gaze caught on the image even before he handed it over.

But it was the blond hair and bright, vivid smile reflected back at her that had Claudia's breath catching in her throat. It was like looking at a photo of herself.

"Who is this?"

"That's Annalise Krupid."

Chapter 3

She was too calm about this. That was all Hawk could settle on as Claudia walked in front of him into the coffeehouse. There had been that one, lone eerie moment in the car when she'd held the photo, her gaze seeming to memorize the image of the woman, only to hand it back, her own face an impassive mask.

Had he gotten through to her?

The photo was hard to argue with—it had been the biggest connection he'd made once he'd seen a photo of Claudia on the *Everything's Blogger in Texas* website and made the connection to his case—but it could still be dismissed.

Anything could be dismissed if you refused to believe.

He'd spent two very long years of his life reinforcing that fact. He'd spent the next two trying to do something about it. Regardless of how you handled things—or didn't—life had a way of smacking you in the ass. And if you didn't choose to fight against it, it would take you down right along with it.

He'd spent too long in the bottom of that well, helpless.

Hopeless.

Claudia seemed anything but as she placed her order, then turned to him expectantly. "What would you like?"

"Coffee. Room for cream, please." He already had his wallet out and before she could protest, he added, "It's the least I can do."

"Guilt, Mr. Huntley?" She hadn't said much since climbing out of the car, but he couldn't fully dismiss the light tease beneath her words.

"Just my good old-fashioned Southern gentlemanly charm."

"We'll see about that." She smiled before moving down to wait for her coffee at the bar.

Once again, he was struck by her beauty. More, by her *presence*. He'd seen it in the photo—a small one taken from a distance on the *Everything's Blogger* post—but was even more captivated by the same since walking into her store. She looked like something out of a fashion magazine, yet as natural and real as the Hill Country that stretched out for miles.

It was a strange juxtaposition. Texas was known for its beautiful women—he'd been fortunate enough to marry one—but there was an artlessness in this woman that drew him in.

Hawk didn't miss the way the barista looked at Claudia while he built her coffee, his gaze drifting toward her as he juggled the staring with the coffee making. And how could he blame the guy?

Her hair fell around her face in glossy waves and the outfit she wore seemed to highlight every single curve of her body. Even the summer heat that had followed them into the air-conditioned coffeehouse couldn't wilt her.

How was it possible?

Livia Colton hadn't managed to spoil her, either. Neither had living in one of the world's largest cities, working in one of the world's most competitive industries.

So how was it she could remain calm in the face of her possible parentage, as well? More, how would someone reach adulthood as one person and then just take it on faith when a total stranger suggested it had all been a lie?

He'd assumed she would rant and rail, fighting off his suggestion that she wasn't Livia Colton's daughter, but Claudia had been understanding, warm and downright casual about it all.

Had life with her mother been that hard?

Or maybe money went a long way toward paving the path to easy living?

Whatever he supposed, none of it would compare to the reality of growing up in the home of a life-long criminal whose network literally stretched across the globe.

Since making the connection on the *Everything's Blogger in Texas* website, Hawk had spent quite a bit of time digging into the Colton family. Livia's crimes were considerable, holding a candle to Matthew Colton, her serial killer brother. The man had reportedly said that the only person he feared on earth was his half sister Livia.

What did that say about the woman?

Hawk took his own coffee and moved to the small station by the door to doctor it to his preferences. The wide-open window showcased the main street of Whisperwood, its storefronts surprisingly similar to Shadow Creek. A few small shops. A general store. The post office which seemed to share space with a feed and seed.

Small-town Texas life at its very best.

The coffee shop sat at the end of that street. The papers scattered on the small tables nearby appeared well-read and the trash can next to the door was close to full. Coffee had clearly become a good business here in small-town Texas. Fortunately, the rush had died down, the midmorning timing working in their favor.

Claudia had chosen a table in the back, out of earshot of the waitstaff, and he headed in her direction. She'd settled into a fluffy armchair, her gaze focused on her oversize cup.

"This is a nice place." He settled into an equally cushy chair. "Unexpected, but nice."

"We could use one in Shadow Creek. The drive over isn't bad, but I'd like to have my latte fix a bit closer."

"Do you miss New York?" If it seemed like he was delaying the inevitable discussion, she didn't appear to mind.

"Some days I miss it terribly. And being here during Fashion Week is going to kill me. But it is nice to be home. And it's incredibly wonderful to be with my brothers and sisters and Mac again."

"Mac?"

"I thought you said you read the blog?"

That light tease was there again, yet there was something more in her words. A subtle challenge, as if she wanted to see just how honest he'd be.

"I did read the blog."

"The sordid life and times of Livia Colton."

"I suppose."

Her eyes rose as she lifted her coffee to her lips. "You just suppose?"

"It was an exposé, I'll grant you that. But I saw a bit more there, as well."

She snorted at his reference to an exposé, but waved him on. "Do tell."

"For all the gossip—"

"Sordid gossip," she reminded him.

"So noted. But for all the digging the reporter did, I took a few things away beyond the story of your mother's life."

"Such as?"

Hawk had read the article so many times he nearly had it memorized. And while the first few reads had given him the direction he needed to work the Krupids' case, making the connection between Livia, Claudia and Annalise, it had been the later rereads of the article that had stuck with him.

Livia's six children were a unit. Even as the story had painted them—born of different fathers—there was still a sense about the siblings. A closeness. A bond.

Heck, it might have even been the simplicity of shared battle scars growing up under Livia's influence.

Regardless of the reason, he'd walked away from that article convinced there was a vibrant, well-tended support system that was a by-product of the lives Livia had created, quite likely beyond her intentions.

"You and your siblings are tight. I got that sense."

"We are."

"You're also close with Thorne's father, Mac."

She smiled at that, a genuine smile that filled her face, softening the slightly wary edges. "Mac has been a surrogate father to me, too. To my siblings as well, but especially me and my younger sister. He took us in after my mother went to prison. He's an amazing man and he's been all the father I've ever needed."

"From all I can see, he's done a damn fine job."

"He's perfect on all counts." A small frown marred her lips. "Except his willingness to ask Evelyn out."

"Your store assistant?"

"One and the same. They're perfect for each other and both are stubbornly resistant to being fixed up."

He couldn't hold back the low bark of laughter, or the subtle delight at the clear grimace on her face. "Think you know best for them both?"

"On this I do. They're bright, wonderful, vibrant people. And there are clear sparks between them on the rare occasion I can manage to get them in the same room. It's a match. I'm sure of it."

"Most people like to decide that for themselves."

"Most people aren't as stubborn as Mac and Evelyn."

"Pot? Kettle?" The words fell from his lips, light and easy.

But it was the answering smile that touched something inside of him, lighting a spark of its own.

"Or maybe just the unwavering hopefulness two

people I think the world of can find each other and live happily ever after."

The easy camaraderie faded, her words a swift, harsh reminder that there was no happy ending. No blissful fade into the sunset. He'd believed it once. Hell, he'd *had* it once. Happy ever after.

Jennifer had even placed a small wooden plaque prominently on their kitchen counter, proclaiming they'd live the rest of their lives that way.

And it had all been shattered in the course of one horrific, haunting evening.

Claudia knew it the moment she'd overstepped, yet had no idea why. Although she was curious about the photograph Hawk had showed her in the car, she wanted a few moments of equilibrium.

A few quiet moments to process the information that had whirled into her morning, along with an attractive, virile man who tugged at something inside of her she'd believed buried.

Or, at minimum, on hold for a while.

The conversation about her family and the easy shift to Mac and Evelyn had flowed, a fun discussion in a quiet coffeehouse. Yes, it had been a distraction, delaying the inevitable discussion about her mother, but it had been fun. Light.

Sweet, even.

And then he'd seemed to crash.

If it were just the mood change she might have shrugged it off and moved on, but it was the utter bleakness that seemed to cover him. A blizzard-like whiteout of anger and sadness and grief.

"Is something wrong?"

"Of course not."

"Since I believe you about as much as I believe the caramel in this latte isn't fattening, you might as well tell me."

"It's nothing."

His tone was sharp—pointed—yet she didn't feel threatened. She'd faced that with Ben, especially in the last few months they were together. The change in conversation and the lightning-quick shifts in mood.

She'd learned to fear those moments.

Hawk continued on before she could say anything. "Sorry. I'm sorry. And it's not nothing, either. I lost my wife a few years ago. There are moments—" He broke off, hesitated. "There are still moments that rear up and remind me. Of her." A sign he was even less like Ben.

Claudia quickly cycled through their conversation before landing on the moment. "The happily-ever-after part?"

"Yes."

The images she'd carried all morning—the first few moments in the shop, her impulsive decision to drive him in her car, even the light teasing over coffee—cycled through her mind, as well. Each had combined, leaving an impression of a capable man who was on a determined mission to find her history and heritage.

But it was this man—the vulnerable one with grief and scars and pain—who spoke to her the loudest.

Losing a loved one was always hard, but to lose one's spouse—their love—and at such a young age… She'd already placed him in his early thirties. The news that he'd lost someone so young was a terrible shock.

"I'm so sorry." She reached over before she could

check the impulse, laying a hand over his. "How long since your wife died?"

"About four years."

Claudia added the time to her age assessment before nodding. "I am truly sorry."

The hand beneath hers was warm and solid, exactly what she'd expected when she'd given him the surreptitious glances in the car. When his gaze drifted over that same place, she began to pull her hand back, aware of how quickly she'd leaped to such intimacy.

But as he laid his other hand over hers, she sensed his need for the simple connection.

"Thank you. I don't talk about my wife much but I usually don't freeze in the middle of a conversation, either."

"You're welcome."

She debated her next step, but knew the time for the personal had passed. Even if she was curious about his wife and how the woman had died, they weren't there to explore his past.

Nor did she need that added wrinkle of awareness that whispered across her senses, reminding her Hawk Huntley was single.

"Since you didn't accompany me here to drink lattes and while away the morning, why don't we discuss what's really going on. Namely this family you're working for."

"The Krupids."

"Yes."

"They're from Russia but live here now?"

He nodded, the lines that grooved around his eyes fading at the shift in topic. "They do now. They did eventually manage to emigrate from Russia. It was several years after Annalise had vanished, but they've never given up hope or the desire to find her."

"And you've not told them what you suspect? About me?"

"No, not yet. They know I'm following leads on their behalf but have given me carte blanche to manage the investigation as I see fit."

"And you found me because of a blog article?"

That damned article was responsible for more pain than anyone could have imagined. From the initial hurt and damage it caused her sister Leonor, to the broader family embarrassment they'd all suffered because of the exposé on Livia, she'd be happy if she never heard mention of the internet or its contents again.

But what if it was the pathway to your own personal truth?

The question whispered through her mind, more tantalizing than she wanted to admit.

She loved her sisters, brothers and Mac without bounds, but even their love for each other had never been able to assuage that pervasive sense of never belonging. The idea that there was an answer for that— one that went beyond basic embarrassment she'd come from a woman who thought the rules of life simply did not apply to her—was heady.

And far too enticing.

"The blog article was the missing link. I'd had several leads, all centering on sex trafficking, but couldn't get that last piece."

"The baby piece?"

"Yes." He nodded, pulling out his phone and opening up a note-taking app she loved. "Here's the trail

I've followed. You can scroll through, but you can see the basic path."

Claudia took the extended phone, surprised by this facet of his personality, as well. Mobile phones were such personal devices, yet he'd surrendered his as if it was nothing.

"Start at the top?"

"You're welcome to read all of it, but if you begin at the notation after she left Russia, you can work through the high points."

The heat of his body was still imprinted on the phone and Claudia did her best to ignore it. Instead, she read the carefully detailed entries, a picture forming in her mind of a young woman, suffering and alone. To have gone from Russia and the only home she'd ever known, essentially kidnapped and moved through the world like a piece of property...

Add on a pregnancy and the loss of her support system and Claudia couldn't hold back the rising anger.

Or that continued sadness that refused to abate when she thought about all her mother's bad behavior and all the myriad ways she'd ruined lives. A hundred lifetimes in jail could never fix or repair what she'd damaged.

No, Claudia amended to herself. What she'd broken.

The entries at an end, the photo from the blog his last entry on the screen, she handed back the phone. "You make a convincing argument, I'll give you that. But it still doesn't explain why my mother would take on the responsibility for a baby."

"It can't be that hard to figure out."

"What do you mean?"

"All we have to do is ask people if they remember her pregnancy or her behavior at that time."

"It's not a secret my mother met my father, Claude, in a whirlwind rush while visiting Europe."

Hawk persisted. "Yes, but did she completely abandon the young children she had here? I know they're not close, but would Mac remember?"

"I could ask him."

"Could you do it now?"

For all she loved Mac, the man didn't handle surprises well. That went triple when the surprise had anything to do with Livia. She'd worry him unnecessarily if he couldn't see her face when she asked the question.

"We can go see him, but I'm not calling him with that."

"Why not? It's a simple question."

"Nothing about Mac or his relationship to my mother is simple."

"I guess I can see that."

Hawk reached for his coffee, impatience telegraphing off him in waves.

"You want to go this morning?"

A wry, sheepish expression crossed his features. "Can we?"

"Can I finish the errands I came here for?"

"Of course."

"We'll swing by his ranch on the way back into Shadow Creek."

An image of bringing a man home to meet her surrogate father filled her mind's eye.

And somehow, despite all the surprises they'd suffered over the past few months since her mother's escape from jail, Claudia figured Hawk's suspicions were one surprise Mac had never seen coming.

Hell, she had to admit to herself, neither had she.

She had a protector.

Those words whispered over and over in the mind of the Forgotten One as Claudia traipsed down Main Street.

Wasn't this a surprise?

The weeks of planning and waiting, plotting and calculating were coming to a close and now she'd found someone to guard her?

Tall and stoic, he had the classic Texas cowboy look down to a T. He even swaggered, his long strides eating up the sidewalk beside the princess. But make no mistake about it; that was no hayseed cowboy walking beside the newly crowned queen of Shadow Creek.

That man was there to watch over her.

The Forgotten One knew that—sensed it—and wouldn't make the mistake of underestimating him. Or the appreciative look that rode the man's gaze as he stared at the figure she made as she walked down Main Street.

Which meant months of planning needed to be adjusted. Refined. It was simply a matter of regrouping and reassessing, identifying a new opportunity to get Claudia Colton alone. One of those quiet, early mornings when she let herself into her pretty new shop. Or maybe late at night when she drove herself home from dinner with family.

Or maybe outside her brother's wedding.

The thought struck, swift and hard as the Forgotten One reassessed.

Regrouped.

And settled on a new plan that was far more exciting than the old.

Chapter 4

Acres of farmland spread out before them as Claudia took the turn onto Mackenzie land. Hawk studied the area, assessing as both first-time visitor and as someone who'd read the blog article.

He'd give the writer credit. Of all the things the blog had gotten wrong or insinuated or flat out made up, the beauty of the Mackenzie property wasn't one of them. Several head of cattle roamed on the front pasture while a horse corral took up a place of prominence on the opposite side of the long driveway. The land was wide-open, yet there was an intimacy, too.

And a fierce pride that reflected from the gleaming fence that rimmed the corral or the perfectly placed posts that made up the enclosure for the cattle. This was a working ranch and, from what Hawk could see, the place hummed.

"He's probably with the horses this time of day." Claudia pulled into a small lot on the back side of the barn and cut the ignition. She turned toward him, and for the first time that day Hawk saw real nerves in her expression.

"Let me tell him why we're here," Claudia added.

"You think I'm going to blurt it out?"

"No."

"Then trust me when I tell you I will handle the situation with absolute discretion."

In the same way his back had stiffened at the coffeehouse, Hawk knew it the moment the conversation shifted.

"Trust you? I don't know you."

"No, you don't."

"It's hard enough to trust the people you do know. Of all the things you can ask me, Mr. Huntley, don't ask that."

Before he could stop her, she'd sailed out of the car and headed for the big man standing watch from the middle of the corral.

"Well played, Huntley." He muttered the words to himself before he swung out his side of the car. He ignored the sense of having overstepped and followed her to the corral. The man she lovingly referred to as a father figure already had her in a big bear hug, his smile deep and loving as he laid his head against hers.

Mac Mackenzie.

Hawk filed through the details he knew of the man. Although slim, they all painted the same picture. Mac was a man of his word. Proud and determined, he'd made a home for his son, Thorne, and the rest of Livia

Colton's children, including taking in Claudia and her sister Jade before they turned eighteen.

"And who's this young man?" The words boomed his direction as Hawk slipped into the corral.

Mac and Claudia had already begun walking toward the fence so Hawk stilled, waiting with an outstretched hand. "Mr. Mackenzie."

"Most folks call me Mac." The man extended his hand, his grip firm as Claudia jumped in with the final introductions.

"Hawk paid me a visit this morning. A few things he wanted to discuss about Mom."

"Oh?" Mac's eyebrows rose but his dark brown eyes remained hard. Unyielding. "What is this about?"

"I'm a private investigator based out of Houston." Hawk already had a card out which he handed over. "I've been working a cold case for the Krupid family."

Again, he dropped the name, curious if it would ring any bells. And yet again, he was met with a blank stare and an absolute lack of response.

"You're a detective?"

"No, sir. I've remained in private practice my entire career."

Mac had tucked the card into his pocket, but pulled it out once more, reviewing the face. "Cards can be faked."

"They can and I've investigated more than a few people who've proven that in spades. If it'll ease your mind, I'm happy to share the references of a Captain Andrew Radner of the Houston PD."

The card disappeared back into his breast pocket as Mac returned his steady gaze. "I'll take your word on it for now. What can we do for you, Mr. Huntley?"

Hawk walked Mac through the same details he'd shared with Claudia, saving the picture for the end. From Annalise's trip out of Russia, to her travels into Mexico and then on into Texas, Mac listened and nodded, adding a few questions where he wanted clarity.

But it was the photo that had the man going still as a block of Texas granite. "This woman looks like you, Claudia."

"I know."

Mac wrapped an arm around Claudia's shoulders. "We'll figure this out."

Claudia laid her head on Mac's shoulder, peace and relief welling in her gaze. "Everyone's got a twin, right?"

The question may have been a grasp at straws, but she wasn't entirely incorrect. A photograph wasn't foolproof, nor was a hunch.

"Of course, sweetie." Mac's eyes met Hawk's. "I suppose there are only so many faces in the world."

"Besides," she said. "There's an easy way to figure this out."

"What's that?"

"Tell me what you remember about Mom's pregnancy."

"She was—" Mac broke off, his gaze narrowing as if he was trying to focus on something far into the distance. "Well now. I suppose I don't remember that time."

"What don't you remember?"

"Any of it. She wasn't here."

Claudia stood up straighter, her spine going stiff at Mac's pronouncement. "Wasn't here?"

"No. She was in Europe. Came home with you once she came back to Shadow Creek."

When she was a small child, Claudia had fallen into the large pool that occupied the back lawn of her mother's home, La Bonne Vie. She'd been told repeatedly by the housekeeper not to go near the edge because she didn't know how to swim, but she'd stared at that welcome pool of water day after day, longing to go in.

Good manners and the subtle sense that always pervaded their home of needing to obey in her mother's domain had kept her away from the pool for several days, but she'd finally given in to the longing one hot afternoon. A small window of opportunity had opened up when the adults had left the room and she'd taken it, slipping into the backyard and heading for the welcome of cold water on a hot summer afternoon.

Claudia had known the moment she broke the surface that she was in trouble. The T-shirt and shorts she still wore wrapped around her, stifling in the way the material instantly clung to her body, and the water, instead of being welcoming, covered her head and face, suffocating in the way it was suddenly everywhere.

She'd tried to scream, only to have that water fill her mouth and every movement—each thrash of her arms and kick of her legs—seemed to drag her farther down instead of buoying her up.

It had been Mac's shout and the solid hold of his large hands as he pulled her out of the water that she still remembered.

But it was the languid claws of the water that haunted her nightmares, even to this day.

She'd taken lessons, of course. She'd been forced back into that pool to learn, day after day. Her mother had been ruthless about it and the staff had followed her orders, scared to do anything that would smack of defiance or disobedience. But it had been Mac who'd sat by the side of the pool, keeping watch lesson after lesson, to see that she was safe.

That memory wove in and out of her thoughts as she, Hawk and Mac settled into the warm, welcoming kitchen in Mac's home. The news in the corral had come as a surprise—her mother had spent months away from her family in Europe?—but it was the story that Mac wove that was the real surprise.

"Mac, how is it I don't know this? I've always heard the fanciful story of her European romance, but in what had to be nearly a year to have a relationship and a baby, Mom never came home? How long was she away from Knox, Leonor, River and Thorne?"

"She always claimed she was wrapped up in her whirlwind marriage and then was devastated when it didn't work out. And it's not like I spent much time around her, questioning the truth. Not like I'd have gotten it, anyway." Mac grumbled that last part and it went a long way toward calming the racing thoughts that kept swirling in her mind, finding no purchase.

He was shaken, too. And whatever calm she'd had when Hawk initially shared his suspicions on their drive into Whisperwood, she couldn't hide the increasing swirl of panic at Mac's reaction.

"But did she ever say anything about her time away? She always told me she'd had a falling-out with my father."

"That's what she claimed. Said Claude was a rebound after divorcing her husband Wes, and that the only good thing she got out of the marriage was you."

Claudia suspected her mother had said a whole lot more—the divorce from Wes had been in no small part because of her affair with Mac and Thorne's subsequent birth—but she kept her thoughts to herself. Mac had done his own penance for getting mixed up with her mother and even for all the pain Livia had caused, Claudia knew with everything she was that he'd never trade his son, Thorne. Or the rest of them.

That fierce devotion had only increased—if it was even possible—when Wes had come back last month to exact his misplaced vengeance against Mac. Yet one more by-product of her mother's hurtful choices.

"Mr. Mackenzie. Did Livia ever say anything to you about that time?" Hawk asked.

After sharing his suspicions about the Krupids' daughter and her mother's subsequent actions, Hawk had quieted as Mac recounted what he remembered of that time. It had only been the bombshell about her mother's time in Europe—her extended time—that had made Claudia finally begin to see the possibilities in Hawk's suspicions.

For all the gleaming temptation she'd felt at the idea of *not* being Livia Colton's daughter, the increasing proof points were something else entirely.

Life just got real, as her brother River was fond of saying.

Very real, she amended.

Anxious to do something, she got up and went to the fridge, pulling out the canister of coffee that sat perpetually full on the bottom shelf. She washed out the dregs from the morning's brew and started them on a fresh pot. Coffee might not solve the world's problems, but she'd always suspected that armed with it she was a hell of a lot more prepared to handle what came her way.

The twin expressions of gratitude as she brought mugs, the sugar bowl and a fresh bottle of cream to the table only reinforced the thought.

"That's my girl." Mac patted her arm, his touch real and comforting as they both tried to process the truth.

"Tell me about this family, Mr. Huntley. The Krupids, you say?"

Once again, Claudia was struck by the innate kindness in Hawk's voice and his deep respect for Mac. For all his deliberate purpose in pushing toward a conversation and a quick resolution, he seemed well aware of the tornado he'd unleashed into their lives.

"The Krupids are good people. Quiet people who've worked to make a life for themselves here in America."

Mac stilled from where he doctored his coffee. "Why do you think this?"

"For starters, they were hesitant to come to me. They've never given up hope of finding their daughter, but they'd been scammed a few times in the past."

"Too damned many people who are too quick to prey on others' misery," Mac said, his voice quiet.

"Yes, sir. That's been my experience, as well." Hawk finished stirring the cream into his mug and continued on. "Even with all their disillusionment, they'd saved more money and were determined to try once more to find some comfort in the loss of Annalise."

"So why did you take on the case?" Mac asked. "Apart from it being your job. I suppose you have a choice on what cases you take on?"

"Yes, I do. And there was something about the photo

of Annalise that captivated me. Something about her parents' grief, as well. I work cold cases as a personal mission and I knew the moment I heard this one I needed to do something."

Cold cases?

Was that what she was?

The thought struck with swift, heavy punches, the blows slamming into her with steady force. She'd spent her life as a Colton, yet there was a possibility to someone else—to an entirely different family—she was a mystery to be solved.

A well of pain and sadness that had never been filled.

Whatever had carried her through the morning— the vague sense of unreality at Hawk's suspicions juxtaposed against the strange reality that had always been her life as a child of Livia Colton—vanished like smoke.

And all that remained was the very real and mounting evidence that her entire life had been a lie.

Claudia excused herself from the table and headed down the small hallway that speared off the kitchen. Hawk knew she needed space and Mac seemed to sense the same, as both men remained in their seats. Her footsteps faded as quiet filled the kitchen. Hawk took in the hard set of Mac's features and his hunched shoulders and for the first moment since taking the case, felt shame. What had he done to this family?

He knew the pain of having your world destroyed, ripped away from you with nowhere to land. An unopened parachute of emotion that laid you out flat, killing the life you had and the world as you knew it.

And now he'd done that to these good people.

Whatever he may have imagined in his mind— or fabricated after reading the *Everything's Blogger* site—he had to reframe and rethink. The Coltons he had met were good people. And Mac Mackenzie was one of them.

"I've brought this on all of you."

That dark, enigmatic gaze stayed on his, not giving an inch. "Yes, you did."

"I'm sorry for that. More sorry than I can say."

That direct stare softened, but didn't lose any of its power. "Were you serious about what you said? About the Krupids being good people who were given a bad deal."

"Serious about every word. They just want closure and some sense of relief."

Something Hawk understood with every fiber of his being.

"I believe you. You strike me as an honest man. The way you talked about that family. The way you look at my daughter." Mac waved a finger. "And make no mistake about it, that woman is my daughter as sure as if she were born to me."

"I know it, sir. I can see that."

"Then answer me something. Why is this case so important to you? There's a fire in you. I saw it outside when you recounted the story of this young woman's life. This poor Annalise."

"I want to make it right."

"Why? Lots better ways to make a living than hunting down trails that have gone cold. In fact, I'd imagine it's the worst sort of job for an honest PI trying to make a living."

"You're right. And I do take the hot ones that close faster, too."

"So tell me why. I'll grant you, the Krupid family deserves answers. I even understand they deserve those answers, whether or not it hurts my family in the process. But you owe me the truth."

Whatever he was—whatever had brought him to this moment—depended on his honesty. And his willingness to open up. Claudia Colton deserved that.

And so did the people who loved her.

Hawk knew it as surely as he knew he'd been living like a ghost for the past four years. Knew it equally as surely as the fact that he'd felt some sense—some *stirring*, really—the moment he'd seen Claudia's photo on that damnable blog post.

"I lost my wife four years ago. She was kidnapped and murdered, then abandoned in a field in a big suburb outside of Houston."

The words were scratchy—raw—and rarely spoken, but it didn't make them any less true.

"No one should have to live with that or lose their loved one that way. There's a sadness in me for your wife, Mr. Huntley. For you, too. A true, deep sadness."

"Thank you." He believed Mac, saw the sincerity in the quiet, grooved lines of the man's face. "I've never found who did it. I was on the force at the time and the police worked long and hard, but every lead they pursued went cold. Every damned lead I pursued did the same."

Hawk drew in a breath, willing himself through the rest of the telling. "It took me two long years to accept that. To pull myself out of an empty life and decide I could die in the bottom of it or I could give Jennifer closure in another way."

"So you work others' cases."

"Others that have a chance of being solved, yes." Hawk ran a finger over the handle of his mug. "I'm sorry if this news hurts your family. I'm sorry for that, more than I can say. But it's why I'm here."

"Livia Colton ruined a lot of lives. She tried to ruin mine and it ripped her a new one when she realized she'd only made mine infinitely better."

Hawk laughed at the wry smile and the epitaph Mac added to punctuate his point.

"She's the reason I have my son and the amazing women and men who I think of as my children. Livia gave me that and nothing can take that away. Nothing can change that, including any lies she told along the way. You do what you need to do. You find the truth for this family and you find the truth for my Claudia. She's tough. She'll stick."

"Thank you." Hawk thought of the woman he'd observed all morning and knew Mac's words for truth.

"I only have one question for you, then."

"What's that?"

"Are you tough? Will you stick?"

"I'll do both, sir. And I appreciate the opportunity to prove it."

Chapter 5

The bedroom walls had long since been painted over, from cotton candy pink to a soft gray that matched her mood. Claudia had shared this room with her sister Jade, and she could still see the two of them, perched atop their matching bunk beds Mac had built with his own two hands. He'd crafted desks into the bottom portion instead of beds and she and Jade had giggled from their chairs over homework, gossip about boys and all the things young girls worried over.

The beds had been moved over to Knox's house and his son, Cody, slept in one of them. The sturdy oak had done her and Jade well and it was nice to know another generation of Coltons slept on Mac's solid and loving work.

Instead of the bunk beds, she sat on the end of a large double, moved in after this became a guest bedroom. She still used it from time to time, as did the rest of her family.

But boy, there were days she missed those bunks.

Life had been confusing back then, in the days after her mother had been arrested, but it had been safe, too. And just like Mac's soothing presence during her swim lessons, as long as she stayed underneath his roof, she knew no harm would come to her.

The knock came first, quickly followed by that voice. Rich and deep, it sent an involuntary shiver down her spine.

Hawk.

"May I have a minute?"

She waved him in, moving over to give him room on the end of the bed, but he chose to remain standing.

"I'm sorry for what's happened today." He held up a hand. "That's not true. I'm sorry for what happened so many years ago that has made today possible."

"It's not your fault."

"Maybe not, but I'm the face of it. And I'm the one who owns the responsibility for connecting the dots."

"Maybe." She considered the large man who stood in the doorway of her room. The weight of responsibility hovered around him and she saw the genuine grief that he was responsible for finding answers. Odd how that thin layer of regret helped her deal with her new reality.

It was also comforting to know he'd not shown up out of a sense of vengeance or self-righteousness or even some sort of professional mission. So many others—especially in the early days after her mother had first been accused—had marched through town and on into her mother's home, La Bonne Vie, with a barely veiled sense of glee.

Hawk Huntley had simply shown up to do what was right. To make another family whole.

"Carrying the news doesn't make it any less true that my mother created those dots." Claudia laughed, the sound wholly unexpected and sort of creaky as it bubbled to her lips. "If I can even call her my mother anymore."

"Nothing can change that. Nothing can change your family, Claudia." Hawk did move forward then, taking the seat next to her on the edge of the bed. The mattress tipped with his weight and she was struck immediately by the warmth of his body and the solid reassurance of having him next to her.

"And even if you were adopted, we don't know Livia's reasons for it. Annalise is dead, so you weren't simply taken from her if she is your mother. Her body was identified when it was delivered to the county morgue in Houston."

"What was her cause of death?"

"She was never autopsied. And her body was cremated before the Krupids could claim her. But the coroner had photos and the proper proof. She did die."

"So who rushed through the paperwork? Why wouldn't the next of kin have been given her body?"

"One more mystery that kept the family certain something else had happened to their daughter."

"And likely at the hands of one more public official my moth—" she stopped, amended "—Livia paid off."

Claudia did some quick math. She was twenty-six and Livia wouldn't have been much older than her at the time of Annalise's death. Her mother's crimes had begun at a shockingly tender age, along with her early marriages, the births of her children and her endless string of affairs.

Had love been a part of any of it? She wanted to think better of her mother, but Claudia doubted it. Livia's string of romances had been about manipulation and greed and money.

The capture of her uncle Matthew had made huge news in Texas after he'd been caught as one of the state's most notorious serial killers. And even with all he'd done, he'd counted his sister among one of the few people he'd never cross.

What did that say about all her mother was capable of?

"So what comes next?"

"Until your mother escaped from jail, the first step would have been a conversation with her. Since that avenue's closed to us we need to see what we can find out from others."

"She wouldn't tell the truth, even if she was still in jail."

That fact stung, but Claudia knew it all the same. Matthew had played similar games with his children throughout the long years he'd spent in prison, the withholding of information one more source of power.

Or believed power.

No, Livia would never voluntarily reveal her choices or what she might have done to influence the course of Claudia's life.

"You believe that?"

"I know it. She can't be persuaded or cajoled. And there is simply no reasoning with her. If I'm going to get the truth, I'm responsible for finding it."

"Then a DNA test is the next step."

"But Annalise is dead. How could we do that?"

"Her parents have mementos. And a small keepsake of her hair from when she was a baby. We have what we need to do the test. But DNA technology is also sophisticated enough to test off the grandparents, as well."

"Then I guess that's the next step. I want to know the truth, Hawk. I want answers."

"Then you can count on me to help you find them."

Midday sun streamed in through the bedroom window, backlighting him with a golden glow. The attraction she'd done her level best to ignore rose up, heightened by their close proximity and the headiness of the moment.

They'd only just met, yet the power of all they'd shared had such weight. Such tremendous heft.

It was her life. And the lives of several others that had stayed in some sort of imbalanced stasis for far too long.

And this man was finally the one who had the power to shatter that immobility.

Drawn in by the firm lines of his jaw and the stiff set of those broad shoulders, she wanted to reach out and touch him. Wanted to pull him close and lose herself for a few glorious moments in time.

How could someone who'd thrown her life into such turmoil seem so appealing? And so very, very right?

Breath suspended, Hawk stared into warm gray eyes that promised a host of things, from welcome to surrender, to the one emotion that scared him the most.

Redemption.

He didn't deserve it and never would. He'd once

been fortunate enough to have the total trust of another person. More, he'd had the total trust of a woman who believed he'd protect her. Always.

Only he'd failed.

He'd failed to keep her safe. He'd failed as a police officer tasked to keep his community safe. And he'd failed in all the time since, unable to bring Jennifer's killer to justice.

He had no right seeking redemption or anything else in the eyes—or arms—of Claudia Colton.

More, he had no right taking advantage of her as he did his job.

Standing, he moved away from the bed and the temptation that filled him at their nearness. "I can make the calls about the DNA test. There's a facility about a half hour from here I've used before. All I need is a cheek swab and your permission."

Confusion replaced the warmth he'd seen in her eyes before they rapidly shuttered, closing off any hint of emotion. "I'll go with you."

"You don't need to. You don't need to be involved in this."

"But I am involved."

Hawk struggled to come up with something—anything—to push some distance back between them. "No, you're not. Not unless the test comes back conclusively."

"Now you're suddenly doubting the outcome?"

He didn't doubt the outcome. Not for one moment did he doubt that Claudia Colton was the daughter of Annalise Krupid. But he needed some space. Some breathing room.

Some air.

Before he could come up with any response the heavy slam of the kitchen door and the echo of voices barreled down the hall. The noise grew, followed on quick heels by a small boy who burst into the room. "Aunt Claudia!"

"Cody!"

Claudia shot off the bed, pulling the small boy into her arms. He was a ball of energy and was covered in a layer of grime; a horse smell immediately filled the room. Claudia seemed oblivious to it as she pulled him close. Hawk marveled at the move and her obvious lack of concern for the high-end clothing that was going to need a severe cleaning when the little boy got done.

The boy's attention shifted once more as the hug ran a moment too long for his liking, his focus shifting to Hawk. "Who are you, mister?"

"This is my friend Mr. Huntley."

Hawk wouldn't have said his real reason for being there, but Claudia's death glare over the top of Cody's head ensured he'd keep her secret. There was no use adding to the pool of people who knew anything until they were sure.

"Are you Aunt Claudia's boyfriend?"

Claudia's skin blushed a delightful pink and Hawk decided to see if he could heighten that shade a few degrees. Even though he already knew the small sprite who stood before them, he decided to play the moment as if he were new to meet the family. "I am. And who are you?"

"Cody. Cody Raff—" The little boy stopped and shook his head before his smile grew wide in his face. "I'm Cody Colton."

"It's nice to meet you, Cody Colton." Hawk stuck

out his hand, charmed when the handshake that came back was firm and solid.

"Cody! You can't just barrel on in to someone's room. You need to kno—" The female voice, tinged with exasperation, faded as a tall, slender woman, clad in jeans almost as dusty as her son's, came around the corner. Pretty hazel eyes widened, her eyebrows inching toward her forehead as she took in the room, and Hawk easily recognized Cody's mother from the blog.

"Allison!" Claudia rushed forward and gave the woman a hug, that sweet blush maintaining its steady wash of pink over her cheeks. Hawk ran through the players in the Colton family in his mind before settling in on the newcomers. This had to be Claudia's sister-in-law Allison.

Allison kept an eye on him, her smile growing as she pulled from Claudia's arms. "I'm Allison Colton. And you are?"

"Hawk Huntley. I'm a friend of Claudia's."

"A New York friend?"

"He's her boyfriend, Mom!" Cody shouted the words before adding, "And he doesn't look like a New Yorker to me. He's wearing boots."

Claudia ran a hand over her nephew's hair before pointing him toward the door. "Why don't we go see what Grandpa Mac has in his cookie jar and we can all sit down and get to know each other."

"I think that's a great idea." Allison crossed the room, her hand extended. "I can't wait to get to know Mr. Huntley a bit better."

As Hawk took her hand in his, he had a feeling his already interesting morning had nothing on his afternoon.

* * *

Where had the boyfriend reference come from? And why hadn't she corrected Hawk once Cody's face lit up in glee at being the first to know a secret? And why, oh why, did that small devil perch on her shoulder, whispering that she really didn't want to correct her impressionable nephew?

Claudia busied herself fixing Cody a plate of cookies from Mac's cookie jar. The man baked them himself and had a wide repertoire of deliciously fattening recipes, rotated regularly through the jar that looked like a cartoon version of the Lone Ranger's horse.

She added extras—no one was immune to a cookie from Mac—and already began calculating all the sit-ups she was not going to do after eating one of Mac's chocolate peanut butter beauties. Allison had already marched Cody to the sink to wash and the boy was busy pouring himself a glass of milk.

"Why don't you ask everyone else if they'd like some milk?"

Cody's eyes darted to the table and back to hers. "Mr. Huntley drinks milk?"

"Why don't you ask him?"

Cody walked over to the table, suddenly shy. She'd seen that swing in his demeanor several times over the past few months. Although they were all so grateful to have him back safe and sound after one of her mother's goons had kidnapped him, Cody still had moments of apprehension around adults. The encouragement to think of others and interact with adults had been a quiet focus for all of them.

"Um. Mr. Huntley. Um. Would you like a glass of milk?"

"I'd love one."

"Okay." Cody smiled and marched back to the counter, reaching for a fresh glass. Claudia couldn't resist leaning over and whispering in his ear, "Nice job. Now maybe you could ask me and your mom if we'd like some, too."

"What about Grandpa Mac?"

"He's back out with the horses so maybe we'll save his for later."

Cody dutifully made the requested round of milk, then dropped off each glass around the table. Claudia didn't miss the way Allison kept trying to catch her eye but she kept her focus on her nephew and off the pointed stares.

"I think you've earned first pick of the platter." Claudia extended the plate to Cody before reaching for her milk.

"So. How did you two meet?"

Whatever subtlety Claudia hoped her sister-in-law might exhibit was nowhere in sight. Instead, Allison seemed to revel in her role as first family member to get the scoop.

Hawk reached for a cookie, his voice smooth and easygoing. "We met through a mutual friend."

"A fix up?" Allison's eyes narrowed. "Because you told me you hated those."

"This wasn't a fix up. Not exactly." Claudia squirmed, almost ready to give up the game, but then thought better of it. Livia had created so much heartache and havoc—and Allison had borne the brunt of that as she'd spent endless days worried she'd never see her son again. It would hardly do to add one more to the list of her mother's sins if Hawk ended up being incorrect.

No, it was better to hold on to this one for a while. And if she had to come clean later, well, her family would just have to understand.

Swallowing back the urge to tell the truth, Claudia skirted Allison's questions with as much honesty as she could muster.

"I never said I didn't like fix ups. I said I didn't want to be fixed up with the three choices you gave me."

Allison gave Hawk a pointed stare before adding a quick wink. "And now I see why."

"Are you coming to Uncle Thorne and Aunt Maggie's wedding?" Cody mumbled around a mouthful of cookies.

"Don't talk with food in your mouth." Allison's reprimand was stern, but the gentle hand she laid on her son's arm softened the criticism.

Claudia didn't miss how Allison's hand lingered there or how love and a subtle longing filled her eyes.

She knows what she almost lost.

Claudia swallowed her bite of cookie, humbled by the thought. And surprised by how quickly her mind shifted to the Krupid family and how much worse it was for them, never to see their daughter again.

They never got one more moment or one more smile or one more plate of cookies.

They never got *her*. Annalise. The woman who was, quite possibly, her mother.

"So are you here for the wedding next weekend?" Allison picked up where her son left off, an impish smile playing about her lips.

The distraction of her parentage faded as Hawk

caught her eye. Since she was unwilling to mention the real reason for Hawk's arrival in Shadow Creek, it looked like she had a date for Thorne's wedding. Her subtle head nod was all he needed.

"I certainly am. We're both looking forward to such a happy day." Hawk reached over and laid a hand over hers. "Aren't we?"

"We're counting down the minutes."

Allison and Cody whirled out of the house nearly as fast as they'd whirled in and in less than a half hour after they'd sat down at Mac's kitchen table, Claudia was putting empty glasses and a plate full of crumbs into the dishwasher. Hawk carried over his and Cody's empties and added them to the top tray.

"Your nephew is a great kid."

"He's wonderful. Knox adores him and I'm so glad they've all found each other again. He and Allison nearly lost Cody a few months ago."

"Lost him?"

"Right before I came home from New York. Cody was kidnapped waiting for the bus. As horrible as it was, the experience brought Knox, Allison and Cody back to each other as a family."

"And the kidnappers?"

"One kidnapper. A man who was in league with my mother. He helped her escape from jail and when she didn't pay up he figured he'd get to her through her grandson."

The haunting thoughts from earlier came back in a rush and the swirl of emotion that she'd battled since coming to Mac's house caught up with her. Tears she hadn't even realized were so close to the surface spilled over with little prompting.

"Hey. Hey there." Hawk was gentle as he reached out, his hands resting on her shoulders. "What's wrong?"

"It's just that—" Her breath caught and she hiccuped around another thick layer of tears. "It's Cody. Something could have happened to him. I knew it. I mean, I understood it. But until I saw him before and realized—"

Claudia broke off, at a loss for how to put into words the myriad of emotions that didn't want to let go.

The large, gentle hands that gripped her shoulders tugged, pulling her close so that she was flush against his chest. Before she could check the impulse, she wrapped her arms around his waist as he pulled her close.

"It's going to be okay." The words were whispered against her head, a promise she tried desperately to cling to through her tears.

"But what if it isn't? She's—" Another tearful hiccup gripped her. "What if it's not? My mother's still out there. People are still at risk. My family is still at risk."

Her fears raced faster than she could keep up with them. The questions that whispered late at night through her mind, wondering where her mother was since escaping from prison. The continued fears that Ben wasn't done with her, determined to wend his way to Shadow Creek to come after her. And now the possible news of her own birth.

When had it all gone so wrong?

And would any of them ever be free from the diabolic influences of Livia Colton?

The tears that had pushed her into Hawk's arms

faded as the rush of adrenaline and emotion worked its way through her system. In its place was the haunting realization of just how good it felt to stand in the circle of Hawk's arms and lean on him. She was a tall woman and she'd always had a figure her mother had kindly—and not so kindly, pending her mood—dubbed "big boned."

How humbling, then, to realize he still had several inches on her and his big, strong arms were more than long enough to wrap around her soundly.

She felt protected.

Safe.

And for the moment, she was fighting an increasing attraction to a man she had no business wanting. Aside from the fact they didn't know each other, Hawk had plenty of baggage of his own and a life he likely wanted to get back to. His visit to Shadow Creek had a purpose.

A goal.

And once he reached that goal, he'd leave Shadow Creek and all its depravity and deceit in his dust.

Chapter 6

Although her crying jag was nearly over, the stiff spine and loosening of her arms indicated Claudia was about to pull away. He should let her go. Hell, he *needed* to let her go.

But the longer she'd stood there, warm and safe in his arms, what he needed to do was fast losing out to what he wanted to do.

And what he wanted to do was kiss her.

"Shh. It's okay. It's all going to be okay, Claudia."

"How can you know that?"

"I don't know it. But I do know you have a family who loves you. Who stands by you and will continue to stand by you, no matter what. And I'm here."

"You got here this morning."

"Yeah, well." He had arrived into her life only this morning. So why did it feel like she'd been a part of him for so much longer?

He had a tendency to get involved with his cases, but the discovery of the Colton connection and the woman who might be Annalise's daughter had happened only recently.

Yet it was her photo—the grainy one that had reached out and grabbed him from the website—that had started it all. Something about her haunted him and whatever it was, it had gripped him from the first.

The pretty curve of her cheeks and the warm smile that seemed to light her up. The attractive, feminine lines of her body that made his hands itch. And the light that shined from her when she was with the people she loved.

He'd seen it in her concern over upsetting Mac and then again in the careful way she watched her nephew.

Claudia Colton was quite a woman.

"Yeah well, what?" She tossed his words right back at him.

"Yeah, well, I'm not going anywhere."

"Since when?"

Her nephew had inadvertently provided an opening and Hawk jumped on it like a drowning man on a life preserver. "I've got a date to your brother's wedding. I can't go anywhere."

"You don't have to do that."

"What if I want to? Cody already thinks I'm coming, and so does Allison, for that matter. What would it hurt?"

"It's not about hurting, it's about us taking you away from your life. Or me taking you away. I can't believe a DNA test takes all that long. A quick match and you can be on your way."

"A fashionista and a scientist, all rolled up into one delicious package?"

The image was a powerful one—and he had no doubt the woman could do anything she set her mind to—but the slight tease drew the smile he was hoping for.

"When you put it like that, I suspect the DNA experts would be a bit insulted by my simplification of the process."

"It'll be our secret."

Her expressive eyes went from storm gray to light gunmetal, to bright and steely once again. Liquid silver swirled in their depths, a hypnotic invitation just before he leaned in to capture her lips. To taste.

To savor.

Unwilling to resist the invitation one moment longer, Hawk bent his head and captured her lips. Soft and pliant beneath his, she opened immediately. He took full advantage of the welcome acceptance, deepening the kiss and satisfying the curiosity that had dogged him since the moment he'd looked at that photo.

She was perfect. Soft. Responsive. And as into the moment as he was.

Hawk let himself go, all the anguish and emotional torment he'd experienced earlier fading away. He would pay for this later—when she wasn't there, in his arms all warm and giving, he'd pay—but for now he let himself feel.

Feel the beauty of a woman's body, curved against his.

Feel his blood heat as her mouth moved beneath his.

Feel his pulse race as she took him places he'd believed long forgotten, never to be discovered again.

* * *

Claudia pulled Hawk tight against her, her initial surprise quickly giving way as she sought to take all he could give. Her arms wrapped around his powerful body and she poured all the emotion she felt into the kiss.

His tongue thrust against hers, a sensual feast as she matched his movements. Matched his ardor and passion.

And his need.

Great, glorious waves of it rolled from Hawk to her and right back again.

She'd missed this. The delicious play of male and female, want and desire. She and Ben had had it at the start, but that had faded quickly, replaced with the dark and the ugly.

An ugliness that had no place in these tender moments with Hawk.

Yet even as she knew not to bring Ben into her head, he'd arrived, spoiling the tender interlude.

The heavy stomp of boots on the porch added to the urge to pull away and Claudia thought perhaps it was a good thing her mind had overruled her passion. Having Mac walk in and see her making out with Hawk would have been awkward.

Even if they were now pretending to have a relationship for her family.

Mac knew the truth.

She stepped from the circle of Hawk's arms and back on the other side of the dishwasher. The door was still open, the top shelf pulled out, so she rearranged everything, straightening just as Mac walked into the kitchen.

"That child would question a rock if he thought he'd get answers." Mac shook his head, his smile from ear to ear. "Wants to know where the ponies came from. I told him to ask his mother when she drove him home."

"I'm sure Allison will thank you for that one," she said with a smile.

Mac reached for a fresh glass above the sink and turned on the tap. "Better her than me."

"Evelyn mentioned a similar conversation with her grandson recently."

"Curious minds." Mac took a long sip of water, oblivious to her mention of Evelyn.

But it was Hawk who wiggled his eyebrows across the kitchen that had her standing to her full height and slamming the dishwasher door closed with extra force. The man was infuriating. One moment he was kissing her brainless and the next he was teasing her for her matchmaking efforts.

Mac and Evelyn *were* a match. A damn good one, if she did say so herself. She clearly needed to up her game.

Filing that one away for later, she moved back to where she'd settled her purse on the counter. "Hawk and I should get going. I need to drop him off and then I need to finish up some items on Maggie's dress."

"Best get to it and finish what you can. And both of you should plan to head back for dinner tomorrow. Leonor called a few minutes ago and says it's all set and that I should spread the word. Allison jumped on the idea."

"I can't do dinner this week. I have to work on the dress."

Mac finished off the water and stared at her. "How much is left?"

"A lot."

"A lot or a few stitches you could do in your sleep?"

Since she'd gotten so much done that morning, she had precious little to do besides finishing a few spots on the bustle and working additional seed pearls into the train. And until Maggie came in for her final fitting, her work on the dress was nearly finished.

"It's a big project."

"Well, after the show you two just put on, you've got a bigger one."

Claudia's eyes darted to Hawk before resettling on Mac. "What show?"

"The Claudia's-got-a-new-boyfriend show. It's all Allison could talk about."

Hawk inclined his head, the cocky smile hovering around his lips absolutely *not* helping. "She did seem rather excited."

"Excited. The woman kept up a brisk pace against her son. And she's now organized a family dinner with your sister for tomorrow night so everyone can meet your new beau. So you, sweet pea—" Mac chucked her on the chin "—had better save that dress excuse for another time."

The closest thing she'd ever had to a real and true parent sauntered out of the kitchen and headed for the back bedroom that had been his forever, tossing over his shoulder as he went, "Leonor is making a lasagna, so she said you can take care of the garlic bread."

"What about me?" Hawk called after his back.

Mac's answer came winging down the hallway, along with a long, low chuckle. "Bring a bottle of wine.

For yourself. You're going to need it for the inquisition."

Claudia took a small moment of petty glee at Hawk's open-mouthed expression before checking herself. If Allison's curiosity over cookies was any indication, the two of them were both about to go before the firing squad.

Goodness above, what had she done with that little white lie to her nephew?

And why did she still feel more excitement than dread?

Hawk's grin had faded but his deep blue eyes still danced with mischief. "So that means you'll say yes?"

"Yes to what?"

"Being my guest at Thorne and Maggie's wedding."

"You mean *you're* my guest."

"Hey, woman." He held up his hands as he moved toward the door. "Don't beg."

Don't beg?

Hawk still questioned his sanity using that one as he jumped into his rental car the next afternoon. The question he couldn't answer was how shockingly easy it had been to fall into an easy banter with Claudia Colton.

Or how much easier it was to wrap her into his arms and kiss her senseless.

She'd been quiet on the short drive back to her shop and he'd figured he'd be better off cutting and running than sticking around to push his luck. She'd played along with the improvised boyfriend routine, but everyone had their limits.

Since he wanted to check in on a few other cases, one of which had required a quick drive up to Waco that morning, he'd made excuses and left her at her shop. Yet none of his innate practicality had kept her from lingering at the very forefront of his mind.

He shouldn't have kissed her.

That had been ill considered. Because now he knew what she tasted like and one taste was not enough.

Aside from the bender he'd gone on about six months after Jennifer's death, he had no love life to speak of. His monk-like existence had seemed like appropriate penance, but it was only now, the memory of Claudia Colton's body pressed to his, her mouth opened to his explorations, that he realized he'd only been playing at penance.

It was easy to repent when there was no temptation.

Hawk pulled into the parking lot of the liquor store he'd seen on the drive into Shadow Creek. He still needed to pick up his wine for the dinner at Mac's. The lot had a few scattered trucks and he estimated he'd get in and out in quick order.

That was until he walked into Knox Colton, staring in confused silence in front of a large wine display in the entrance.

Knox turned to him with a droll smile. "What happened to red and white? All this choice is enough to make a man's head explode."

"We'll fumble through it together." Hawk extended a hand, aware he had the advantage. "Hawk Huntley. I'm half the reason for tonight's impromptu dinner and your current wine dilemma."

Knox's easy smile faded as he moved into big brother mode. "You're dating Claudia?"

"I am."

The answer spilled out, quick and easy, and he couldn't deny to himself just how good it felt.

"This was a surprising development."

Since agreement wasn't an option, Hawk played it easy. Loose. "Oh?"

"How'd you two meet?"

"Through a mutual acquaintance."

"Claudia hasn't mentioned you." Knox's fierce expression faded ever so slightly. "But with all that's been going on around here, I'm not sure there's been a lot of time to talk about private matters, either."

"It's a new relationship."

"It might be new, but you're coming to my brother's wedding Saturday after next."

Although he was more than willing to take the required family ribbing, he wasn't going to fully roll over. "Word travels fast?"

The comment was just enough to fully break the ice and Knox's easygoing smile returned. "My wife and nine-year-old son are key grapes on the Colton family vine."

"He's a sweet boy. We shared some cookies and milk yesterday. I think it's possible you've got a horseman on your hands. He couldn't stop talking about Mac's stable."

The same wistful look he'd observed in Allison's eyes filled Knox's, no doubt an all-too-recent recollection of the boy's kidnapping, before his smile went positively electric. "He's the best. And if given his druthers I think he'll be Texas's first horseman slash astronaut slash dinosaur digger."

Hawk remembered those days, was surprised how easy they were to summon back. "It's good to be nine."

"That it is."

"It's also good to be over twenty-one and able to ease into a family dinner. Shall we pick our poison?" Hawk pointed toward the assembled racks before them.

"I think you mean family inquisition." Knox clapped him on the back. "So let's do it."

Claudia finished tying off the last thread for the last loop on Maggie's bustle. Mac had been more spot-on than she'd wanted to acknowledge and the dress was basically ready for the bride's final fitting.

Although she typically preferred a bit more time between the final fitting and the actual wearing of the dress, Maggie's pregnancy had ensured they needed to manage the final size to a bit of a game time decision. Her future sister-in-law had worried that she'd be "a house" by the time she walked down the aisle and no amount of protesting, soothing or convincing had changed the woman's mind.

So they'd do the fitting next Tuesday before the wedding and give her one less item to worry about before the big day.

Not like she hadn't dealt with crazy deadlines before. The rush leading up to Fashion Week had always meant a few weeks of sleepless nights. It was part of the job and, more to the point, part of what made it so much fun.

It was surprising to realize that while she missed it in a general sense, she'd begun to look forward to new sorts of fun. Dinners with her family. More Colton nieces and nephews to spoil. And the joys of owning her own business.

Evelyn had already shared the morning's receipts

and Claudia had needed her to repeat them twice, the number had been such a surprise. Shadow Creek had embraced the Honeysuckle Road boutique and she was beyond grateful for the quick reception.

A loud noise outside her workroom window startled her, the heavy, clamoring echo a cross between a car backfire and a gunshot. She leaped off the small rolling stool she used while she worked and raced for the door that led out to the alley behind the entire row of buildings that occupied Main Street, still trying to process the noise.

Who would be shooting guns off in the middle of the afternoon?

Hot air slammed into her as she opened the back door, the fine Texas June afternoon pushing a wall of heat into her face. The back parking lot looked calm and she couldn't see anyone, let alone any movement that would have indicated there'd even been a person outside.

Claudia stood there a moment longer, her gaze on the far side of the parking lot when the buzzing of a fly had her swatting it away from her face. It was only as she shifted her gaze, her eyes dropping as she shooed away the pest, that she caught sight of what lay just beyond her back door.

A pile of dead rodents lay there, a rat on the top of the heap, a bullet hole in its side.

"Who? Why?" The words mingled with the scream that rose in her throat and she backed toward the door.

Hands pressed into her back, stopping her progression, and Claudia screamed once more as she turned, only to find Evelyn standing there, her hands now up. "Honey! What is it?"

Claudia struggled to drag in big gulps of air. "It's… I mean." She stopped, shook her head as she reached for Evelyn's hand. "Look there. Over there."

The blend of emotions that crossed the older woman's face went from concern to open horror before transforming into a contained rage. "Who on earth would do something like this?"

She pulled Claudia close against her small form and walked her back into the building. "I want you to sit down."

Evelyn kept one hand on her while she used the other one to firmly close and lock the door. She then moved them back toward the work space before Claudia stopped her. "No. I don't want to be near the dress."

Evelyn nodded and moved her toward the far side of the room, near a rack of material and threads. "Sit down here for a few minutes. Let's catch our breath."

"Is the front door unlocked?"

"Yes." Evelyn stilled, considered. "I ran back here so fast. Let me go do that."

Claudia sat down as her friend left, only to pop back up. The image of what lay out back—*still* lay there— wouldn't leave her mind and she tried desperately to process what she'd just seen.

Was it a prank? A cruel joke?

The kids in town were forever running up and down Main Street, especially now that school was out, yet she couldn't see them responsible for such a horror.

Sure, kids enjoyed a good trick on their elders every now and again, and summer boredom could lead to many things. But what she'd just seen was disgusting. Stomach turning. And unspeakably cruel. She was no fan of rodents, but she was less of a fan of anything innocent being tortured or mistreated.

The urge to walk to the back window beckoned her, but Claudia stayed on her side of the room, suddenly fearful to stand near the outer wall.

Had someone else done this? Someone with a far darker motive than a simple prank?

Ben?

His name bombarded her senses, an immediate rejoinder in her mind.

He'd been so cruel there at the end. So dark and mindless every time he got angry. Every time he felt any perceived slight or disagreement from her. Was this his work? They'd broken up before the holidays and he'd spent the entire season reaching out and trying to get to her through friends. He'd even showed up at the New Year's party she'd attended, drunk and belligerent.

Her friend's boyfriend had dealt with him, adding several threats to keep away, and she'd thought it had done the trick. After that he'd only sent her two texts and an email, the time between those contacts growing longer and longer. And then she'd packed up and headed home to Texas and hadn't heard from him at all.

Was it possible he'd only been biding his time? Worse, had he come for her?

Shivers racked her spine and she wrapped her arms around herself, trying to hug the warmth back into her bones.

Evelyn came back in, her earlier anger channeled into bustling energy. "I locked the door and put up a sign that we're closed. Then I called the cops and my son-in-law."

"Cops?"

Another wave of nausea coated her stomach as she pictured the Shadow Creek police force. There was no love lost between the Shadow Creek PD and her family. Even the recent events that had proven her siblings were not in league with their mother hadn't swayed anyone in law enforcement over to the cause of the Colton family.

In fact, she'd begun to question if anyone with the name of Colton would get a fair shake from the Shadow Creek police department.

Certainly not as long as Bud Jeffries was town sheriff.

"Lot of help they'll be."

"Which is why I called my son-in-law, too." Evelyn nodded, firm in her resolve. "He'll keep watch and will help clean up that disgusting mess, too."

"Thank you."

Claudia stilled as another wave of nausea filled her. "Did you hear it? Before?"

"Hear what?"

"The gunshots. That's why I went out there."

"I didn't hear anything, honey. But then again, I was ringing up Priscilla Todd and that woman would talk her way through the apocalypse."

The joke was enough to ease the moment and Claudia laughed in spite of the tension that still gripped her stomach with tight claws. "Pris is just excited to have a new shop in town."

"That she is. That was her second trip in. She dithered over the new accessories when she bought herself a new outfit this morning and then came back after convincing herself over lunch that she needed them."

"Nothing like a happy customer."

Evelyn was prevented from saying anything by the hard knock on the back door. She walked to answer it, her steps tentative until the unmistakable shout of "Police, open up" echoed through the door.

At the thick twang, Claudia braced herself. Sheriff Bud Jeffries had apparently come to handle the issue himself. The man was no fan of her family and the sentiment, unfortunately, was mutual. She needed every ounce of manners that had been drummed into her over the years in order to manage a base civility to the man.

But regardless of how she felt, she couldn't deny she needed his help.

"Please let him in, Evelyn."

Her assistant opened up, the beefy figure of Bud Jeffries standing sentinel on the other side. He had a deputy with him and Claudia vaguely recognized the guy from high school. If her memory served, he had been in between her and Jade. Tommy Jackson; that was his name.

"Thank you for coming, Sheriff." Evelyn stepped back from the open door. "As you can see, Ms. Colton has had an incident."

"More suspicious events hovering around the Coltons." Bud tossed a glance over his shoulder. "Are we surprised, Tommy?"

"No, sir." Tommy's voice was quiet, but his obedience was absolute.

"Let's get some statements, then." Bud pulled out his notepad as he stepped through the door. He spoke to Evelyn first. "You called this in?"

"I did."

Bud held back a barely veiled sneer as he walked

into Claudia's workroom. "Looks like a lot of ribbons and fuss. Women's work."

Claudia caught Evelyn's eye and gave a shake of her head. It would do no good to take the bait Bud was dangling. And make no mistake about it, he *was* trying to bait her. He'd done it to Mac, to her siblings and to her on prior occasions. It didn't matter how they reacted, he had the security of his badge backing him up and he knew it.

So she'd tamp down on her temper and let him do his idiotic strut through her workroom. And if ignoring his boorish behavior was a small prick to his enormous pride, well, she could live with that.

Bud came to stand beside her, his gaze traveling the length of her body before he returned his attention to his notebook. "When did you find that little death zoo out there?"

"About fifteen minutes ago."

"You haven't seen any rodents before? Cities are full of 'em."

Claudia didn't miss the insinuation—or Bud's deep desire for her to tell him Shadow Creek had nothing on New York—so she gave him as straightforward an answer as she could. "No. And I know we've done a lot of construction around here recently, getting the shop ready. We haven't seen any rodents nor have my fellow businesses been complaining of problems."

"Hmm." Bud jotted down a few notes before his gaze darted to hers. "That makes it all the more suspicious, then."

"Suspicious?"

"Yep. Awfully suspicious." Bud's eyes narrowed, their depths menacing, the look not unlike a rattler she'd seen in the back field of La Bonne Vie years ago. "Be easy enough to round up a few field rats. I bet they hang around barns all the time. You collect 'em up and then place 'em outside the back door. Easy peasy."

"Sheriff Jeffries." Evelyn's tone was full of warning from where she was, still over by the door. "I knew your mother and she was a good woman. Do not tell me she raised you to talk such nonsense."

"She raised me to look for the truth." With Bud's attention caught by Evelyn, he didn't see the figure that poked its head in the back door. "And it's true that Ms. Colton here comes from a family with loads of farmland. Stables, too. Perfect breeding ground for rats and other rodents."

"The truth? Is that what you call spouting nonsense and innuendo?"

Claudia's heart squeezed as that sure, steady voice filled the cavernous room.

Bud whirled at the intrusion, his back stiffening as he caught sight of Hawk. The impressive Mr. Huntley had Bud on both height as well as an innate confidence that only came with the personal knowledge you could hold your own. "This is a private investigation on private property. I suggest you move along."

"Not at all, Sheriff." Claudia slid around Bud, giving him a wide berth, to head over and intercept Hawk. She put her arm around his waist and laid her free hand over his chest. That firm, hard expanse was all delicious heat beneath her palm, but it was the steady, true heartbeat that went a long way toward calming her racing pulse.

"Mr. Huntley is my friend."

"Your friend. Right." Jeffries snorted.

"Is there a problem with that?" Hawk's tone was low but the subtle menace beneath was more than clear.

Well aware Bud heard it, too, Claudia quickly pushed on. "Why yes, he is. He's come to town for a visit and is going to be my date to my brother's wedding."

"Sounds like more than a friend to me."

"We've been keeping things quiet."

Evelyn's eyes widened behind Bud's back but she said nothing. One more set of amends Claudia would need to make later.

"But you can't stop the real thing." Hawk hugged her tight against him. "And now that I'm here, I can manage the little mess outside."

"See here, now. My deputy and I came over to manage that mess."

Hawk hitched a thumb toward the outside wall, well aware he held the upper hand. "Then you'd best get to it."

Chapter 7

"Did you see his face?" Evelyn's low laugh punctuated her words as she idly tidied up the counter in the work space. Her son-in-law, Dan, had arrived as promised and he and Hawk had disappeared outside to deal with *the death zoo*, as Jeffries had so ineloquently put it.

Claudia was still shaken by the events, but Bud's arrival had given her a suitable outlet for her frustrations and Hawk's arrival had gone a long way toward assuaging her fears.

Not that she wasn't scared.

Despite the sheriff's innuendo, she hadn't been the one to put that mess outside her back door. And she *had* heard a gunshot, of that she was now certain. Even though Bud didn't think it was possible for anyone to have gotten off a shot that no one else on Main Street heard or observed. Claudia wasn't so sure, but arguing with Bud Jeffries only made him dig in harder and it wasn't a big enough point to matter.

She'd manage this herself. She'd been meaning to get perimeter cameras for her business—had already made the investment for the front door—and now she'd just need to get them for the back, as well.

One more investment in a long line to get her business up and running, but if it meant peace of mind, then it was well worth it.

"So now that we're alone, you want to tell me how you went from an introduction to dating in the span of a morning?"

Evelyn had been quiet up to that point, giving Claudia space, but clearly her grace period was at an end. "I'd like an answer before Hawk and Dan get back in here."

"There's not that much to tell."

"Right. And I'm the first lady of Texas." Evelyn snorted. "Spill it."

Claudia shot one last glance toward the back door, her fervent hope Hawk would walk back in dashed. And based on the muted discussion she could hear coming from the other side of the door, she didn't think he and Dan would be back in before she could stall Evelyn.

"He had some news for me yesterday morning."

"What sort of news?" Evelyn was across the room in a heartbeat. "You're okay? Is it your mother?"

"Yes. And no." Claudia answered the questions in order. "Well, it sort of is my mother but not how you mean."

When confusion only added to the worry in Evelyn's

eyes, Claudia pointed toward the stiff-backed chairs that sat around the small table where they took their breaks. "Let's sit down and I'll tell you."

Claudia reiterated the same details Hawk had shared with her over coffee the day before, then further relayed to Mac. "And Mac's the only one who knows, so I need you to keep this between us for now."

"How'd he take it?"

"He's Mac. He took it all in stride, just like he does everything else."

"I'm sure he's worried about you." Evelyn ran a hand over Claudia's cheek. "Just like I am."

"Maybe you can call him. See if he needs to talk about it."

"Well, of course I can—" Evelyn stopped and snatched her hand back. "That's so manipulative!"

"I'm a woman on a mission."

"A futile one."

"Why? Give me one reason and I'll stop."

"I've already given you three. My age. My stage of life. And my grandchildren."

"Mac's older than you. He's in the same 'stage'—" Claudia made air quotes "—as you call it. And he has Cody and a new grandbaby on the way. Should he sit home dateless?"

"Of course not."

"Then give me a real reason."

Evelyn shook her head but was saved from saying anything when Dan and Hawk walked in the back door.

Hawk had remained quiet after Bud Jeffries left, his faithful deputy in tow, but his eyes had said it all. She might have only met the man the day before, but it wasn't hard to read raw, furious anger in the depths of

Hawk's sky blue eyes. The time that had passed since the sheriff had departed hadn't appeared to lessen the fire and fury that burned in those azure depths.

Dan spoke first. "Since I'm guessing you're not going to open back up today, can I take you home, Mom?"

Claudia loved that Evelyn's son-in-law called her "mom." She'd marveled at it the first time she'd heard it and had smiled each and every time since. How lovely would that be? To marry into a family where you had so much love and devotion for your spouse's parents?

Unlike hers.

She couldn't imagine Allison calling Livia mom, or Leonor's new fiancé, Joshua, doing that, either. And Maggie would no sooner speak to Livia than attempt any moniker that suggested the woman was a parental figure.

"Get out of here." Claudia waved them on. "Hawk and I can run your car by your house on our way to Mac's tonight."

Evelyn looked about to argue before her gaze drifted to Hawk. Although he kept his smile light and easy, his anger radiated off him in waves as he paced near the door. "That would be nice. I'll just get my things."

In moments, Evelyn had her purse and handed over her keys.

"I'll see you later, then." Claudia pressed a quick kiss to her cheek before pulling her in for a tight hug. "Thank you for everything."

"Of course, sweetie." Again, Evelyn ran a hand over Claudia's cheek, the moment sweet and motherly. More motherly than Claudia had ever experienced from Livia. She reveled in that soft touch and knew Evelyn was one more example of the gifts that had come back into her life with the move home to Shadow Creek.

Claudia closed the door and flipped the lock behind Dan and Evelyn. She'd deftly ignored the industrial trash can that sat behind her store, focusing her gaze on her friends instead. The pile from her back sidewalk had likely been swept up in there and she didn't want to remember the disgusting image or think of it still so nearby.

"Are you okay?"

"I'm fine." Claudia leaned her back against the door, pushing the revolting image from her mind. "Better now knowing that…pile is gone."

Hawk moved closer and placed a hand on the door, just beside her head. "Dan and I disposed of everything. You don't need to worry about it."

He was close, but not touching. Even with the small distance, she could feel the heat emanating off his body. Despite the summer warmth of the day, a bone-deep cold had settled beneath her skin as she dealt with the dead animals and then the sheriff's visit. It was only with Hawk's closeness that she began to feel that chill fading.

"How did you know to come?"

"Word travels fast through town. I'd met up with your brother at the liquor store and then headed on to—"

She interrupted him. "You met my brother?"

"Knox was at the liquor store picking out wine. I introduced myself, then we spent a riveting half hour arguing over wine neither of us understood."

"Oh. Okay." He didn't make any sense but she figured Knox was the lead part of that statement anyway. "And then what?"

"Then I headed to the mercantile to see if I could get some flowers when the call into the police station made the quick rounds as I stood in line."

"It made the rounds?"

"I've only been here a few days, but it's been long enough to know that anything Colton-related is hot gossip around town."

She sighed. "Sad truth. But still true all the same."

"Hey." He brushed several strands of hair behind her ear. "I'm sorry. I didn't mean to be insensitive."

"It's not insensitive when it's the truth."

"I'll take that under advisement." He traced the shell of her ear before trailing a path down the column of her throat. "But right now I'd really like to kiss you."

"I'd really like that, too."

The last vestiges of fear that lingered at the afternoon's events faded as Hawk lowered his lips to hers. With his body pressed to hers and the door at her back she should have felt claustrophobic.

Trapped.

She felt anything but as she wrapped her arms around his neck and clung.

Simply clung as the touch of his hands, the warmth of his body and the sheer power of his kiss carried her away from all the pain, trouble and confusion that was life in Shadow Creek.

And life as a Colton.

Hawk savored the warm taste of her lips and the lush curves of her body that filled his hands. He wanted this woman. Like he wanted his next breath, he wanted her.

Claudia moaned in his arms, her hands drifting over his back before settling at his hips. Her fingers stilled there, pulling him even closer against her and he fought the desperate desire to strip them both bare.

How had this happened?

He'd spent so many years with this part of his life on hold, every bit of feeling seemingly vanished from his body, that it was a shock to have it all rush back at once.

He wanted her. No, he *needed* her. It gripped at him with fierce fangs, a desperate yearning that wouldn't be sated. Their stolen moments in Mac's kitchen had given him a taste, and he was unable to resist taking more.

Even if you had to rush in here to deal with a threat to her safety.

The castigation blindsided him, the swift smack upside the head enough to have him pull away.

"Hawk?" Desire stamped itself in the smoky depths of her eyes, along with a rapidly dawning confusion as he pulled away from her. "What's wrong?"

"You're in danger. And here I am ravishing you against the door."

"Ravishing me?" A silly, lopsided smile tugged at her mouth. "That's a new one."

"I'll give you another one, then. Try *taking advantage* on for size."

The grin faded. "Taking advantage? Since I'm standing right here feeling quite advantaged all by myself, why don't you look for a new description that's more appropriate? I'd suggest you start with *consenting adults*."

Claudia pushed off the door and stomped across the room. Her heels clicked on the hardwood, short little stabs of irritation marking each and every step.

"I know we're consenting adults. That's not what I meant."

She whirled on him. "Oh no? Why don't you explain it to me, then?"

"You were in danger." He jabbed a finger toward the door. "A half hour ago you were calling in a threat and dragging the police out here. I hardly think I should be kissing you after something like that."

"If not after something like that, then when?"

"I—" He stopped and choked back whatever he was going to say next. He wanted to kiss her, damn it. He didn't need any further encouragement to act, no matter how determined she was to absolve him of guilt.

Because he *was* guilty.

He'd failed in his ability to protect Jennifer and now, damn it, he'd failed again. Had he brought this to her door with his suspicions?

Had they somehow gotten back to Livia Colton?

Because someone had threatened Claudia. He and Dan had gotten the full story out of her and Evelyn after that bumbling ass of a sheriff had gone on his way, and with each piece of the story, he'd grown more and more upset.

Dead rats? Gunshots?

What the *hell* was going on here?

This was a fashion boutique. And yet something dangerous and horrible had found its way to her door. Literally found its way to her door.

"Have you been threatened before this?"

"No." She shook her head, angry color still riding high in her cheeks. "Not here."

His attention sharpened. "What do you mean, 'not here'?"

"I mean, not here. I haven't had any incidents since I've been back in Shadow Creek. Sadly, my family can't say the same."

"Did you have any incidents in New York?"

"Look… I…" She stopped. "It's a big city."

He might have believed her—he almost did—until those expressive gray eyes dipped, avoiding his stare.

"What happened?"

"It's nothing. It hasn't happened in a while. I mean, it just can't be related to this."

"Damn it, Claudia." He stomped across the room, following the same path she'd trod on her heels. "What aren't you telling me?"

"I dated a guy last year. Ben Witherspoon. He got nasty at the end. Possessive. And then the last time we were together, he took a few swings. Smacks, really."

She was calm as she related the incidents—robotic, almost—even as Hawk felt his blood vessels constricting at the image of what she'd endured. "He hit you? Slapped you?"

"At the end. That was it. I was going to end things but that was the final straw and I walked away."

"Has he contacted you here? Did you tell the sheriff? Does your family know?" The questions spilled, one after the next, each generating several dozen more.

Had he hurt her?

Where did he live?

And where could he find the freaking ass to destroy him?

"Hawk, it's fine. My friend's boyfriend talked to him and he's left me alone. I don't think he even knows I moved out of New York."

"Oh no? Because it looks like he's shown up with

a dead pile of street rats. Feels like a piece of home, doesn't it?"

He saw the moment his words penetrated, her head whipping toward the door before she turned back to him. "Sheriff Jeffries insinuated it was Mac's farm and that I'd made it all up, anyway."

"Sheriff Jeffries is an ass. I saw that coming the moment I saw the piss-poor way he parked out front. But putting that aside, why the hell would you drum up a pile of rats and put them in the back of your store?"

"No one said he was a *smart* ass."

A small laugh bubbled out as she made the connection between her words and Hawk fought a smile of his own. His heart still felt too tight in his chest and he wanted to punch a hole in the wall, but the juxtaposition of words *was* funny.

And the laughter felt good. Far better than thinking about some jerk threatening her and slapping her around.

"You sure you're okay?" He closed the small distance between them, pulling her close once again. Her head nestled just beneath his chin and he stood there for a moment, his eyes closed as he breathed her in.

Dangerous ex-boyfriends and threats in the middle of the day?

He'd been a cop long enough and around law enforcement even longer. Abuse, mutilation and death of animals was a bad sign, rodents or not.

A very bad sign.

Which meant he needed to put all his skills to use to track down Ben Witherspoon and find out what the man had been up to for the past several months. As Hawk held Claudia tight against him, he could only hope for the asshole's sake that he had stayed far away from Texas.

Far, far away.

Hawk followed the long, narrow driveway Claudia had navigated the day before, the late afternoon sun high against his windshield. He'd kept Claudia company in her shop for another hour before she'd slipped to her apartment upstairs above the shop to change for dinner.

He'd wanted to follow her, but had stayed in the shop instead, armed with the knowledge that seeing where she lived would only add one more tick in the fascination column that was rapidly forming in his collective conscious about Claudia Colton.

Damn, but the woman tied him up in knots. Even now, his hands firmly against the steering wheel, he could feel the softness of her curves and the heat of her body against his palms. His senses were full of her, the light scent of honeysuckle that pervaded her shop seeming to cling to her with delicious sweetness.

And her lips.

A man could die happy after tasting their rich, lush softness.

Drunk.

He was positively drunk on her.

Unbidden, a memory of his early days with Jennifer swatted at him. He'd been in love before. Had married his love, convinced they'd find their way to old age together. Was he so fickle he could forget that?

Even as the thought wormed its way through the sensual feast that had accompanied him all day, he had to acknowledge he was being unfair. He'd loved

Jennifer. Still did. And if things had been different, he'd still be faithfully married to her, honoring that love and their vows. His attraction to Claudia wasn't a black mark on his marriage or his love for his wife, and he did both Jennifer and Claudia a disservice for thinking it.

Whatever pain or continued self-loathing he carried for his inability to keep his wife safe, he wasn't cheating on her, memory or no. His wife had been far too pragmatic for that.

Besides, he remembered with a small smile, hadn't she teased him mercilessly when he was on the force that if he ended up dead she was going after George Clooney for round number two?

"What's so funny?"

"Hmm?" Hawk navigated around several parked cars to find a space on the far side of the paddock.

"Your smile. It looked like something was funny. Is it some nervous reaction to my five brothers and sisters?"

"No, I was actually thinking about my wife."

"Oh?" Curiosity stamped itself in those deep gray eyes, even as a subtle wariness seemed to grip her as she folded her hands in her lap.

"I um—" He broke off, the sudden reality of the situation—and his big mouth—filling him. "I haven't dated much since Jennifer died."

"I'm sorry. Truly sorry."

"It's fine. It's just, well. I loved kissing you earlier. I wanted to kiss you earlier. And yesterday. Both times." He stopped again, his ham-handed sharing as embarrassing as a teenage boy on his first date.

He inhaled a deep breath and blew it out. Took another and did the same as he put the car into Park. "Let me try this again."

"Alright."

"I loved kissing you. And I wanted to kiss you. I want to kiss you again, as a matter of fact. But I haven't wanted that in a long time. That longing that comes from wanting a woman. It's an adjustment. And as I was getting down on myself for wanting those things with you, I realized that Jennifer would have smacked me upside the head for thinking so."

"You think so?"

"I know so. She was a special woman. Warm and caring and wonderful. And she had a funny practical streak that was oddly endearing, even as she cut you off at the knees. And for those reasons, I know she wouldn't be upset by my kissing you."

"That's a beautiful way to speak of her. To remember her."

"She also told me on several occasions that if I ended up killed in the line of duty when I was a cop, she was going after George Clooney for her second husband."

A small smile curved Claudia's lips. "I suppose she wasn't going to let his wife stand in her way?"

"She died before he got married, but knowing Jennifer, I suspect not."

Claudia laughed then, the subtle nerves fading as she turned more fully to face him. "I'm glad you told me that. If we're being truthful, I have to admit I've never dated a man who lost his wife. It's not something you expect." She took a deep breath of her own. "It's not something you expect at our age."

"No, it's not."

Although he'd shared the details of Jennifer's death with Mac, he sensed even before she spoke that Claudia was going to ask him how she'd died.

How did he share that?

All the shame and embarrassment he'd managed to push aside rushed back at the thought of sharing how badly he'd failed his wife. Just like he'd failed Claudia today.

The muted sound of feet and a big shout interrupted the moment just as Cody slammed his palm on Claudia's window, shouting for her. "Aunt Claudia!"

"We're coming!" She laughed, their discussion fading in the face of youthful exuberance. She tapped on the window. "Stand back so I can open the door."

He tumbled back like a puppy, letting her out before racing around to Hawk's side. "Mr. Huntley! I have to tell you what happened. Grandpa Mac gave me one single horse to groom and take care of every single time I'm here! And not just a pony, but a big mare!"

Cody danced back around the front of the car, regaling Claudia with the same news as if she hadn't heard him.

"A mare? Already?"

"She's over here. He's letting me work with Bunny to ride and train and work with when I'm here. But he says I have to learn how to take care of her, because that's just as important as riding her."

Claudia was already out and following behind Cody. She waved a distracted hand in the direction of the car. "We'll get the food in a minute. Let's go see."

Once again, Hawk was captivated by the easy way she was with her nephew. She'd changed for the evening into a printed sundress and a pair of summer heels and seemed oblivious to both as Cody marched her determinedly toward the paddock.

He stopped at the rails, content to simply take in the sweet moment as Cody whistled for Bunny. The horse's ears perked immediately and she trotted over toward the small boy. Claudia helped him as Bunny joined them, petting her nose and making a general fuss over the pretty bay mare.

"Come on, Mr. Huntley!" Cody waved him over. "Come meet Bunny."

Hawk moved toward the excited boy, the pretty mare and the gorgeous woman, the early evening sun highlighting them all in a golden tableau.

The scene captivated him, the pleasure of the moment erasing all that had come earlier in the day.

Here there were no vicious attacks. No questions about parentage and birth. No death.

Right here, right at this moment, there was joy.

He'd be a fool to miss the opportunity to reach out and grab it with both hands.

Chapter 8

Claudia washed her hands at the sink, scrubbing off the visit with Bunny before helping Cody to do the same.

"I'm not dirty." The words slipped out, yet another stream of happy chatter as he squeezed soap onto his hands. "Bunny is pretty and clean. Grandpa Mac and I washed her earlier so she had a bath."

While she appreciated his nine-year-old logic, she figured she couldn't play the softie all the time. "While I believe you gave her a very good bath and she's quite clean as horses go, she's not quite human clean. Especially when we're about to eat."

Hawk came up behind them, reaching around her back to get his own squeeze of the soap. "My mom had a rule I try to live by. Any time spent outside the house or inside the bathroom means the hands get washed."

Cody nodded, his gaze growing serious. "That's a pretty good rule. Makes it easy to remember."

Hawk winked at Claudia before flicking a wet hand at Cody. "That was her point."

Her nephew squealed at the water and quickly retaliated, shaking his hands like a dog climbing out of a tub.

"Now you've done it." She giggled as she sidestepped to get out of the way, only to find Hawk's arms tight around her and positioning her as a human shield. "Hawk!"

He only laughed behind her and held her still as Cody shook his hands one more time.

"Cody Colton!" Allison hollered as she walked into the kitchen. "Stop that."

Hawk dropped his arms and turned to Allison with a good-natured grin. "I'm the guilty one. Got a little carried away with getting clean."

Allison's eyebrows rose as she took in the three of them. "Remind me not to put you on dishwashing duty."

Hawk winked again before offering Cody a high five. "Works every time, my man."

Before she could protest or stop them, Cody was dragging Hawk toward the family room and what sounded like an active baseball game in progress.

Allison watched them leave, her smile wide. "And I thought he had a case of hero worship for Knox. My husband had better look out."

"Oh, I don't think Knox has anything to worry about."

"No, he doesn't." Allison pulled her close for a hug. "But it's wonderful to see yet another adult male figure in his life. He's been so anxious for that. And has just blossomed with the opportunity to have it."

Claudia heard the light sniffle and hugged her sister-in-law a bit tighter before pulling back. "Things have a wonderful way of working out."

"They do, don't they?"

Before she could reply, Leonor and Maggie came into the kitchen, both arguing about a call in the game. "The shortstop has had his head so far up his butt it's amazing we're even still in this."

Claudia went to Maggie first, giving her a hug. "Salty language for a bride and a mother-to-be. I like it."

Maggie hugged as tightly as Allison before pulling back and laying a protective hand over her belly. "Much as I want to be a good role model, I don't think there's any motherhood gene that'll knock out my loathing for a bad sports call."

"Note to self," Leonor added before snagging her own hug, "buy the baby some tiny earmuffs."

"Already on my list," Allison added and grabbed some pot holders on the stove. "Also on my list, digging into this lasagna."

"It needs to cool off." Leonor pulled out a seat for Maggie, then gestured to another one for Claudia. "Which gives us enough time to bug little sister here about her new, sexy-as-sin boyfriend."

"Hey!" Claudia protested as Leonor shoved her into a seat. "I thought you were madly in love with Joshua."

"I am madly in love with Joshua. I also still have a working pair of eyes. The man sitting in Mac's living room is gorgeous. He's also kind, sweet and a natural with Cody. So spill."

Spill that I met him yesterday? Or that I might not really be your sister? Or that I'm beginning to think he's the best thing to ever walk into my life?

Claudia discarded each and every question, unwilling to dwell too hard on any of them.

Or the implications of her answers.

"He's a great guy."

Maggie reached for a carrot on the table and smothered it in a heap of spinach dip. "I didn't even know you were dating anyone."

"It's new."

"And there is that delicious feeling when it's new. Like you want to shout it from the rooftops but you also don't want to risk spoiling it by telling everyone." Leonor sighed. "I love that part."

Maggie waved her half-eaten carrot at her. "You love all the parts."

"I do." Leonor got up to poke at the lasagna. "I really do."

Allison turned from the stove, giving Leonor room to poke at dinner. "So, Claudia. Which parts have you gotten to?"

"Allison!" Leonor swatted at her arm with a pot holder which their sister-in-law neatly sidestepped.

"I'm the objective outsider, able to ask the questions everyone else is dying to know."

Leonor rolled her eyes from behind Allison's back. "You're nosy and you know it."

Claudia decided it was time to step in before the collective estrogen in the kitchen had her walking down the aisle to meet her fake boyfriend. "I'm going to agree with Leonor and say that things are still new and fun and I'm not ready to share all the details. I will also say that he's a wonderful man and I'm happy he's here tonight to meet everyone."

"Cop-out. But fair." Maggie leaned over and pressed a quick kiss to her cheek. "We've all been there. Recently, too."

They had all been there recently. It was what made it so hard to sit there and lie to all of them. But how much worse would it be to tell them the real reason Hawk was in her life?

That she wasn't really their sister. That she was, instead, the child of just one more victim of Livia Colton.

The happy, buoyant spirit that had carried her into the kitchen and into the arms of her family dimmed, replaced with the sorry reality of what her life might become.

A lie.

One that grew bigger by the moment.

Hawk filed into the kitchen with Mac, his son, Thorne, and Claudia's brother Knox. His earlier meeting with Knox at the liquor store had given them a shared bond to talk about and they'd taken a ribbing from Leonor's fiancé, ex–FBI agent Joshua Howard, about their ineptitude in selecting a cabernet over a merlot. Hawk was familiar with Howard by reputation only and the guy was solid. He was also building his own private security firm and it gave them a ready area of discussion.

They'd spent a good hour getting acquainted over baseball, shared case stories and a dancing Cody, whose excitement about the horse was infectious.

Which made the wall of anxiety wrapped around

Claudia that much more jarring the moment he cleared the entryway.

"Hey there." He waited until everyone had lined up to make their plates at the kitchen counter to carry into the dining room before he moved in behind her. "What's the matter?"

"Nothing." She reached for two plates, handing him one with a bright smile painted on her face that fooled no one. "Nothing's wrong."

He took the plate, quickly taking her hand before she could snatch it back. "What's really wrong? I can tell you're upset."

"Come on, Hawk. It's nothing. I mean it."

He was about to drop it when she pulled her hand away and put her plate on the counter, then headed for the front door. The kitchen had cleared, with only Joshua and Knox still there fixing their plates, and he was able to escape with minimal fuss or notice from the men as he followed her.

The evening sun was still high as he sat beside her on the big bench swing that hung from the ceiling of Mac's wide front porch. Sounds from inside were dim but he could hear the laughter as it filtered through the windows.

"Did something happen before? In the kitchen?" he asked.

"Not really."

She'd slipped out of her heels and tucked her legs up beneath her on the swing. Her position gave him the opportunity to put them in motion and he slowly pushed them back and forth with his foot. "Then what didn't happen?"

"It's silly."

Hawk kept up the steady back and forth of the swing. "It's not if it upset you."

"That's just the problem. I have no reason to be upset. It's just—" She exhaled a hard breath before beginning once more. "The girls were asking me about you. And it got silly, the way that women do."

"What way?"

"We tease and poke a bit about a new guy. And then we give off a whole lot of innuendo. At first it was okay. I mean, they think we're dating and they're excited for me." She darted a glance at him. "For us. But after a while it just felt like I was lying to them."

"Lying about what?"

"About being a Colton. About being your girlfriend. About faking my way through the day when all I really want to do is bury my head under the covers and come out once they've caught Livia."

"There's a lot in there. I'm going to take it point by point." When she only stared off into the distance, he took her silence for acceptance and continued on. "First, you are a Colton."

That was enough to pull her attention away from the head of cattle that grazed in Mac's western field. "How can you say that? I'm likely Annalise Krupid's daughter, which makes me very much not a Colton."

"Biology can't change who you are, Claudia. If anything, it will add to your life because Annalise's parents are anxious to be reunited with their granddaughter, but it won't change the bonds you have with your siblings. With their spouses. With Mac or Cody, either. You don't stop being their sister. You don't stop being Cody's aunt Claudia. And you certainly don't stop being the daughter Mac loves deeply, just because of something Livia Colton did over a quarter century ago."

"I don't want to lie, but it feels pointless to say anything until we know."

"I agree. So does Mac."

"And even though I know that, I don't want to feel like I'm hiding it."

She wasn't hiding anything—she was dealing with it—but there seemed to be no convincing her of that.

"But if it's true—" She stilled, that gray gaze drifting back toward the field. "If it's true, then I need to decide how to tell them. And a week before Thorne and Maggie get married is not the time or the place."

"So stop beating yourself up over it. You're not deliberately lying. You're waiting to get more information on a situation you're still processing yourself."

"Okay." She brushed a few strands of silky blond hair away before she turned to face him. "So I'm not lying about the DNA test, only omitting. I am lying about you."

"How so?"

"You're not my boyfriend, Hawk. Forty-eight hours ago we didn't even know each other. Now I'm parading you around to meet my entire family."

"For the record, I don't parade." When she didn't smile at his lame joke, he kept on. "And you might not have known me, but I knew you. I knew you the first moment I saw your picture."

"How can you say that? And how could you possibly know me from a photo?"

How did he explain it without sounding like an absolute nut job? Even as he questioned himself, he couldn't stop the words that rushed into his throat.

"I know it doesn't make sense, but I knew you, Claudia. It was that damned blog. I read the article. I scoured it for details of your mother and her actions, seeking a clue to Annalise's disappearance. And then I saw you. Read about your background and your history as the daring Colton daughter who struck off for New York and I was captivated."

How did he explain the way that photo had seemed to supercharge his emotions?

That it had brought him back to life.

Working cold cases had helped him deal with the pain of losing Jennifer, the hunt for answers for others a type of penance for the answers she'd never get. But none of them had affected him like the Krupid case.

None of them had felt personal.

His reasons for handling them had been personal, but the work—the research and interviews and effort— that had all been straight down the line investigative work.

Until Annalise.

Only the moment he'd seen Claudia's image, the urgency to find answers—the sheer need that coursed through him every time he thought about the case— finally made sense.

He wanted answers for the Krupids but he wanted Claudia Colton for…himself?

"I got an alert on the article because of the references in it to sex trafficking, and I expected one more dismal walk through human depravity. And then I saw your photo and it woke something in me. And the more I looked into you and your background the more I wanted to know you. Your work. The way you've contributed to the fashion industry. Even in your short time back here in Shadow Creek, you've made an impact."

He watched her face for any sign he was scaring the heck out of her, but all he saw was that continued bleakness, her eyes the color of an impending winter storm.

"You've made an impact on me."

"But we didn't know each other. A person isn't a photograph. They're flesh and blood, full of creativity and ideas and soul. A photo doesn't have any of that."

"Yours did."

Again, he knew he veered dangerously close to weirdo territory, but it was the truth. And the more time he spent with her—the more time that flesh and blood and creative soul became tangibly real—he was hooked.

And utterly captivated.

"Before I completely embarrass myself, let's take the last point."

She arched one delicate eyebrow. "The one where Livia Colton is on the lam, out to do as much damage as she can for the first time in a decade."

"That one."

"She's a problem, Hawk. Even today. I know you think Ben had something to do with that incident outside my shop, but I don't know. The more I think about it and the more distance I get away from the shock of it all, it doesn't smack of Ben."

He fought the urge to growl at the mention of her douche-bag ex and instead listened to what she said. He'd spent enough of his life on investigative work to know instinct mattered. "Okay. Walk me through it, then. Why don't you think it's Ben?"

"I'll admit, it's one of the first places my head went.

Ben found me. He's here. But as I keep thinking about it, it seems less and less possible."

"Because?"

"The rats, for one. That was a nasty heap of animals and there's no way the man I know would get his hands dirty with that."

"You don't have to touch them to create that pile if you use tools."

"Oh, come on, of course you do. A pile that neat? It's gross. And it's the sign of someone who's gone really far around the bend. Ben was violent, but I used to be the one to kill spiders in his apartment."

As arguments went, it had some merit. While he wouldn't put any act past anyone, her thought process was fair.

"Is that all?"

"It's also the way it happened. Whatever else he was, he was an in-your-face sort of abuser." She laid a hand over his clenched fist. "I know those are harsh words, but hear me out."

"Yeah. Right."

The words were harsh—the image of the man laying a hand on her even worse—and he took comfort when her fingers slowly pried his open, her hand slipping into his.

"Ben was never secretive. Other than the fact that his behavior came on some months after we were dating and fully in the relationship, he was deliberate about it. I just feel that if it was really him today, he'd have made sure I knew it. Would have gleefully let me know he'd found me in Texas."

"And you can't think of anyone else who'd leave such a violent calling card?"

"None. Whoever was responsible ran off like the coward they are."

"So who can it be?"

The heavy tread of boots on the edge of the porch stilled his feet, the swing coming to a halt at a deep voice saying, "That's exactly what I'd like to know."

"River!" Claudia flew off the still-quivering bench swing, her bare feet slapping on the porch as she ran to her brother. He'd only been back a few weeks, his return from the marines fraught with an air of danger and menace that hadn't faded the longer he was home. In fact, it seemed to work the opposite way, eating at him as he tried to readjust to civilian life.

She knew he struggled with the loss of an eye and whatever hell had caused it, but other than the outward scars that marked the incident and grooved deep into his face, he refused to discuss it.

Heck, he was barely willing to acknowledge it.

Claudia knew it bothered Knox and Thorne, Mac, as well. She'd attempted to get them to open up about it and share their thoughts, but they'd blocked her with a wall of solidarity and stubborn male pride.

And silence.

Which had left her, Leonor and Jade to do their level best to prod and poke their brother, all to no avail.

His hug was extra tight before he pulled away, holding her at arm's length. "You're okay?"

"I'm fine."

"I'm talking about what happened today," River said.

"About what that happened today?" Since the last couple days had included the arrival of Hawk Huntley, the news she might not be a Colton and the incident on her back driveway, she mentally figured she had a right to ask for clarification.

"A pile of rodents? One with a hole shot clean through it."

"Oh. That."

"Yeah, little sister. That." River's good eye darted from her face toward Hawk and back again. "Who's this?"

Hawk had crossed the porch behind her and now moved up to wrap an arm around her shoulders. She swallowed back the guilt and turned into him, placing her hand on his stomach. The move was more comfortable than it should be and she nearly snatched her hand back, but Hawk must have sensed her move because he captured her hand beneath his, holding her still.

"Hawk Huntley. I'd like you to meet my brother River Colton. River, my boyfriend, Hawk Huntley."

"Your boyfriend?" River's disbelief was palpable. The first genuine surprise she'd seen in him since his return, even as he extended his hand to shake.

"You have a problem with that?" she asked before she moved aside so the two men could shake hands.

"No." Seeming to catch himself, he added, "Of course not."

"He's also my date to Maggie and Thorne's wedding. Leonor thought it would be fun to have a family dinner tonight so we could all get to know each other before the wedding."

"How…familial."

"We are all Coltons." The words slipped out of their own accord and Claudia fought the deep urge to wince.

Where had *that* come from?

Since she needed to cut bait while she was ahead, she gestured to the kitchen. "Leonor made her famous lasagna and Cody's been dancing around with news. Let's go back inside."

"Sure."

"And maybe you can skip the part about the incident at my shop."

"Keep dreaming, little sister." River's chuckle was long and low. "Keep dreaming."

Dreaming? Yeah, right. More like a nightmare.

But she kept the thought to herself as she headed back into the house to fix their plates. True to his word, they'd barely cleared the entrance to the dining room when River started in on the events of the day. "Claudia had an incident at the shop earlier."

Knox attempted to speak first but it was Mac who stood, his quiet presence shutting them all up fast. "What sort of incident?"

Claudia set her plate on the table, meeting Mac's direct gaze head-on before shooting a pointed stare at Cody. "It was really nothing."

"It was an incident big enough to call Sheriff Bud." River's derisive tone only added fuel to the moment, but Mac held his ground, his voice never going above a loud whisper.

"And you've kept this quiet despite being here for over an hour."

"I'm sorry. Look—"

He held up a hand. "Look nothing. We're a family and we share things. Something like this is something you share."

Before she could say anything in her defense, Mac turned to Hawk. "You, too. You're welcome in my home but you play by my rules. Especially when it comes to my family."

"Yes." Hawk nodded. "Of course."

On a satisfied head nod, Mac sat down. "Now walk us through it."

She and Hawk both shot a pointed stare toward Cody, who'd suddenly grown interested around his mouthfuls of lasagna.

"The high points," Mac added, clear on the message.

"It was an unfortunate prank outside the back of my shop. At the base of the stairs up to my apartment."

"What sort of prank?" Knox's focus was as unrelenting as Mac's. "One that required a call to the police."

By unspoken agreement, Allison began to distract Cody, culminating in a whisper to help her pull out the dessert. The promise of scooping out chocolate ice cream was sufficient enough to draw his attention from the conversation and he quickly followed his mother from the room.

Once the small footfalls had faded into the kitchen, Mac nodded his head. "Now please tell us everything."

Her family had a right to know. First, because they loved her and second, because they needed to be on watch themselves. Her mother's sins were numerous and if anyone was seeking payback against the Coltons, each and every one of them was fair game.

It was a haunting thought, but it also confirmed why she had to share what happened.

They *all* needed to be on their guard.

"I was back in my workroom finishing up a few things and Evelyn had the shop covered. I was puttering around, taking care of a few items when I thought

I heard something out back." She refused to mention it was Maggie's dress she was working on at the time.

While Claudia had never considered herself terribly superstitious, there was no way she was telling a bride anything about her day connected with something so dark and ugly.

She sped through the story, the dead animals still creepy but also a disgusting dinner topic, then closed with the sheriff's visit and Hawk's arrival.

Hawk took over the story then, wrapping up the details. "The news traveled fast through town and I got there before the sheriff was gone."

"What did our old friend Bud Jeffries have to say?" Knox asked.

Although he was clearly shaken by the conversation and angry on her behalf, her brother also had no love lost with the town sheriff. His outright disdain was further proof of just how much he resented the Shadow Creek PD's handling of his son's kidnapping and anything related to the Colton family.

She knew it was going to inflame an already tense situation, but she also couldn't sit by and keep her family ignorant of the details.

"He made a few insinuations."

Other than his initial demands she and Hawk share the details, Mac had remained quiet during the telling. "What sort of insinuations?"

"He suggested a pile of dead rats could easily be rounded up in a farmer's field. That perhaps I was attempting to drum up sympathy or create an incident."

"Why would you do that?"

"Who knows?" Claudia threw up her hands, her dinner forgotten. "Maybe he thinks we're covering for Mom. Or that we want to win the town over to our way of thinking."

"Shadow Creek takes care of its own and a lot of people were mad with our mother's behavior and what it said to the town she called home for so many years." Thorne reached out and took Maggie's hand. "But people aren't blind or stupid. They know we're not responsible for her actions. And they know we've been as affected as anyone else. Cody's kidnapping." Thorne's gaze drifted to his father. "Dad's, as well."

"But Livia did those things," Joshua pointed out. "Directly or indirectly, each has her stamp."

Leonor took her husband's hand, the move so like Thorne's. "Then the sheriff should be concerned with protecting us instead of making empty accusations."

Heads nodded around the table, but it was Hawk that spoke first. "I agree with you all. But if the man I met is any indication, you'd all better be prepared to weather this storm without the support of the Shadow Creek PD."

Whatever she'd thought earlier when Jeffries was in her shop, never had she believed the man wouldn't do his job. "You think Jeffries, for all his small mindedness, would fail to do his duty?"

Hawk's gaze was grim, his eyes dim with concern. "I'm a man who likes to hedge my bets. And Sheriff Jeffries is a rather sizable long shot."

Chapter 9

Hawk hated the bleak notes that had colored the last half of dinner. Regardless of the danger that swirled around the Colton family, they were at Mac's house to celebrate Maggie and Thorne's upcoming wedding.

Instead, they'd all finished the dinner on a morose note that even Cody's happy chattering couldn't fully assuage. They grew even more morose when he encouraged Claudia to tell her family about Ben. She might not believe the man capable of the rats and possible stalking, but he wasn't taking any chances. If her family knew what to look out for, they were that much stronger as a united front.

It was only when they were back in the car, bumping down Mac's long driveway, that Hawk gave voice to the thoughts troubling him.

"Your family's dealt with a lot these past few months."

"Having a violent criminal for a mother will do that to people." The sentiment was unbearably bitter and once again, Hawk was struck by what Claudia had survived up to this point.

What her entire family had survived.

Knox and Allison had spent most of their adult lives separated, finally reunited before the near loss of their son. Leonor had suffered a terrible betrayal which had led to the *Everything's Blogger* article before she found Joshua. And Thorne and Maggie had barely begun a relationship with each other when Mac was almost killed out of misplaced vengeance. Claudia's life had a series of challenges they were just beginning to get to the bottom of and her brother River was nursing a world of hurt behind his wounds.

And then there was Jade.

"Where was your younger sister tonight—Jade, isn't it?"

"I asked Leonor earlier and she said that Jade declined, the last-minute invite not a match for her plans. She said she'll see us at the wedding."

As reasons went, it was more than fair. Dinner had come together quickly and it was a wonder they'd been able to confirm so many of them for the meal on such short notice. "That makes sense."

Hawk didn't give it another thought as he came to a stop at the end of the long driveway, waiting for a car to pass until he turned onto the farm-to-market road that led to Mac's ranch.

"If you buy that BS." Claudia's frown flashed in clear relief in the light of the passing headlights.

"Excuse me?"

"My sister has been out of pocket for weeks, one

excuse after another for all the reasons she can't spend time with us."

"Did something happen to her?"

"Besides bad taste in clothes and an obsessive love for her horses?" Claudia stopped and blew out a hard breath, her chin dropping toward her chest. "That's horrible. Really, truly horrible of me. And I don't mean it. Honest, I don't."

He'd pushed and prodded on so many other topics, Hawk was hesitant to go after something that sounded so personal. Yet it was obvious Claudia had a deep, recessed anger at her youngest sister.

"Didn't Mac raise you and Jade after your mother went to jail? I'd have thought the two of you were really close."

"I did, too. I guess I was wrong."

"Has something happened to her?"

"What hasn't happened to her? Happened to all of us? My mother imprinted her legacy on all of us and it's hard to run from that. But instead of running toward us, she's turned away."

As someone who had checked out of life—and who still had considerable guilt about checking back in—Hawk knew what it was to avoid those who most wanted to help you. He'd alienated Jennifer's parents after her death, unable to spend time with them and look them in the eye. On the few occasions they'd attempted to spend time together, the memory of Jennifer had hovered like a ghost around the periphery.

Or a demonic reminder of all he hadn't done to keep her safe.

"A lot has happened. Maybe Jade's trying to deal with it in her own way."

Claudia nodded, the light shrug of her shoulders rustling against the fabric of the passenger seat. "Maybe that's it."

"You could go talk to her. Before the wedding. See if there's anything she needs."

He'd never considered himself a particularly encouraging sort of fellow and he sure as hell wasn't anyone's psychotherapist. But he'd seen the Colton bonds tonight, forged in adversity along with a certain "screw you" attitude the siblings had used to connect them against the world. It would be a shame to ignore the depth of those bonds if there was an opportunity to help her sister.

"I haven't seen her very often since returning home."

"Think about it." *And disregard the fact that a man who absolutely refused to deal with the pain of his past is the one giving you advice.*

It was humbling, those dark thoughts that swirled in the background, waiting for the opportunity to rise up and knock him down a few pegs.

The drive to town passed quickly and in moments Hawk was pulling into the parking lot behind Honeysuckle Road. The small apartment above the shop where she lived had a bright light reflecting down on them and she'd left the light burning above the back door.

"Home sweet home."

"I'd like to walk you up."

Although he'd resisted the temptation earlier to see where she lived, after the rats, there was no way he wasn't walking her up to her home. If given the chance, he'd like to check the place out, too, to satisfy himself no one had intruded.

If it meant he'd later torture himself with images of her living space or the even more intimate ones of her bedroom, he could live with that.

Ensuring her safety was priority number one.

"I'd like that."

He cut the engine and the lights. The small parking lot was quiet, but hardly empty. There were still several cars parked behind the Whiskey Sour and Hawk could see a few people milling in pairs. There was a quiet safety in that, the idea that there were people around.

People who could come running if she screamed.

"Hawk?" She stood on the opposite side of the car, her gaze steady across the roof. "Everything alright?"

"Of course."

He came around the car and followed her up the wooden steps that led to her apartment. A burst of laugher echoed from the direction of the bar, eerie in the languid evening air.

They reached the top of the stairs, her keys jingling from her hands. "Thank you for everything tonight. You've been nothing but kind to me and my family."

"You're easy to be kind to. Your family, too. I enjoyed meeting everyone."

"That was entirely mutual. Everyone loved you."

The lightest breeze swirled around them, just enough to lift several strands of her hair, blowing them in his direction. He wanted to reach out and touch all that soft silk, fascinated with the way it formed a pretty blond halo in the moonlight.

Before he could act on impulse, she pushed open the door, leaving him at the threshold. The lamp she'd left on emitted a quiet glow from the corner of the living room. His training kicked in and Hawk moved in front of her, his focus on clearing each room. "Wait by the door."

"Oh, for goodness' sakes."

He shot her a smile over his shoulder. "Wait by the door, please."

A small, petulant moue marred her features, but she listened, folding her arms as she stood sentinel by the entrance.

The apartment was small, the living room and kitchen combination forming one oversize space, with a single bathroom and bedroom farther down the hall. She'd left several lights burning so it was easy to find his way, clearing each large, square room as he went. The apartment was neat—pin neat—until he hit the bedroom. It was there that he saw the distinct imprint of the woman he'd spent the day getting to know.

Color splashed the walls, matched to additional accents in the bedding. Clothes were spread across the bed, from dresses to summer blouses and slacks, to a discarded skirt. It looked like someone had exploded color everywhere.

In short, it looked like her. It was life and color and even in the mess he saw an active sense of motion that enticed and enchanted.

"You're taking an awfully long time in here." Claudia barreled through the door, almost slamming into his back.

"I'm just observing."

"What, exactly, are you observing? That I'm a horrible slob who can't put anything away?"

"Does it usually look like this?"

"No."

"I didn't think so."

She grew speculative. "Are you in here angling for a peek into my underwear drawer?"

"Tempting, but no. I was actually thinking how the rest of the apartment, while lovely, isn't a depiction of the real you. And then I walked in here and saw all the color and fabrics and life and I knew this was where you create."

"I do more work in my studio downstairs than in the apartment."

"You don't design here? Dream here?" He pointed toward the large sketch pad that filled her nightstand.

"Well, yeah, sure. But it's not like this is where I do my actual work."

He didn't agree but knew he was already on tenuous ground standing in her bedroom, so close to her he could reach out and touch her. Could run his fingers through that lush, gorgeous hair that beckoned a man to touch—to take. Could take her lips once more with his, his arms wrapped around her as they moved toward the bed.

No, Hawk cautioned himself. He had to tread carefully or risk losing himself in the arms of a woman who was quickly driving him mad.

"I'd better let you get some sleep."

"Are we going to go on Monday? To that center that does the DNA testing?"

"We can wait until after the wedding."

"I'd rather go sooner. Get it over with, even if I don't share the results until after the wedding. I'd like to know what I'm dealing with. What my family is going to have to deal with. Armed with that, I can begin to work toward an answer instead of living with all these questions."

"You're talking like it's a done deal. That you're Annalise's daughter."

"Aren't I?"

He marveled at how quickly she'd come around to the idea of her parentage. "You've accepted it more quickly than I'd have expected."

"You can't be that surprised."

"Oh?"

"You met my family tonight. You saw everyone. My sister Leonor is slender, with red hair and green eyes. I know you've not met her yet but Jade is dark and petite. Both have the same willowy frame as my mother."

"So that means you're not related?"

"It means I'm not a physical match. And while I don't disagree that body shape isn't a conclusive point of proof, it's always been the physically outward sign that reinforces how I feel on the inside. I've never fit. Not really."

"Your family loves you."

"And I love them. What I'm talking about isn't love or familial bonds or even an adverse reaction to my mother's behavior. It's the real, true feeling that I don't belong. That I'm not a fit."

Not a fit.

Was it possible she knew, in some innate way, that she wasn't the biological child of Livia Colton? Would it make this upheaval in her life a relief? Or further reinforcement of all the years she'd spent feeling different? Removed, somehow.

"You will get answers, Claudia. I'm determined to help you find them."

"And what happens once I do?"

He moved in then, unable to leave even the slightest

distance between them any longer. He bent his head, his lips brushing her cheek before they drifted up to press lightly against the shell of her ear. "Then I'll help you live with them, too."

I'll help you live with them, too.

Claudia still shivered, even with a weekend of distance, as she thought about Hawk's tender words. The light press of his lips against her ear. The gentle heat of his breath as he whispered the support and encouragement she needed to face whatever was still to come.

She'd sent him home, even as her body begged her to ask him to stay, and he'd gone easily enough. But it had only been after she'd closed her door, his low voice still echoing in her ear, that she'd finally understood what it was to want another.

One day, one year or one lifetime, she'd want Hawk Huntley through all of them.

She'd lain awake long into the night, thinking about him and the havoc he'd managed to create in a matter of days.

Was *still* thinking about him, after a long, restless weekend where she hadn't been able to settle, despite ruthlessly cleaning her already-immaculate stockroom, dithering over Maggie's dress and aimlessly drawing up several new designs.

How was it even possible?

Even as she asked herself that question, she couldn't deny the wild swings of raw emotion and odd hopefulness that wouldn't stop seesawing through her mind. Emotions he'd managed to unleash.

Be a Colton. Be a Krupid.

Find your birth family. Find proof Livia Colton was your birth mother.

Dismiss feelings for a man you've known less than a week. Cling to the one man who seems to have the answer to your future.

Over and over, around and around, those emotions swirled.

And as she'd struggled to understand what needed to happen next, small snippets of their drive home Friday night found a gentle place to land.

Didn't Mac raise you and Jade after your mother went to jail?

A lot has happened. Maybe Jade's trying to deal with it in her own way.

You could go talk to her. Before the wedding. See if there's anything she needs.

Once she pushed aside the crazy reality of her own life, the questions about Jade's had begun to haunt her. And by Sunday night, the subtle resentment she'd harbored had begun to fade, replaced with something far darker.

Was something going on with her sister?

Whatever self-righteous BS had kept her from finding out needed to end, and there was no better time than this morning to get started. She was already up and her sister was an early riser, awake at dawn to care for her horses.

Armed with an outfit she'd set aside for her sister as a possible choice for the wedding, Claudia got ready and headed for Jade's farm on the outskirts of Shadow Creek. She'd allowed her own anger and hurt that Jade hadn't spent much time with her since her return to Texas to dictate her behavior and it needed to stop.

This was her sister. Of the heart and of a lifetime, even if the blood part was questionable.

The sign for Hill Country Farms came up about a quarter mile before the formal turnoff and Claudia slowed to make sure she didn't miss it. There was a four-way stop up ahead which she remembered, but then the turnoff was slightly hidden if you weren't looking for it.

An old car pulled up behind her at the stop, the front bumper seeming a bit too close in her mirror. Claudia inched forward, then proceeded through the four-way, surprised when the car behind her didn't even wait its turn. It just sped up, close enough again to be on her tail.

She didn't want to miss the turnoff and knew it was soon, so she edged forward, speeding up slightly to let the person know she was paying attention and put on her blinker.

The indicator didn't help. Instead, the car behind her swerved slightly as it moved up even closer.

A dull panic crawled up her throat as Claudia accelerated a bit harder. "What the hell is wrong with this person?" Her muttered words ended on a high-pitched yell when the car tapped her rear bumper.

"Slow down!" She screamed it, waving her arms at the driver. Although she tried to keep her eyes on the road and still get a glance of the driver behind her, each time she looked the person seemed invisible, somehow. Between a thick visor hanging low and a weird shroud of some sort hiding the person from view, she couldn't get a handle on what the driver looked like.

Was it a man or a woman?

And what had them so worked up and angry on such a bumpy back road?

The road grew even bumpier—a fact Claudia remembered from her last trip there—but it didn't deter the driver behind her who sped up again, tapping her rear bumper harder this time.

Claudia accelerated a bit, frantically searching for the small turnoff that led to Jade. It was close. So very, very—

The car behind her slammed into her once again, the move hard enough to fishtail her car. She put everything she could into the turn of the steering wheel, attempting to turn herself out of the swerve without ending up in the narrow gully that ran along the side of the road for rain runoff.

Anger still burned inside of her, but the rapid realization that the person in the other car was deliberately trying to push her off the road added a slick layer of fear that coated her throat with acid.

The car behind her moved up closer and as she saw the acceleration in her rearview mirror, the entrance to Jade's flashed about twenty yards ahead on the right-hand side of the front windshield. Although her driving over the past eight years living in the city had been sporadic at best, Claudia had been raised driving over these roads.

She could *do* this, damn it.

She had to.

Carefully calculating the remaining distance to Jade's, she focused on the road and off the car behind her.

"Focus, Colton. Focus!"

On a hard acceleration, she gave herself the advantage of some momentum to head into her turn. The car shot forward, dirt flying beneath the wheels, just before she made a hard turn to the right. The tires scrabbled for purchase and she felt the car shudder as she bumped over the rutted edge where Jade's driveway entrance narrowed over the rain gully.

The car seemed to suspend momentarily and Claudia refused to look at the car behind her, instead bracing for a rear right impact when the driver continued to plow forward at high speed.

Blessedly, the hit never came.

That realization was met with another one before her eyes widened at what still lay before her. While her calculations into the driveway had been accurate, she hadn't accounted for the obstacle—a deep set of ruts grooved into the dirt driveway.

The car had too much momentum and it carried her over the grooved ditch, shuddering and shaking as her tires struggled to find purchase on the combination of dirt and rocks.

She slammed on the brakes, suddenly desperate to stop the forward momentum she'd so recently needed.

And felt herself lose control of both the brakes and the steering wheel as the car slid toward the edge of Jade's driveway, the ravine beckoning her over.

Chapter 10

"**Y**ou're okay. You're okay. You. Are. Okay." Claudia whispered the words to herself as her car hovered over the edge of her sister's driveway. She'd come to a complete stop, but her right front tire was off the edge of the dirt, dangling above the ravine that rimmed the property.

The acidic smell of burned rubber filled her nose and she gave herself a moment to simply sit there, her foot firmly on the brake.

Park. Put it into Park.

The thought whispered through her mind but she was too scared to make any move so she sat there, her foot unmoving against the brake pedal.

She fumbled for her purse on the passenger seat and her phone, shocked when she realized that her hands were shaking. Even more shocked to realize the foot still positioned over the brake pedal was attached to a leg that was gripped in trembling spasms.

Park!

Her mind screamed the word once more and something finally kicked in. Her phone slipped from her hand and she lifted her quaking fingers toward the gearshift.

What was she supposed to do?

The shaking intensified in her foot and a hard sob rose in her throat as she tried to remember how to shift gears.

Park, damn it!

She lifted her hand to the gearshift, depressing the mechanism and moving the car into Park. The rapid thump of her foot continued as she gently lifted it off the brake, settling into the narrow space between her seat and the pedals.

What was that about?

A hard heavy shout beside her head had her jumping, another scream on her lips when she realized it was her sister who stood on the other side of the driver's side window.

"Claud! Are you okay?"

Claudia nodded as a thick wave of relief washed over her. She fumbled with her seat belt, dragging what felt like a noose off of her body the moment the lock snicked open. Pushing on the door, she practically fell out of the car and into her sister's arms.

"Jade. Oh, Jade!" Her sister pulled her close, her slim frame a wall of strength and solidarity.

"Shh, sweetie. You're safe now. You're safe."

Claudia still shook intermittently as she wrapped herself in a blanket while sitting at Jade's kitchen table. Her sister had helped her turn off the car and lock it before they walked down the long driveway, Jade's horse, Feather, trailing in their wake.

"Are you sure you don't want me to call the cops?" Jade took the seat next to her, her hand immediately reaching over to cover Claudia's. "I know Sheriff Jeffries isn't exactly a friend, but he has a right to know what happens in his jurisdiction."

"No. Not yet." Her throat was raw, the same acid that had ridden her stomach creeping its way north. No amount of swallowing or hot tea could seem to ease the feeling.

"Can I call anyone?" Jade smiled, a small spark lighting her brown gaze as her fingers gave a friendly squeeze. "Your new boyfriend, perhaps?"

"News travels fast."

"It does when it's good, happy news that you have a hot boyfriend you've been hiding from all of us."

"You should have come to dinner Friday night. You could have met Hawk along with the rest of the family."

The smile faded from Jade's face, her dark eyes going flat as she pulled her hand away. "I had plans."

"I know. You seem to have a lot of them lately."

"Come on, Claudia."

Whether it was the events of the morning or the anxiety that had settled in when she'd realized something might actually be wrong with her sister, Claudia didn't know. But she was done sweeping this under the rug. "No, you come on. I've been back what, four months almost? And I've seen you a few times. We have family events and you don't come. When you do, you breeze in and breeze out so fast it's hard to know you were even there."

"I've been busy."

"We've all been busy. That's not an answer."

Jade stood up and walked her mug to the counter, pouring a fresh cup of coffee. "It's the only one I have for you."

"It hurts. Whatever it is you feel you can't share with us—with me. It hurts."

"I'm not hiding anything. I've just been busy, keeping the ranch afloat and all the work that comes with owning the farm. It's a big job. One I want, but one that keeps me busy all the same."

The DNA results might ultimately reveal she and Jade weren't sisters by blood, but one thing she didn't need a test for was to know they were both some of the most stubborn women in all of Shadow Creek. Mac had teased them both mercilessly about that fact.

Claudia liked to think it was a big reason she'd had the gumption to go to New York in the first place. And even now, with her return home, owning and running a business scared her silly but she was doing it anyway.

Stubborn Colton pride.

Jade leaned back against the kitchen counter and stared over her coffee mug.

"So are you going to tell me about Hawk? Maybe a few details like how his blue eyes would rival Paul Newman's or he's lean and strong and sexy like a movie star."

Claudia laughed in spite of herself or her desire to remain stern.

"Who called?"

Jade's eyes widened in mock innocence. "What do you mean, who called?"

"Was it Leonor, Maggie or Allison?"

Jade smiled, her expression straight-down-the-line

cat-in-the-cream. "The better question would be what order they called in."

"All three of them called?"

"Yep. Allison got me first. Leonor rang through on call-waiting. And Maggie texted me furiously, complaining she had a busy signal on my line."

"Wow. News really does travel fast in the country."

Jade leaned over and pressed a kiss to her forehead. "You have no idea, city girl. No idea at all."

Mac finished loading up his order at the Shadow Creek Mercantile and allowed his gaze to wander over toward Honeysuckle Road. The bright sign he'd helped Claudia with looked pretty as a picture winking out from the top of the store and he could see a few women laughing with each other as they walked inside.

The daughter of his heart had built something. Something strong and solid and sure. Something with roots.

How disappointing, then, that those roots might be ripped from her before they even had a chance to take purchase.

What on earth had Livia done?

He remembered those days when she'd escaped to Europe. He'd been panicked as all get out because Thorne was still small and he'd convinced himself that he might do something in his ignorance to harm the boy. But Livia had gone off and the children had needed tending and he knew damn right well Thorne was his son and not Wes Kingston's.

Their temperaments were the same. And the bow of his mouth that had noted a Mackenzie for five generations marked his son as surely as it marked him. He might have conceded to Livia's wishes and allowed her to give Thorne the Colton name—as she'd insisted for all her children—legitimizing his birth and his position in Shadow Creek, but he knew in his heart his son was a Mackenzie.

But Livia had made up yet another one of her stories. She twisted up the truth about what really went on over at La Bonne Vie, claiming any number of horrible lies about Wes, ultimately driving him away from his family.

Then she'd vanished.

When she said she was going to Europe, he'd assumed she went to the same places other rich women went. The French Riviera. London. Paris. Geneva. Wherever it was, she'd left and given them all some peace and he had been given a chance to raise his son.

To fall in love with being a father.

How humbling it had been to realize that River, Knox and Leonor had hungered for a father figure, too. And they'd clung to him as closely as Thorne did, his little ducks all in a row as they followed him around the ranch.

A year. He'd had a lone, wonderful year with his little ducklings, spending time with them. Teaching them. And raising them in ways nannies, tutors and house staff never could.

He'd raised them as his own and every time a nasty thought about Livia Colton entered his mind, all he had to do was look at those children and understand he was the one who'd been given a gift.

Then she'd returned with Claudia. She'd claimed a husband while in Europe, discarding him as easily as she'd done with every other relationship in her life. And just like that, Mac had fallen in love again.

Only this time, it was with a small, tiny package that sported angel-soft blond hair, big gray eyes and the sweetest smile he'd ever laid eyes on.

Oh, how he'd fallen in love. And in Livia's disinterest in her children and her home life, she'd given him two more opportunities to become a father, first with Claudia and then with Jade.

Nothing could keep him from the children.

Nothing ever would.

The bell over the door jingled as he walked into Honeysuckle Road. The shop was cool, the air-conditioning a welcome respite after the midmorning Texas heat. He gave himself a moment as his eyes adjusted to the interior light, the racks of clothing bright and vivid as his gaze scanned the room.

Oh, he was proud of her, his Claudia.

He'd been so sorry to see her leave for New York, but had been so proud of her and her work. So excited for her to make her way in the world, doing something she loved. That love had bloomed over and over, each email she'd sent home and each phone call she'd made signs that she was happy. Productive. Engaged in her life.

And then it had all stopped. A year before, the calls had slowed and the emails had gotten more sporadic. "I'm busy" had been the ostensible reason, but work had never kept her away before. Nor had she ever before characterized the work she loved to do as if it were a chore.

Mac had known something was wrong. And now he knew the reason why.

Ben Witherspoon.

He'd been damn near ready to take off after the coward last night. It was only Knox's and Thorne's steady hands—and whatever new trouble they were dealing with—that kept him firmly in Texas.

"Can I help you—" The soft voice faded out as Mac turned from his study of an artful display of summer dresses. "Oh, Mac. How are you?"

"Ma'am." He nodded his head. "I mean Evelyn. Hello."

He cursed himself for nearly fumbling her name. And wondered, not for the first time, how such a lovely, petite woman could tie his tongue up in knots.

Livia Colton hadn't even managed that all those years ago. He'd fantasized about Livia, but he'd never fully lost his head. And he sure as heck hadn't lost his ability to speak.

So what was it about this one sweet woman that made him think of apple pie and lazy afternoons sitting on his porch swing? She made him think of other things a gentleman had no business thinking about.

His hands full of her feminine curves. His mouth full of the taste of her. And coffee-flavored kisses the morning after...

"And how are you this morning?"

"Fine, thank you." He coughed long and low. "Just fine."

"If you're sure?"

He let his gaze roam around the shop once more, desperate for something to say that didn't sound as inane as he felt. "Brisk business this morning."

"This morning and every morning. We're usually rearranging racks by lunchtime there's such a rush to try things on. You should be so proud of Claudia." Evelyn's smile fell. "Of course you're proud of her. How silly of me."

"I am. And I understand. Is she here?"

"Why no." Evelyn's smile fell. "She texted me this morning. Said she was headed over to Jade's for a quick visit and if I could open the store."

"Oh. Well, good, then."

The news was a pleasant surprise and he wasn't about to argue with the idea of Claudia visiting with her sister. But why did something feel off about it?

Silly. He was being silly. Whatever challenges might be headed their way, her visiting Jade was a good thing.

"I'll just give her a quick call. I had a stop off at the mercantile and figured I'd say a quick hello."

"I'll also let her know that you stopped by."

"Thank you."

Evelyn hesitated for the briefest moment before she rushed on. "I look forward to seeing you at the wedding on Saturday."

"I'm delighted you can join us." He had that insane urge to clear his throat once more. "Will you, um, be bringing a guest with you?"

The words were like spikes on his tongue, but he forced himself to be civil. She no doubt had a string of men she could ask at any time to join her for an evening out and a wedding was one of the occasions when it was so much better to go with someone.

"It'll just be me."

"Well, then. You be sure to save your first dance for me, Evelyn."

Inappropriate and demanding. Yet as the words escaped, he found he couldn't call them back.

And then as her pretty brown eyes widened before filling with a smile, he was glad he hadn't.

"Why, I'd love to."

"You were what? Run off the road?"

"Practically, Hawk. I said I was *practically* run off the road." Claudia's voice was a tart echo in his ear as he slammed the lid down on his laptop and leaped to his feet.

He'd already showered, had breakfast in his room at the B&B and had been puttering for a short while on a few other cases until it was time to leave and pick up Claudia for the trip to the clinic outside of Austin.

Damn it.

He cursed himself as he jotted down Jade's address and the short list of directions, along with the admonition that her sister was hard to find on GPS, and disconnected.

He might not know Claudia Colton all that well, but he'd heard the fear layered beneath her words.

The woman was scared.

And right about now, so was he.

He followed the directions, racing through town toward her sister's ranch. The four-way stop she'd outlined came up about ten minutes later, and he slowed as he went through it, his focus on the final turnoff into Jade's driveway.

As he crept along the road, scanning for the entrance, he needn't have bothered. Claudia's car was visible at the edge of the Hill Country Farms property the moment he turned the last bend toward Jade's home.

The car sat at an odd angle, a front tire hanging off the edge of the driveway, dangling over the ravine that ran the edge of the property. The drop wasn't steep, but she'd have done some damage to the car if she'd fallen into it.

She'd have done even more damage to herself if she'd hit the ravine at any rate of speed.

The helpless rage that had gripped him as he'd cleaned up the mess of dead animals had nothing on that moment as he slowed to look at the car. Scratches and a deep dent lined the bumper, another indicator of what she'd shared on the phone.

But it was that dangling tire that kept him riveted to the spot, unable to look away.

Who had done this?

She hadn't been planning the trip to her sister's— their tense and loaded conversation about Jade on the way home from Mac's had been proof of that. So whoever had tried to run her off the road had followed her.

Which meant they'd been watching her.

Hawk drove on past the car and down the long driveway. The stretch was narrow and long, similar to Mac's but not as smoothed over. In fact, everything about Jade's property looked a bit like a work in progress.

Like a business that was in its early days instead of one that was well established. He understood that. Had lived it, building his own business from scratch, case by case. Maybe it was that knowledge that had him looking at the possibilities in Hill Country Farms instead of the work still to be done.

But even with that rose-colored outlook, it couldn't diminish the bone-deep fear that gripped him as he pictured the car hanging over the unpaved drive pitching toward the ravine.

A small, unassuming ranch house sat at the end

of the drive and he could see Claudia standing at the kitchen window. She waved at him as he drove up and the breath he'd held all the way to Hill Country Farms finally expelled from where it had lain, pent-up in his lungs.

She was alright.

Yes, he'd heard her voice on the phone. And yes, he knew if she had been really hurt they'd have called for help. But as he slammed the car in Park and raced for the house, all he could think about was getting her in his arms.

A weekend away from her had been torture. But the fear that had kept him company on the drive had simply shredded him.

"Hawk!"

She flew out the front door and launched herself at him. He held tight, his heart racing as images of what could have happened to her filled his mind's eye.

"You're okay." He whispered it over and over, the words part prayer, part reassurance.

"I'm fine."

"What happened? How did it—"

And then her mouth was on his and there were no more questions. No more worries of what could have been or what might have happened.

There was only her. Claudia.

Hawk put all he felt back into his response, his mouth flowing over hers as a waterfall of emotion spilled from deep within him.

He'd lost someone before. In the most awful, horrible, devastating of ways. He couldn't do that again.

Couldn't live through it again.

A heart wasn't made to go through that once, let alone open up and try a second time.

What was he thinking?

He was gentle as he held her arms, but pulled back from the kiss. They had an audience, anyway, and it wouldn't do to give in to something so deep.

And so very, very needy.

"Ma'am." He nodded toward the slim, smiling figure on the porch. The woman was pretty, but there was no mistaking her resemblance to Knox and Leonor. The arc of the cheekbones and the firm set of jaw.

"I think we're past the ma'am stage." She sauntered over, her smile welcoming as she pulled him in for a hug. "You can call me Jade."

Chapter 11

"Do you need to go back to the store or to your apartment?"

"No." Claudia's gaze hung on her car as Hawk maneuvered them out of Jade's driveway. He'd already called a tow shop in town to come deal with the vehicle, all while instructing her to reach out to Mac and then her siblings.

She'd resisted at first but when the threat had come down—swiftly—that it was Mac, then her brothers and sisters, or another call to Sheriff Jeffries—she acquiesced.

And had to admit he was right when it gave her the opportunity to control the story through its telling.

Mac had struggled the worst with the news, but they managed to reassure him when Hawk got on and relayed the details, as well. He'd also promised to get

them out of Shadow Creek for the day for their errand
to Austin and Mac had seemed subtly relieved.

So here they were, heading out of Shadow Creek,
on a mission to determine if her life was a complete
and total lie.

The back roads of Shadow Creek gave way to the
main drag through town before they were traveling
down better-used highways with signs indicated Austin was their next major stop.

"You know your way around."

"You navigate one small Texas town, you can navigate them all."

While she'd spent a long time away, she had to admit
he was right about that. She'd easily fallen back into
small-town living and had found it equally easy to
head for the highway into Austin or up to Waco if she
needed larger shopping or entertainment opportunities.

"I've always wondered why my mother chose
Shadow Creek. She's a city girl through and through."

"I bet it killed her to know you were in New York.
Living it up in the big city."

"I don't know if it did or not. I avoided visiting her
once I graduated."

Claudia thought back to those early days, shortly
after Livia was put away. Mac had dutifully driven
her up to Gatesville to visit. Jade hadn't wanted to go
and Mac hadn't pushed her, but Claudia had felt it was
something she should do. The good daughter routine.

"When was the last time you saw her?"

"I went the week before I graduated high school. I
told her I was going to New York and she'd given me
a few pithy remarks about watching out for myself and
being careful in the big city. More than anything, she'd

seemed distracted, her gaze following the goings-on in the room more than on me."

"Setting herself up. Reading the room."

Hawk's words were murmured, but something in them stuck. "What do you mean by that?"

"Your mother is the quintessential player. She's always looking for an angle and always on the hunt for the person who can give it to her. You were superfluous by then."

"Cheery thought."

"Actually, it sort of is. Staying off your mother's radar is the very best thing you can do."

"I guess I never thought about it that way."

While it was excellent advice, none of them knew when Livia would decide to make her presence known. Or when one of them would land on her radar for some twisted purpose only she knew. Cody's kidnapping was a perfect example of that. So was the way she'd watched Leonor from a distance.

Her mother was still out there. And while it would be wonderful never to see her again, Claudia didn't think her mother was done with any of them.

Or if they'd ever be free.

Regardless of what her DNA said.

"What happened before?"

"Before when?"

Hawk picked up speed as the highway opened up, his acceleration matched to the increased speed limit signs posted on the side of the road.

"Before, when you got to Jade's house. I was kissing you and I thought you were kissing me back and then you went somewhere."

"I think I was there. Right there with you, as I re-call. It was my lips on yours."

"Don't do that. Please don't do that. Don't pretend you don't know what I mean."

She knew it the moment she got through to him, by the hard clench of his jaw and the way his gaze nar-rowed on the road. "Alright."

"Did something upset you?"

"Several things, actually."

While she appreciated the honesty, the swift curse before he brought the car to a skidding halt was an aw-fully large surprise. The car slowed, a carefully con-trolled motion so at odds with what she'd experienced earlier that morning at Jade's, and once stopped, he shoved it into Park and turned toward her.

"I lost my wife. It was every terrible thing you'd think, then about a million more that no one braces you for."

She nearly responded, but it was that urgent need to speak that had her keeping quiet. He needed to say this—needed to get it out—and she had to give him the room.

"You know it would be horrible. Empirically you know losing someone you love will be the worst thing that could ever happen to you, and then it does happen and it's like your imagination was a child's, limited by all the things of the world you know nothing about. My wife died and there was nothing I could do or say or try or ask for that would make it better."

He stopped at that, a hard sob lodging in his throat.

"For four years I've lived with that. I've never got-ten used to it, but I've lived with it. And then somehow you find your way into my life, first with the picture in that blog post and then you, Claudia. It's like something happened. And everything—every damn thing—I'd shut down in order to cope, to survive, came rushing back to life."

"Hawk—" Emotions of her own lodged in her throat and all she could do was reach for his hand, take it with her own.

"I'm not ready for this. For whatever it is between us. I can feel it and I want it—you have to believe that I want it. But it scares me. And it has the power to end me. Do you get that?"

He turned his hand up beneath her palm, linking their fingers. "Do you get that?"

The tears that lodged in her throat stayed there in a hard lump and all she could do was nod her head.

But for the moment, there by the side of the road on a pretty summer morning, it was enough.

"That's really all there is to it?"

"That's all there is."

"Seems a bit anticlimactic relative to the expected results on the other side."

The pale woman Hawk had come upon at Jade's was nowhere in sight as he and Claudia walked out of the medical clinic. Instead, she'd been replaced with a woman who'd gotten some of the swing back in her step. Or perhaps "clip in her heels" was a better description, based on the summer skirt that currently had his attention. Along with the pretty long legs that peaked out from beneath the hem.

The DNA test had taken the promised five minutes—the paperwork had taken longer to fill out than the actual test—and they were already on their way.

FREE Merchandise is 'in the Cards' for you!

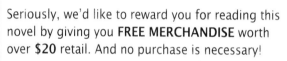

Dear Reader,

We're giving away FREE MERCHANDISE!

Seriously, we'd like to reward you for reading this novel by giving you **FREE MERCHANDISE** worth over $20 retail. And no purchase is necessary!

You see the Jack of Hearts sticker above? Paste that sticker in the box on the Free Merchandise Voucher inside. Return the Voucher today... and we'll send you Free Merchandise!

Thanks again for reading one of our novels—and enjoy your Free Merchandise with our compliments!

Pam Powers

Pam Powers

P.S. Look inside to see what Free Merchandise is **"in the cards"** for you!

W

e'd like to send you two free books like the one you are enjoying now. Your two books have a combined cover price of over $10 retail, but they are yours to keep absolutely FREE! We'll even send you 2 wonderful surprise gifts. You can't lose!

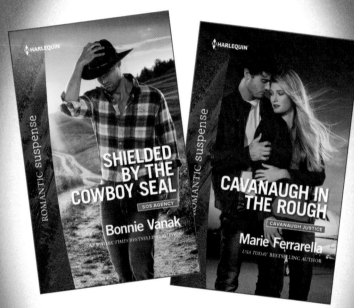

REMEMBER: Your Free Merchandise, consisting of **2 Free Books** and **2 Free Gifts**, is worth over $20 retail! No purchase is necessary, so please send for your Free Merchandise today.

Get TWO FREE GIFTS!

We'll also send you 2 wonderful FREE GIFTS (worth about $10 retail), in addition to your 2 Free books!

Visit us at:
www.ReaderService.com

YOUR FREE MERCHANDISE INCLUDES...

2 FREE Books **AND** 2 FREE Mystery Gifts

▶ Detach card and mail today. No stamp needed.

FREE MERCHANDISE VOUCHER

2 FREE
BOOKS
and
2 FREE
GIFTS

Please send my Free Merchandise, consisting of
2 Free Books and **2 Free Mystery Gifts**.
I understand that I am under no obligation to buy
anything, as explained on the back of this card.

240/340 HDL GLTJ

Please Print

FIRST NAME

LAST NAME

ADDRESS

APT.#   CITY

STATE/PROV.   ZIP/POSTAL CODE

Offer limited to one per household and not applicable to series that subscriber is currently receiving.
Your Privacy—The Reader Service is committed to protecting your privacy. Our Privacy Policy is available
online at www.ReaderService.com or upon request from the Reader Service. We make a portion of our mailing
list available to reputable third parties that offer products we believe may interest you. If you prefer that we not
exchange your name with third parties, or if you wish to clarify or modify your communication preferences, please
visit us at www.ReaderService.com/consumerchoice or write to us at Reader Service Preference Service, P.O. Box
9062, Buffalo, NY 14240-9062. Include your complete name and address.

NO PURCHASE NECESSARY!

® and ™ are trademarks owned and used by the trademark owner and/or its licensee.
© 2016 HARLEQUIN ENTERPRISES LIMITED.   Printed in the U.S.A.

RS-517-FM17

Perhaps it was the earlier emotion that had spilled over both of them at the start of the drive. Or maybe it was just the freeing feeling of getting out of Shadow Creek for a few hours, but he felt lighter than he had in days.

And more prepared for whatever his future held.

"What's that look for?" She eyed him sideways as they headed for the car.

"I was thinking about your shoes."

One lone eyebrow rose at his comment. "My shoes?"

"Less the style and more the volume. Just how many pairs do you own?"

Her voice was breezy as she slipped on a pair of sunglasses. "I have no idea. I lost track a long time ago."

"Come on. It's not like counting decimal places after Pi."

"Oh, it's far better. But seriously, I don't keep count. It's a number that's always going up and down anyway so why bother?"

He pulled the passenger door open for her and shook his head as those most excellent legs swung into the passenger seat. "Don't mistake my message. I'm more than appreciative of their effectiveness. I just don't understand how you can lose track."

She clucked her tongue and laid a hand against his cheek. "Sweet, silly man."

He gave those long, smooth legs one last, longing glance before closing the door. Who was he to argue with her logic?

He climbed into the rental car and hit the ignition. "Do you have to be back to the boutique?"

"No. Evelyn's working today and she's training a

part-time associate we just hired, so I'm good for a while."

"How about we play hooky from Shadow Creek for another few hours and go get some barbecue in Austin?"

"I'm in."

He headed for the interstate, already imagining the food at one of his favorite places off of Congress Street. They weren't too far outside of downtown but Austin's legendary traffic had them at a standstill as they crept toward the city.

"At the risk of putting a sour taste in your mouth before you eat the food of the gods, why don't you tell me a bit more about this morning? What happened with the other driver?"

"It was awful. He came out of nowhere just as I neared Jade's farm."

"You didn't see anyone before then? Or anyone during your drive?"

"No. That was the odd part. Once I got off Main Street I saw no one. Besides, it was early so I think I'd have known if there was anyone else around, but I don't remember seeing another car. And then this guy just came out of nowhere."

"At the four-way stop?"

"Yes. That's when I noticed him first. The car was too close while parked behind me at the stop sign. I had that claustrophobic feeling you get when you look in your rearview mirror and the person feels like they're on top of you."

Hawk considered her words as he maneuvered into another lane. "You keep calling the driver a he. Was it a man?"

"Yes, it had to be. Well, now. Wait."

"What do you remember?"

"That's the weird part. I did try to see the person. The view's not perfect, but you can almost always see the person who's driving behind you when you look out your rearview mirror. And I couldn't see this person. The visor was pulled down low which was the first block, but then there was this sort of drape up."

"What sort of drape? How did the driver see?"

"That was what was so odd. I could see a slit in it of some sort, but it was like they deliberately concealed their face." She waved a hand. "That's not entirely right. I knew there was a person there, but it was like there was just an additional layer of something blocking the view. Almost like a thin material."

"Could you describe it?"

"That's the problem. I know what I saw, but I don't know how to explain it. It's like I knew there was someone in there, but the details were just too hazy to define."

"We can work with this."

"How?"

"Whoever tried to hurt you followed you this morning. All we need to do is get some film off of any camera in town, on a building or on the streetlights."

The heavy indrawn breath had him glancing over, away from the mess of traffic. "Followed me? This person followed me?"

The sheer insensitivity of his words had him reaching for her hand. "I thought you knew. That you understood that part. That's why they showed up out of nowhere. Because they followed you to Jade's."

"I didn't make the connection."

Connection. *Connection.*

What was the connection here?

He'd been so damned focused on Claudia's ex-boyfriend or on Livia that he hadn't considered who else might be involved.

"What have the authorities uncovered so far about your mother's prison break?"

"Why does it matter?"

"Hear me out. I think we may be looking at this all wrong. Think about all that's happened since she broke out of prison. Cody was kidnapped by one of your mother's associates."

"Right." Claudia nodded. "But the man is dead and by Livia's hand, no less."

"And then there's Leonor. She mentioned something last night there at the end of dinner after we told them all about the dead rats and the conversation drifted to Livia and her choices. She said that she believes she saw your mother in her hospital room."

"After Livia took care of the other man trying to hurt Leonor, killing him, too."

"Don't you see the pattern?" Hawk asked. "Your mother is tying up loose ends."

"And I'm a loose end?"

The horrified look negated any of the good feelings that had carried them to the car. When they'd left the clinic, he'd sensed a renewal in her spirit. Like the search for answers—real, tangible answers—would help them move forward.

But now?

The fear was back and along with it that frustrated anger that Livia Colton seemed to generate in all who knew her.

"You're not a loose end, but her known associates are. What if they've ganged up and decided to harm her children as a chance to get back at her?"

"But why would anyone think that? You said it yourself, when I described going to see my mother in prison. She uses people for what they can give her. How they can advance whatever agenda she has. Her children don't have that. Even if you put aside the fact she never cared all that much for any of us except maybe Leonor, we're grown adults. It's hard to see us as objects of revenge."

"But the people she's worked with don't know that. They think she's the loving matriarch of the Colton clan."

Disbelief was layered beneath her questions, but as they talked it out, Hawk heard Claudia begin to come around.

"What we need to do is find out who is still at large from her pool of known associates. Do they know who broke her out of jail?"

"A few guards were the ones to help with the actual jailbreak. But there are others. Knox is convinced she has a judge in her pocket and Joshua has been quick to verify the same with his FBI contacts."

"It goes that high?" Whatever he'd imagined about Livia Colton's influence and network, it hadn't been contacts like that.

"Joshua's convinced there's another one. Someone big," Claudia added. "Someone who would have the influence and authority to get a lot of folks to look the other way for a while."

"How did she build something like this? A network this large means people will talk."

"Money. Lots and lots of money."

"But her money's been tied up for over a decade. La Bonne Vie, for example. Where's the money there?"

"It's there in the land and the house itself."

"So why hasn't anything been done with it?"

"The Treasury Department is the one who confiscated it. I suppose they have their reasons."

Hawk shook his head, annoyed with himself that it had taken so long to put the pieces together. Was his police work that rusty? Or had he been looking in all the wrong places? While he technically was working for the Krupids, not uncovering Livia Colton's extensive crimes, understanding how Livia made her money would lead him to the answers he needed. For the Krupids and for Claudia and her family.

"Claudia. Think about it. She went to jail and all her belongings were confiscated. Yet the feds have been willing to leave a valuable piece of property sit empty, just dying on the vine."

"Okay, I suppose."

"Her empire has continued to flourish, even though she's been behind bars."

"What empire?"

"The one that helped her break out. The same one that has given her a place to hide now that she's free. There's a reason she keeps showing up. And why trouble keeps following you and your sisters and brothers."

"Now you've lost me again. What do a pile of dead rats and someone trying to run me off the road have to do with my mother's jailbreak?"

"It's all part of the same. She's going after her network and her network's trying to fight back. And when people are desperate, they'll use anything at their disposal."

"You mean coming after me and my siblings?"

"That's exactly what I mean."

Once again, Claudia tried to shake off the sheer roller coaster of emotion that seemed to haunt her at the very thought of her mother. Or her adoptive mother. Or whatever the heck Livia ultimately ended up being to her.

Known associates and criminals out for revenge? Outcomes that could only end in the murder of one human being by another.

Was this the reality of Livia's life?

Because regardless of what she personally called her or how she thought of her, Livia Colton was at the heart of everything that was happening to her and her brothers and sisters.

So even with that knowledge and reasonable understanding, why did Hawk's theory feel off, somehow?

It would be so easy to blame her mother for what was happening. But it didn't fit with the incidents to date.

"How do you explain the dead rodents behind my store?"

"A gross and menacing way to grab attention."

"Risky, too. Who knew I'd be in the back of the shop at that moment to hear the gunshot? And what if one of the other proprietors had showed up first? I realize it's likely it would be me, but I do share that area with other businesses. All I'm suggesting is that it's something of a bet to assume I'm going to be the one to walk out and discover that pile."

"So it's a way to throw us off the scent."

Us.

Something warm and delicious shot through her at his use of the word *us*. And how had that happened?

She knew her recent definition of *us* was tainted by Ben's behavior, but was it possible she actually had an *us* to cling to with Hawk Huntley?

He certainly seemed dedicated. Even his zealous approach to finding Annalise Krupid's lost child had faded in the reality of her and her family's situation. He seemed genuinely focused on helping her. And, by extension, her sisters and brothers, too.

But what if they were beyond help?

The question whispered through her mind, insidious as it swirled like mist, forming and reforming into a dismal fog.

Livia Colton had manipulated everything in her world, ultimately for her own benefit. Even now, long after they'd all believed themselves safe from her, she pulled strings, dancing everyone to a tune only she knew.

They were puppets—pawns in her game—and sadly, Claudia had to acknowledge to herself, none of them knew the rules.

Chapter 12

The barbecue was as good as promised and even a half-hour wait for service hadn't diminished the product. In fact, Claudia thought as she resettled her napkin in her lap and eyed her brisket sandwich for another bite, the wait had only enhanced the experience. That deliciously dark, woodsy scent permeated the air and the rich flavor hovered on her tongue like a fine wine.

"Bet you can't get this in New York." Hawk lifted his own sandwich to his mouth and took a large bite.

She watched, fascinated by the long, strong column of his throat as he swallowed, then again as he took a sip of his sweet iced tea.

Had she actually stooped so low to watching a man eat and liking it?

Yes, came the resounding cry of something wonderfully feminine deep inside of her.

Goodness, the man fascinated her. From eating to kissing, to conversations about their past, nothing was off-limits. Nothing escaped her interest or notice.

"How'd you get into fashion? I know you love it and you're always well put together, but what was the thing that pulled you in?"

"Pulled together?"

"Yeah." He lifted his own napkin to his lips, catching a small dab of barbecue sauce that lingered on the corner of his mouth before his gaze met hers. All warm and beautiful blue; Claudia would swear a woman could fall into their depths and never climb back out. "You're like something out of a magazine, yet you're not untouchable."

He wadded his napkin, then reached for several more out of the metal dispenser on the table between them. "That's not quite right. *Untouchable* isn't the word. Unreal. That's better."

"Thank you. I think?"

"Trust me, it's a compliment. Like yesterday, with Cody."

"When did Cody and I discuss fashion?"

"You didn't. But there you were, all put together and looking glamorous at Mac's and he runs up to you, filthy and smelling like horse."

"He's perfect. And there's no resisting one of his hugs. Besides, why would I want to? They're as perfect as he is."

"Little boys are hardly perfect, especially not when they're covered head to toe in whatever it is they've been rolling around in. But you didn't notice any of it. You just pulled him in close."

"I love him."

"It's nice. And it's a sign that you don't take fashion as an excuse not to be real. I like it. That's all."

"Well, thank you."

"You're welcome."

He dived back into his sandwich and Claudia wondered if she'd ever received such a lovely compliment before. The notice of her—and more, the notice of her behavior—was sweet.

And it made her feel like he saw her. All the way down to what lay beneath the accessories and the clothes and whatever color happened to catch her fancy that day.

Ben hadn't seen it. And if she were honest, the men she'd dated prior to Ben hadn't, either. She was a doll, dressed up and perfect when they were together. There'd been very few occasions when she'd been comfortable pulling off that facade and letting the real Claudia come through.

Yes, she had a true and deep love for fashion. A passion for beauty and the art of putting pretty things on to wear. But no matter how much she loved it, those were still just things. They didn't replace her family. Or her hopes and dreams. Or the hugs of one small little boy who held her heart as surely as the next breath she took.

She wasn't window dressing and not many people beyond her family understood that. So it was nice to know that Hawk did. It was even nicer to hear the words.

"Huntley!" The words boomed from somewhere over the back of her head and she saw Hawk's gaze alight, then grow bright as he quickly stood and extended his hand.

"Andrew!"

She turned in her seat and came face-to-face with a bullish man with military-short hair and a big smile.

"Andrew. Let me introduce you to someone." Hawk came around the table and stood by her side. "Claudia Colton, please meet Captain Andrew Radner, Houston PD."

They exchanged handshakes and Hawk extended the invitation to join them.

"I'd love to, but I'm in line over there with a few of my colleagues. We're up here in the capital for a statewide training session and were able to sneak over for some good grub during our lunch break."

"This place is the best. In fact, come to think of it, you're the one who hooked me on this place for a training session many years ago."

Claudia was content to watch the byplay for a few minutes, their friendship obviously one forged in strong bonds.

A few moments later, Andrew clapped a hand on Hawk's arm, even as his comments were directed at her. "I haven't been successful in winning Hawk back over to rejoining the police department, but it looks like maybe this PI gig is starting to work out for him."

They said their goodbyes and she watched Andrew walk back to the line. For all his strength and heft, the man had an almost regal bearing in him.

He's a guardian. A watchdog.

The thought struck, clear as a bell, and it had her turning toward Hawk as she made the same connection.

That protector personality, so strong and sure, covered both men like the finest suit. It was what made them so likable and so easy to trust. More, it was the juxtaposition between Hawk and Sheriff Jeffries she hadn't been able to put her finger on the day before that now made perfect sense.

Bud Jeffries saw his badge as a shield, allowing him to impart judgment and criticism on all who crossed his path. A tool that he believed made him "better than," instead of understanding what the badge truly promised. Service to others.

Dedication and commitment to the truth.

Hawk had that, even as someone in private practice.

But it was only as she watched, his gaze wistful as he stared at the captain and the small group of men and women he stood in line with, that Claudia finally understood.

Once, Hawk had been a part of that. Had worn the badge and given his life in the service of others. Only he didn't do that any longer. He'd relegated his gifts and his time and his life to cases that didn't have much of a chance.

Yet one more thing that died along with his wife.

She'd bet Honeysuckle Road on it.

The cut-up newspaper lay around the feet of the Forgotten One, squares culled neatly from its pages. The tactic was an old one, but surprisingly effective as the work came to life on the plain sheet of white paper. The old-fashioned smell of rubber cement was a reminder of childhood, but the neat pasting of letters had a precision no child could accomplish.

The path had been laid out, the endgame in sight. The trap was set and patience was required for its ultimate fulfillment.

There'd been no patience this morning.

The opportunity to end things early—to drag the life from Claudia Colton's body as surely as her mother had dragged the life from another child—had presented itself and was taken. But it was a premature act, miscalculated and ultimately ineffective.

There was no room for those sorts of mistakes, especially as more and more people came to Claudia's aide. Even the sheriff had come to lend her a hand, and the rumors around Shadow Creek were that the Coltons had a disdain for law enforcement that couldn't be righted. A belief they were above the law, passed from mother to child.

The Forgotten One knew that.

Knew the depths of that depravity.

Worse, knew the horrors the Colton family was capable of.

Sin came from the mother. It was passed down in the womb and a stain like that could never be righted.

That was why it must be blotted out.

The drive into Shadow Creek had gone a bit faster once they cleared Austin traffic and by early afternoon, Hawk was passing the Welcome to Shadow Creek sign that dominated the entrance to town. It had been a surprise to see Andrew, but good. It was always good to see Andrew.

The one man who'd remained steadfast in his belief in him, long after Hawk had lost his own.

"Andrew seems like a good sort."

"The best."

"You miss him."

"I do. He's a good guy. And he was good to work

for. Honest. Solid. You don't realize how rare that is until you don't have it."

"He sounds like a wonderful mentor."

"That he was. He's also an ass kicker. You don't get to be a part of his department without knowing your stuff and being on point. Always."

"Then I'm forced to repeat *my* point. You miss him."

Claudia's assessment rubbed uncomfortably against him and he tried to shake it off. They'd had a good day—an emotional one, sure—but one that didn't have room for idle hurts and ill-considered responses.

"How long has it been since you worked for him?" she asked.

"I left his team about three and a half years ago."

"Have you considered going back?"

"The PI gig isn't so bad. I make my own hours and I pick my own cases. And I still have my contacts. My network. Private investigation is still detective work." Even if it wasn't the same damn thing as catching a case, working it with a partner and closing it down as one more tick mark in the victory column against the scum of the world.

But he didn't say those things. Instead, he kept his eyes on the main drag through town and navigated around a small road crew as they dug a hole through what had to be blazing hot asphalt in the middle of the afternoon.

"Now there's a job I have respect for. I have to imagine very few days of the year provide perfect weather conditions, yet they take on the job. From brutal heat to bitter cold to spring storms that light up the sky. It's impressive."

"Hmm" was all the response he got. Or thought he

was going to get until she added, "So's your ability to change the subject."

"My what?" She'd waited to drop that little bomb until he was at the main stop sign in town and he turned to face her. "That's harsh."

"And here I thought it was truthful."

"It's something you know nothing about."

"Oh no? Enlighten me, then. Because you keep suggesting there's something between us. And I'm hardly arguing with you because I feel it, too. Yet you refuse to answer some of the most basic questions."

"We haven't known each other that long."

"I might be persuaded to buy that, except you're one of a handful of people, three of whom are medical professionals, who know I likely have a different mother than the one who raised me. This—" she waved a hand between them "—whatever's going on between us. It doesn't play by the rules because there are no rules. So stop tossing them at me as an excuse to keep me in the dark."

A convenient power play and one designed to get him to let his guard down. But how did you remove something that had become such a part of you it had practically welded itself to your personality? He wasn't a cop any longer. Nor was he a husband. Both of those things had nearly killed him and she wanted to talk about them as if they were as simple as discussing the weather.

Seriously?

The knot in his stomach that had nothing to do with eating a pound of barbecue wound itself a bit tighter, until he was nearly mad with the bitterness that seemed to never have a place to fully land.

That never had a place to go.

Until now.

"I don't want to discuss this."

"I'm not necessarily fond of discussing Livia Colton, but I did. I have. Don't I deserve this?"

"Deserve what? To rip me apart? To watch me bleed in front of you?" The words ripped from his chest, all black bitterness and white-hot anger. They raced through him, a fire in his blood that couldn't be quenched.

That refused to be quieted.

"Is that what you want?"

"No."

"Are you sure? Because I'm pretty sure those actually *are* the questions you want answers to." He tore into the parking lot behind her store and threw the car into Park, his tires squealing against macadam. The air conditioner had blasted throughout the ride back, comfortable enough for the drive, but he now found he needed more.

More cool.

More air.

More time.

Only best as he could tell, Claudia Colton wasn't going to give him any.

Nor was she going to back down.

"I don't want answers to hurt you. Nor do I want them to be nosy. I want to know the truth. I want to understand what's brought you to this moment. Damn it, Hawk, I want to know why you're here." Her voice had risen with each word she spoke, part demand, part plea.

And still, he held out.

How did you put into words your greatest failure?

Was it really as simple as screwing up the courage and telling the one person you were already halfway in love with that you didn't deserve them?

That their heart was safer far away from yours.

That the cold, empty life you'd been living—the one that was all black-and-white and bereft of color—was something you needed to remain trapped in as punishment?

It wasn't rational, nor was it simple. But it was terribly, horribly honest.

"My wife was brutally murdered four years ago and I did nothing to stop it."

Murdered.

The implications hung there, dark and twisty, hovering in the car like wraiths. Claudia hadn't responded with words during his outburst, but her body language said everything. Her pretty pale skin had gone paler, a sickly white that made her gray eyes stand out in harsh relief. Her mouth had dropped open before she closed it, the move repeated a few times as she processed his words.

And bastard that he was, he kept on.

"She was mistreated and abused before being killed and left dead in a field outside the city limits."

"Hawk. Oh, Hawk." Claudia reached out for his hand but he pulled his back and slapped it on the steering wheel, seeking some neutral place to hold on to.

"Don't." It was the sympathy that nearly broke him. Hers. Others' before. The piteous glances and the "I'm sorry"s. People were so full of both, he'd long stopped acknowledging them. Had long stopped allowing them to burrow beneath his skin.

He didn't deserve it and he sure as hell didn't want it.

What he wanted was to be left alone, with his dark thoughts and his empty life.

"Was her killer found?"

"No. Bastard disappeared after such a heinous act, never to be discovered. I followed every lead and when those turned up nothing, I dug for more. I hunted everywhere I could, determined to find justice."

"Only none came." Claudia put the truth into words.

"Not a single damn bit of it."

Images of Jennifer's smiling face filled his mind. The big curls that framed her face and the dark brown eyes that had been so expressive. She loved to laugh. She'd had a zest and a love of life that had been infectious.

He hadn't pictured her like that in a long time. Most of the time, when he did see her, his mind conjured up the picture of her at the end. Her body swollen with the ravages of death and the additional brutality of how she'd died.

He hadn't pictured her laughing in a very long while.

Too long.

"How can you say you did nothing to stop it? You can't honestly think you're responsible. There's a killer who is responsible for this. A depraved, horrible person who committed terrible acts."

His earlier words winged back at him but it was the gentle hand, pressed to his shoulder, that offered one more kindness he didn't deserve. Especially when that touch filled him with such longing.

How could he talk about his wife when he wanted the woman sitting next to him? Jennifer's death wasn't some story to be pulled out of a mental box, shared and then snapped closed. A horrifying little anecdote to get under Claudia Colton's skirt.

"Because I am responsible. I made vows to her, before God and our family and friends. I also made a vow to the police department to protect and serve. I did none of that."

"Protecting and serving, just like loving and cherishing, don't apply here." Her hand never lifted from his shoulder. "Surely you can see that."

"I know what I see. It haunts me every night and it tells me every way I've failed. You don't get to tell me different."

"I'm not telling you different. I'm trying to make you understand this isn't your fault. You won't convince me of it, Hawk, no matter what you think. No matter how many times you've told yourself this version of the story, you have to know it's not true."

He'd seen her fire. Her inner light that drew him toward her as surely as he drew breath. Claudia wasn't a woman to back down. Nor was she someone content with accepting things, just because someone told her to.

"Then our time is finished here because you can't change my mind. I've spent the past four years living with the poor choices I made. Jennifer died because I wasn't there to keep her safe."

"Jennifer died because there are horrible people in the world. People who want nothing more than to hurt others and take what they want."

"Then he succeeded. And I let it happen."

Chapter 13

Claudia fixed herself a cup of tea and wondered how the day could have gone so wrong. It had obviously gotten off to a bad start with the drive over to Jade's, but that had paled in comparison to what had transpired on the drive back from Austin.

Hawk's wife had been murdered?

She still struggled to wrap her head around the information, but the internet search she'd run the moment she got back to her apartment had proven the truth of it all. She could practically recite the opening line of the Houston newspaper article and could see the image of Jennifer and Hawk, smiling on their wedding day, from the photo that had been included in the article.

How did a person survive that?

And how many people lived with the same horrors in their own lives because of something her mother had done to one of their loved ones?

That thought had settled in shortly after Claudia had first read the newspaper article and had been a strange accompaniment to the information Hawk had shared. Claudia had asked herself those questions over and over, actual answers nowhere to be found.

But pending the outcome of the DNA test, it was highly possible her very own mother and grandparents had been additional victims of Livia's machinations.

A young woman sold into the sex trade, smuggled out of Russia. A family so desperate for answers they'd withstood numerous scams but continued their search.

She'd paced the length of her apartment, trying to wrap her head around the details but unable to give her thoughts any firm place to land. Unable to truly reconcile the haunting image of Jennifer Huntley lying dead in a field and Livia Colton's brutal approach to all things illegal.

Yet were they really that far apart?

Hawk's wife might have been the victim of apparently random violence, but that made it no less horrifying than something premeditated. Or worse, a crime that was the result of careful planning and hidden behind an architecture of obedience and cultured civility.

Civil?

Just the crimes Livia had been convicted of had smacked of the worst, most heinous abuse. And those were just the things she'd been tried for.

In some ways, wasn't that actually worse?

As horrible as it was, Jennifer was the victim of a wretched, horrifying attack, played out as a crime of opportunity. Claudia meant no disrespect or insensitivity, but there had been an end to Jennifer's suffering. Hawk couldn't find solace, but his wife had, her pain at an end.

What about the women sold into Livia's sex trafficking ring, ripped from their homes at young ages and treated like property? What about the minions kept in Livia's pockets? The government officials paid to turn a blind eye and, if they didn't, putting their families at risk?

Ultimately, it didn't matter, Claudia knew.

She was grasping at straws as some way of convincing Hawk that he needed to look at his wife's death differently. That he wasn't responsible, no matter how he tried to convince himself otherwise.

But it was an exercise in futility. In the end, all that mattered was someone you loved was gone. And for the ones still living, finding equilibrium and balance and an ability to rejoin the world was often just not possible.

"I love it. It's perfect. So perfect."

Maggie beamed before the three-way mirror Claudia had hung in the back of the studio. She'd helped her future sister-in-law into her dress and then gently helped her stand on a small stool so she could finalize the measurements at the hem and make any needed adjustments.

Claudia had arrived early to set up the studio and prep before Maggie's arrival and instead, had barely had time to start the coffee. Maggie had sailed in, flush with excitement and brimming with barely contained energy.

The woman wore her pregnancy beautifully and, just as Claudia had expected, Maggie wasn't a "house." She had gained a few more inches in the bust than

Claudia had anticipated and she'd already marked down a few quick measurements.

"Oh, and the bustle!"

Maggie's exclamations pulled her from her notes and Claudia rubbed at her eyes to wipe out the grit that didn't want to fade this morning.

"It's gorgeous. And it gives the dress an entirely different look."

"Two dresses in one. Oh. Oh, wow." The tears that had been intermittent company since Maggie's arrival welled up again and Claudia helped her off the small stool so she could stand on terra firma when she blew her nose.

"Shh, now. It's okay."

"It's more than okay. And I'm so happy. And we're having a baby and I'm in love with Thorne. Mac and Thorne are even building my dream house, right there on the property." Another hard sob hit Maggie and Claudia led her to one of the chairs at the small break table so she could gather herself.

"Here. Let's settle this over you." Claudia added a drape over the front of the bodice to avoid the tears and the possible addition of Maggie's makeup, then handed her a few more tissues.

"I am sorry for the waterworks but it's just a little overwhelming at times. I'm happier than I've ever been and I've got a stew of hormones racing through my blood. It's the weirdest thing to keep crying pots of tears over all that happiness."

"Weird and absolutely wonderful," Claudia reassured her.

"The hormones have made me strangely perceptive, too." Maggie took one last sniff and turned watery eyes on Claudia. "So why don't you tell me what's going on?"

"Nothing's going on."

"Oh, girlfriend, it's so not nothing it isn't even funny. So come on and tell me, or I'll play the whiny pregnant woman card and mix endless tears with nasty outbursts demanding you get me biscuits and gravy at the Cozy Diner. Take your pick."

Since Maggie's eyes had taken on a diabolical glint beneath the tears, Claudia figured she'd better listen up. Even with that knowledge, she tried one more approach.

"You're wearing your wedding dress. It would hardly be fair for me to say anything in front of it to make it sad."

"It's a wedding dress designed to begin a marriage. One that will be as filled with happiness as it will be with challenges. I think this dress can handle it. And if it can't, I've got no business wearing it."

She loved Maggie—had loved her from the first time they'd met. But in that moment, Claudia understood what a gift this woman was to her brother. Warm and kind, funny and loving, Maggie knew what it was going to take to forge a lifetime with Thorne. And wasn't that something special?

"How'd you get so smart?"

"Natural talent." Maggie laughed before reaching for another tissue. "And now I'd also add experience. What Thorne and I went through to find each other. Almost losing Mac. All we've overcome together makes me that much more sure we have to keep that commitment and that focus on building our future."

"What if something had happened? Would you blame yourself?"

The warm smile faded as Maggie leaned forward over the table. Or as far forward as she could go with her stomach providing a barrier. Her hand held the drape in place but her eyes were flat and focused. "What's this all about?"

The very last person she wanted to have this conversation with was a pregnant woman about to walk down the aisle. So it was strange to realize that Maggie was actually the most perfect person *to* have the conversation with.

She understood the risks of loving. And she'd experienced the dangers of loss all too recently.

"Hawk's a widower going on four years now."

Maggie reached for the box of tissues, pulling out a fresh one for herself, then one for Claudia. As she took hold of the soft material, Claudia felt the overwhelming love and acceptance from her future sister-in-law in that simple gesture.

"Tell me all about it," Maggie said.

And as she started the tale, Claudia knew she had the loving support to share all she'd learned.

The Cozy Diner was doing its usual brisk business when Hawk walked in, hungry for breakfast. He'd skipped dinner the night before, his eyes wide-open and focused on the ceiling above his hotel bed. He'd fought sleep—or it had fought him—until somewhere around four, when he'd drifted off.

The dreams that came when he finally did sleep

were what he'd have predicted. Images of Jennifer running through the field where her body had been discovered, trying to elude her captor. Her inert form out on a slab in the morgue. And the clumps of hair they'd found at the ultimate scene of her death. It was all familiar, the nightmares his steady companions for the past four years.

So it was odd, at the end, when the nightmare had shifted. The soft strands of hair he held in his hand slipped from his fingers, caught on the breeze to dance and flutter just out of his reach.

When he'd looked up, he'd seen Jennifer smiling, dancing before him with her arms outstretched. She wore her wedding dress before it morphed into the black sheath and coat she'd worn that last day to work. Even in the outfit that had been her last, she smiled at him. Waved to him. And beckoned him toward her for a kiss at their front door.

He'd watched her, entranced but confused, knowing even in sleep that she'd fade the moment he touched her.

So it was even more jarring when she'd followed the wave with a small two-step, shimmying toward him in her high heels. And then she'd pressed her hand against his heart, her palm laid against the thick, heavy beats.

He'd woken up then, the hard, insistent pound of the alarm on his phone dragging him from the dream.

But as he sat up, he could have sworn he felt the indentation on his chest. The determined press of a hand where it lay against his heart.

Damned fanciful notions.

All cooked up by an overactive imagination that was

trying to find some sense of order in the crazy chaos that had become his life.

"Breakfast for one?" One of the waitresses he hadn't met yet pointed toward the counter. "I can seat you at the bar or give you a booth in the back."

"I'd like the booth, please." He was in no mood to make small talk with his neighbors at the counter and he'd forgotten to grab a newspaper on his way in, the ability to rustle it an effective shield against conversation.

He'd nearly cleared the long row of booths that ran along the windows when he heard his name.

"Hawk. Good morning." Maggie Lowell, or the soon-to-be Mrs. Thorne Colton, waved him over. "Come join me and save me from the guilt of eating these biscuits and gravy."

"You don't want them?"

"I do want them but I'll feel better if I wave a bit of my personal blend of pixie dust as I do."

The surly attitude that had carried him into the diner didn't have a chance against her pretty smile, even as his stomach sunk toward his knees at the need to make conversation. And what on earth was she talking about with pixie dust?

He and Claudia had left things on a terrible note the day before. He owed her an apology, but couldn't summon up the needed elements to give her one. "I'm sorry" felt way too paltry and simple but he'd yet to settle on anything better.

And no doubt sitting with her future sister-in-law was going to raise some uncomfortable questions.

So it was a genuine surprise thirty minutes later when they'd talked about everything and nothing, his laughter still echoing over the image she'd painted of Thorne attempting to put together the baby's crib, that he realized just how much he'd enjoyed himself.

"I swear he'd have broken the legs over his knees if I hadn't called his father in to help."

"Mac's handy?"

"Oh, and then some. Chaps Thorne a bit, too. Mac offered to make us a crib but Thorne wanted to do it himself."

"Seems like a shame when he's got someone there who can do such a beautiful job. And who would be honored to create a crib for his grandbaby."

"Yes, well, men don't always have the sense they were born with. Women, too, I suppose." Maggie winked. "But men are worse about it. And stubborn men, well, look out."

He had to give her credit. The woman had boxed him in before he'd even realized she was laying a trap. "Is this an example for me to make me see the stubborn error of my ways?"

"Did it work?"

"Can I say it didn't not work?"

She shrugged, those shoulders rising up and down with the motion. "Be my guest."

Hawk took a sip of his coffee and considered her words. "Is that crib story made up? Like some teaching metaphor for how I should proceed with Claudia?"

"That's an unequivocal no. Thorne really did spend the last three nights attempting to build a crib that falls apart with the slightest ounce of pressure." She leaned forward, her gaze urgent. "But if it'll get you to go talk to Claudia and open up to her... Well then, sure, the crib can be as imaginary as you'd like."

As he sipped his coffee, he couldn't summon up one single argument to refute her logic.

"That plum-colored blouse will look gorgeous on you. And I love the cami tank you picked to go underneath. Subtle and sexy." Claudia smiled at the young woman who'd drifted into Honeysuckle Road earlier as she handed over a sturdy paper bag with the shop logo imprinted on the side.

"I had no idea you were here. The few shops in town. Well—" The girl broke off before smiling. "They don't necessarily have things to flatter a gal who likes her biscuits and gravy."

"You don't need to worry about that here. Every woman is beautiful and that includes those of us who aren't afraid to eat a few calories in the pursuit of the perfect meal."

"That's what my boyfriend's always telling me but I don't believe him."

"Let me give you a piece of advice, then." Claudia leaned over the counter. "Give that man a good, solid chance to convince you."

The woman giggled at the advice before turning away, a determined bounce in her step. Claudia gave herself a moment to enjoy that walk, satisfied when she saw the extra layer of confidence that came from buying something pretty. Something that flattered.

She'd lived like that once, when she was younger. Had convinced herself she needed to be as thin as her sisters. That somehow by starving herself she'd manage to get their fine-boned structure, too.

It had been Leonor who'd put a stop to that nonsense. She'd taken her on a drive up to Dallas and they'd walked through several art galleries around the city and then on over in Fort Worth. Leonor had shown her images of women through the ages, captured in painting after painting, by some of the greatest artists who'd ever lived. The paintings had depicted so many different types of women. Tall and short, those with more curves and those with fewer and every shape in between.

When Claudia had only scoffed that they were looking at art and she was talking about real life, Leonor had laid down a challenge.

You want to be a fashion designer. That's a very real form of art. Use it to make women feel beautiful.

The words had carried her on to New York and then into her career. They'd also gone a long way toward how she saw herself after that. She could tell herself she was flawed and imperfect, or she could learn to love her own shape and craft her own style around that.

From where she stood at the counter, Claudia couldn't see the exchange at the front door, but she did see the door hang open a few moments longer as her most recent customer slipped out. It was only when someone new came in the door—his large frame filling the entryway—that her heart caught in her throat.

"Hawk."

He strolled toward her, looking so good her knees nearly buckled. He wore a pair of jeans today over his boots. A black T-shirt hugged his broad chest and narrowed over his slim waist.

Goodness, the man was a vision. She was surprised he hadn't been approached half a dozen times while walking down Main Street.

"That was one happy customer."

"She should be. She purchased a beautiful outfit."

And damn it all. Did that high-pitched, slightly squeaky voice belong to her?

If Hawk noticed, he didn't say anything. Instead, he just continued that slow saunter up to the counter, moving through the rows and racks of clothing like a shark slicing through the water.

As he came closer, she was forced to amend the shark thought. They might have predatory grace, but they weren't gifted with the cheekbones of a fallen angel or the vivid blue eyes of one who still played its harp, content upon a throne of clouds.

She dismissed the ridiculous image and cleared her throat, willing away the squeak, as well. "I'm surprised to see you today. Especially after how we left things yesterday."

"I can understand that."

"Then why are you here?"

"I'm not entirely sure. I mean, Maggie sent me but if I'm being honest, I'd likely have come all on my own. It just might have taken me a bit longer." He laid a hand on the counter but it was his shift from foot to foot that gave her the slightest pause.

Was he nervous, too?

"Maggie sent you?"

"I saw her over at the diner. She invited me to have breakfast with her. Claimed she didn't want the shame of eating a huge pile of biscuits and gravy all on her own."

Since she could see it—and knew from the woman's comments during her fitting that Maggie had practically dreamed about the biscuits—a picture of Hawk's morning began to form in her mind's eye. "Sheesh, that's the second reference to biscuits and gravy just this morning and all this supposed shame they cause. Eat the darn things and be done."

"Can't argue with that."

She busied herself putting away the credit card receipt from her last guest's purchase. "Did Maggie say anything else?"

"She did say something about cribs and stubborn men."

"Oh?"

"Yeah. You had to be there."

"Alright, then."

That shifting from foot to foot continued and it was the only thing she could focus on. The only suggestion that maybe he was as affected as she was.

"I'm sorry. About yesterday. About my comments. About all of it." He stilled and shoved his hands in his pockets. "Look. I've had a long time to get used to my life. My new life. And I can't help the way I feel. I was a cop. And not only did I lose my wife, but I didn't have the tools or the talent to find who hurt her. That doesn't just go away."

"I know."

And she did know. Just like the visit with Jade, when she got over her personal upset, Claudia had admitted to herself that Hawk's situation had a whole lot more to do with his feelings than hers.

"Can I ask you something, though?"

"Sure."

"I know people say they'd want their spouse to move on. Or that their spouse would have wanted them to move on. And I'm not saying this because I want you to move on with me, although I'm not going to lie and tell you I don't enjoy your company."

The slightest bit of humor swirled and eddied in that ocean of a blue gaze. "I'm not going to lie and tell you I don't enjoy your company, either."

"Good."

"But if the situation were reversed. If something had happened to you. Wouldn't you have wanted Jennifer to have a life?"

He shoved his hands deeper in his pockets.

"Yesterday. When we were talking. I had a memory of her laughing. That hadn't happened for a long time. The picture of her there, at the end. I mean, of what she looked like. I was a cop and I know what dead bodies look like. But there's no preparing for it when it's your family."

"No, I suppose there isn't."

She couldn't imagine it. To see a loved one become nothing more than a broken shell, and especially after what Jennifer Huntley had sustained. It was a haunting thought.

"That's the picture that's kept me company for four long years. And then, yesterday, I remembered her smile. It was big and bright and you couldn't help but smile right along with her. And then I dreamed about her, too. Smiling that smile at me as if she had a secret."

Although she'd never given in much to superstition, matters of the world always keeping her far too grounded, Claudia couldn't quell the faint shiver that raced up her spine. Or the feeling of ease that settled in its wake.

Hawk had spent a lot of years grieving and suffering

over a loss he couldn't control. She wasn't silly enough to assume that all just vanished as if it had never been.

But maybe, if he could remember more smiles and more happiness and more joy, then maybe the two of them had a shot.

Chapter 14

River Colton knew when a man was lying. He also knew when he was being played and the phone call he'd just made to his mother's longtime lawyer smacked of both circumstances.

In spades with aces over kings.

Preston Hoffman had been his usual polite self, which meant the man had put on his benevolent dictator voice and no doubt steepled his fingers beneath his chin as he spoke through the speakerphone on his desk.

River would bet his military pension and his good eye that Preston Hoffman knew exactly what was going on with La Bonne Vie and why the government had kept it boarded up so long. The rat bastard also likely knew why it was suddenly going on the auction block.

"No details." River muttered Preston's refrain to himself. "My ass, he has no details."

With that unproductive conversation behind him, he was fast running out of answers. La Bonne Vie had secrets and he'd recently come to understand that the only way he'd ever be free of his past was if he uncovered the lot of them.

Which would be a hell of a lot easier if they weren't all hidden in his mother's shadowy—and well-concealed—past.

The news of the auction had been unexpected. It was information he wasn't even supposed to have, but spilled to him when he'd walked back into the First Federal Bank to open up a savings account earlier that week. The bank manager had handled his account herself, her endless tittering as she walked him through the required paperwork grating on his nerves.

Irritation had turned to gratitude when she let the information about La Bonne Vie slip.

The bank had held the property in trust for the past decade on behalf of the government. Apparently someone new came into the office and questioned why it had sat empty for so long, ordering the house and the lands to auction. In less than three weeks it would be all done, and he and his family weren't even aware of it.

Which smacked of just one more secret in a lifetime that was full of them.

He and his siblings were Livia's only known heirs, yet someone had seen to it—Livia, even?—that they weren't given the details of his mother's affairs.

What else had been kept from them?"

Since that way lay madness, River decided to shake off his bad mood with a visit to his sister. He was still pissed off over the rat issue behind her store and then had gotten doubly pissed when she'd called about the incident at Jade's. She could play it off all she wanted, but something didn't sit right.

And although he'd stopped being a man who got involved a long time ago, he'd decided it was time to make an exception.

"The dress needs to be pressed and then laid in the tissue paper."

He and Claudia had settled into a subtle routine of sorts over the past few days. She was so focused on finishing Maggie's wedding dress that she'd stayed put in her studio. Hawk had set up his laptop in a back corner and worked from there, quietly observing her in between emails and phone calls.

Other than going out to pick up lunch for the two of them and Evelyn, he'd been able to stay close and available. Which had given him a measure of comfort, but had also ensured whatever threat was hovering had stayed away.

"Over there, Hawk." Claudia's hand shot out in the direction of the stockroom and Hawk followed her line of sight.

When he'd offered to help with the transport of Maggie's wedding dress, he had no idea he'd be ordered around with all the finesse of a drill sergeant. After listening to Claudia grouse and shout orders at him for the past half hour, he had to admit a morning running field drills and climbing muddy walls might have been preferable.

"That tissue paper. Over there."

"I have tissue paper."

Hawk looked down at the pale pink paper in his

hands. He'd grabbed a handful behind the checkout counter, only to be directed toward the back of the store.

"The white kind, not the pink kind. I don't want any chance of the colored paper rubbing off on the dress."

He supposed he saw her point, but damn it, what the hell was he supposed to do with an armful of pink paper?

"Just put that back on the counter. I'll use it to stuff a few bags."

Back and forth he went, from the main floor of the shop and then back to Claudia's workroom. By his fifth jaunt, he held up his hands. "Why don't you leave me out here to watch the door and you can get everything set up to your liking?"

"Temperamental much?"

"I am when I'm lectured on the simply staggering differences between pale pink paper and white paper."

"Touchy."

"I believe the word you're looking for is *grouchy*."

"Grouchy, then." She waved a hand over her shoulder. "Oh look, here comes Pris Todd now. She's one of my best customers and always full of the latest gossip. Don't be so grumpy to her you drive the woman away and lose me a customer."

Claudia slipped through the entrance to her studio, the door snapping closed with a sharp finality, just as a middle-aged woman with seriously impressive hair waltzed into the shop. "Why, hello?"

The image of an old *Golden Girls* episode flashed through his mind and Hawk had the unlikely sensation he was being sized up like a piece of meat at the grocery store. Swallowing around his irritation and sudden awkwardness, he put on his best smile. "Good afternoon, ma'am."

"Aren't you a sweet man." The inimitable Mrs. Todd worked her way around the various racks of clothes, one eye most definitely set on him. Hawk did his level best to fade into the background and kept his attention focused on straightening the checkout counter.

But there were only so many ways you could tidy up a stack of neatly pressed bags. And the mess of pink paper he'd made had already been wadded up in some way that made it like a light, fluffy cotton ball and was, even now, in fresh bags standing sentinel on the back counter.

There was nothing to do.

Except sit there like a bug under a microscope.

"You're new to Shadow Creek, aren't you?"

"I'm in town visiting."

"You have kin here?"

She's Claudia's very best customer.

The success of Honeysuckle Road depended on keeping the customers she earned and there was no way he was going to be a part of ruining that. Even if he did have to fight the overwhelming urge to tell the woman to mind her own business. "No, ma'am, I don't."

"So that means you won't be sticking around long?"

"I'm here for a wedding this weekend. Then I need to head home to Houston."

Which had been his plan all along. Get into town. Get Claudia Colton on board with a DNA test. Hit the road.

Only now here he was, already in town for more than a few days. She'd gotten on board, agreeing to the

DNA test. He was the one who'd pushed to stay. And he was the one who decided it would be fun to join in on Thorne and Maggie's wedding festivities.

He had no one to blame for his situation but himself.

So why did the thought of heading back to Houston have no appeal?

It wasn't like he had anything to go back for. The other cases he had in progress had moved forward, even with his travel schedule. And it wasn't like he missed the one-bedroom apartment he called home. He'd sold the house he and Jennifer had lived in three years ago, the apartment feeling like a better fit at the time.

But was it?

For the first time, he was forced to ask himself that. Forced to look at the fact that in his efforts to atone for Jennifer's death, he'd also given up any memories of her life or their life together.

"Well, I hope you enjoy your time in Shadow Creek." Mrs. Todd's suggestion pulled him back to the store, the racks of clothes once again taking shape in his field of vision.

"Is there anything I can help you with?"

"Oh no. Not today. My husband will simply cut up my credit cards if I buy one more thing this week."

"I'm glad you stopped in."

"Me, too, Mr.—?" She left the question hanging there, waiting for an answer.

"Huntley. Hawk Huntley." Hawk extended his hand over the counter, only to be met with a quick wink along with a firm shake.

"It's good you're here. This town needs some new blood. It also needed things like Claudia's shop."

"New blood? But I'm not staying."

"Of course you're not." She turned on her heel and headed for the door, her movements swift and hurried, as if she'd delivered her message and then needed to be on her way. It was only when she got to the door, the bells tinkling as she opened it, that those hurried movements slowed.

"Make no mistake about it—we need a few new things in this town to shake us up. Shadow Creek's stood still for so long it's a wonder we haven't dried up and turned to dust. I, for one, am glad to see the signs of change."

"I guess you are." Hawk said the words to no one but himself, but it was several long moments later when he finally pulled his gaze off the front door.

Claudia hit the off button for her steamer with her toe, satisfied that Maggie's dress had been pressed to perfection. She'd give it a few moments to let the steam evaporate and then it was getting folded to go into the box for one very special delivery.

She'd laughed to herself more than once as she considered how Priscilla Todd's arrival had coincided with Hawk's complaints over the chores she'd given him. And she was just petty enough to admit that it had been great fun to listen at the door as he attempted to keep up with the woman's barrage of questions.

She did miss racking up another sale on the Todd charge account, but figured it was just deserts for tossing Hawk to the wolves.

Not like the man needed any help. Standing around looking like a rock mountain of eye candy shouldn't be all that hard. If she played her cards right, Pris would have it all over town in under an hour that there was a man managing the till over at Honeysuckle Road, and the corresponding traffic would start pouring in.

The thick, heavy box was already open and waiting for Maggie's dress and Claudia carefully folded the long leaves of tissue paper that met her exacting standards into the bottom. The dress box was a vintage find she'd discovered online. She'd liked it so much she'd ordered several more wholesale to decorate her front windows.

"I'm going home." The door to her studio swung open and her big mountain of eye candy filled the frame.

"Okay. I'll see you later."

"I mean home, home. To Houston. I'm heading home after the wedding."

The news shot a small dart into her chest, but she couldn't say it was totally unexpected. The man had been living in a hotel. And he wasn't from Shadow Creek. Nor was it fair to expect him to decide to move there after a week.

But damn it all. Claudia added a few more inventive curses to the first and wondered when she'd begun to think of it as a possibility.

"That's fine. We can call you if we need you and I suppose you'll keep me posted on the Krupids."

"That's all you can say?"

The shifting from foot to foot she'd observed earlier had changed. Morphed, really, as he moved into a pacing movement in front of the studio door.

"I suppose you'll keep me posted, *please*?"

"You don't care I'm leaving?"

"I didn't say that. But your mind seems made up."

Wasn't it?

She didn't dare hope otherwise, but when Hawk shifted from pacing near the door to prowling across her studio, a small kernel of hope speared up from the churning swirl of nerves in her stomach.

Was it possible he didn't want to leave?

"What if my mind isn't made up?"

Claudia chose her words carefully. Hawk Huntley was a free man and she had no business thinking otherwise. "Then I guess you'll need to spend time deciding what you want."

"What if I know what I want but am afraid I ruined it?"

And then she stopped caring if he had a choice because hers had long since vanished. "Do you think maybe you can come over here and put me out of my misery while you try to figure it out?"

The man might be an infuriating mix of stubborn pride and Southern gentleman, but when something dark and dangerous lit in his gaze, Claudia considered herself the luckiest of women.

And when that prowl turned into a full-out stalk as he closed the distance between them, she stood up and reached for him.

The anxiety of the last few days faded as she went into his arms. Whatever they still needed to figure out—and it was a lot—this was right.

Real.

And oh so wonderful.

His mouth crushed hers, his arms pulling her against that hard chest. The interest she'd tried so hard to push aside was given full reign as she ran her hands over his chest before dipping to where his T-shirt hung over his jeans. She ran her fingers beneath the hem, gratified when she finally touched warm, heated flesh beneath her fingertips.

The attraction that had burned between them from the first rose up, the flames flying high as she ran her hands over the muscles of his stomach. Thick indentations outlined the firm barrels of muscle and she plied her fingers over the grooves, practically shivering from the glory of finally touching all that raw musculature.

Hawk's mouth devoured hers and she was rapidly losing any ability to reason when a vague notion filled her thoughts.

"The door." She whispered the words against his mouth before his lips took her under once again. She kissed him back, then spoke louder when she had an opportunity to come up for air. "Hawk! The front door."

He smiled, his mouth curving over hers. "Already locked it."

She did pull back then, a mock sense of shock filling her. "Awfully sure of yourself, aren't you?"

"Nah. Just wildly hopeful."

She leaned in and pressed a firm kiss to his lips. "Consider me suitably appreciative."

"Perhaps you can show me?"

Claudia's last thought as she pulled him close was that she was going to have an awfully short run as a proprietor if she couldn't find a way to keep her shop open.

The warm welcome in her eyes was all Hawk needed as he and Claudia drew close once more. With her back in his arms, he braced himself for the sensual feast that was this woman. She was everything he'd imagined and more, from her warmth, her humor and her deep devotion to family.

She was also gorgeous. Bright and luminescent, she captivated him so that she was all he could see. All he wanted to see.

Even the night before, when he'd told himself he needed to leave her alone so he could continue to fight against the demons of his past, he couldn't deny her heartbreaking beauty. She was an enticing, exiting woman wrapped up in a delectable package.

And God help him, he could not resist her.

Hawk knew he was weak. Knew he'd given in to the need to hold her close and touch her and feel her warmth. But try as he might, he couldn't fully fight the desire that refused to listen to reason. That rejected his self-censure and the monastic existence he'd lived for the past few years.

He fisted his hand in the long wave of blond hair that spilled over her shoulder, the soft texture his for the taking. With his other hand, he explored the curves of her body, tracing the arc from shoulder to breast, to hip and back again. The light moan that had Claudia pressing against him, filling his hands, had him growing bolder in his explorations. But it was the play of her own explorations, her hands fluttering over the waistband of his jeans, that stole his breath.

She knew what she wanted and as her fingers reached for his zipper, parting the material of his jeans, Hawk knew he was lost. Whatever willpower he believed he possessed—and he was red-blooded enough to know he had his limits—Claudia Colton had the ability to destroy them all.

"Why don't we move this upstairs?"

"Hmm?" Her query was a cross between a whisper and a purr, and, when her hand wrapped around him fully, Hawk nearly abandoned his plan to take her upstairs. "You were saying?"

"Vixen." He said the moniker through gritted teeth, his body leaping against her palm without any additional provocation. Head bent, he pressed his forehead to hers as a wave of the most glorious sensation rippled through his body. Like a tsunami gaining power, it started somewhere deep inside, building through him until he was nearly shaking from the effort to maintain his control.

"Do you know what you do to me? And how long it's been?"

The words ripped from his lips and it was only once she contained her movements, her hand still pressed intimately against him, that he realized what he'd said.

More, what he'd implied.

"Claudia?"

What had he done? His body cooled rapidly at the evidence she was sorely unimpressed with his confession. Worse, it was one more reinforcement—delivered by his own hand—that he couldn't get over his wife. Couldn't move past her death.

Only in this sense, he hadn't. Not until now.

A three-month bender after he'd quit the force, with a series of nameless, faceless women, had left him feeling more empty and alone. It had been unfair to them as well as to him and he hadn't touched a woman since that time. Hadn't allowed one to touch him.

So now here he was, three endless years later. A freaking eternity.

"I guess I should—" He shifted to pull away from

her but she didn't let go. Didn't disengage from his arms or remove her hands from the most intimate of positions.

"Shh." She pressed her lips to his, her voice low. "You've just given me a gift and I'm savoring it for a moment. Just for one quiet moment."

"A gift? I just—"

She kissed him once more. "I said shh."

The awkwardness vanished once more, despite—or maybe because of—the intimacy of their position. And it was in the quiet, his heart thundering in his chest, that Hawk had to admit his choice had been the right one.

The women he'd been with after Jennifer's death had deserved better. Jennifer's memory had deserved better. And now, he saw so clearly, Claudia deserved better, too.

He was able to give her that.

He hadn't been capable of all that many good choices over the past four years. The dead-end apartment, the near total focus on his cases and far too many nights spent drinking his dinner from a whiskey bottle. But he'd held his ground on the sex.

And perhaps he'd been rewarded for his patience.

As Claudia Colton's lips moved over his and her hands filled with him, Hawk realized he'd been rewarded in a myriad of ways. With her generous smile. Her innate poise and grace. And with her body, pressed to his in the most carnal exploration of his life.

If he'd only reach out and take what she offered. Accept all of it. The risks. And the glorious rewards.

He wanted to. He wanted to so badly.

With renewed urgency, his lips met hers, pressed

and sought, consumed and devoured, as they pleasured each other. His hands drifted to her breasts, the points of her nipples firm and hard against his fingers. Hawk learned the shape of her, learned what made her moan, and in the meeting of their flesh he gave her pleasure. Received it in return.

He was so hard he marveled that he could still stand upright, but still, the battle for pleasure raged on between them.

How was this possible? For her to come into his life in such a rush, and then open herself so generously. For her to accept him for all he was and all he'd been.

Her voice was husky, her pupils wide black disks inside the gray when she gazed into his eyes. "Now what was that you were saying about going upstairs?"

"Are you sure?"

She gave him a light squeeze in answer. "I'd say that's a yes."

"Don't get grabby." He stilled her hand, gently removing her hold. "And give me a chance to collect myself."

"What fun is that?"

He pressed a hard kiss to her sexy, pouty mouth. "Give me a few minutes to get this under control and I would be more than happy to show you."

"I'm going to hold you to that."

His gaze alighted on the dress. "Can we leave the dress here?"

"It's fine. We'll package it up later. After." Her words were full of promise as she took a moment to rearrange her blouse. "Are you sure you locked the front door?"

"Positive."

"The Main Street business association is going to kick me out." She shook her head but couldn't seem to muster any real apology or remorse in her tone. "Somehow, I think they want their shopkeepers to keep more regular hours."

"Consider it a start-up commitment as you open for business."

"Start-up commitments?"

"You're consulting with your own personal security expert. If anyone asked, he came to help you identify the best places to install perimeter cameras."

"Nice try. I have those out front."

"You need an upgrade out back. And while you were at it, you decided to add on to your apartment security, as well."

"You've got this all figured out."

"I'm a full-service security specialist."

She wrapped her arms around his waist, a sexy smile filling her face as her hands played over his ass. "Is that what they're calling it these days? Full-service?"

"Yes, ma'am."

"That 'ma'am' routine worked on Pris Todd but it won't work on me."

"You prefer something else?"

"I sort of like 'vixen.'"

"I'll be sure to remember that."

Hawk got stuck in her arms once again as they fell into another hot, steamy kiss. At this rate, their first time together was going to be on the floor of her studio and, while the thought wasn't a deterrent, he had something else a bit more romantic in mind.

Softer, too.

"*Vixen* is the perfect word."

"You bet your sexy ass." She added a light swat firmly to his backside before she swung away to grab her purse. The jingle of keys confirmed she had it and Hawk reached for the knob. He dragged open the back door, only to find River Colton standing on the other side, his hand lifted as he prepared to knock.

Chapter 15

Claudia would have laughed at the twin looks of surprise on River's and Hawk's faces if she weren't so disappointed to see her brother standing at her back door.

She loved him, of course. And she was so glad he was home, back in Shadow Creek. They'd worried about him for so long, his time in the marines shrouded in danger.

But could he have picked a worse time to show up?

The burn in her cheeks grew a bit hotter as she pictured what she and Hawk would have looked like, falling all over each other up her apartment steps, and decided River *could* have picked a worse time.

About two minutes later than his actual arrival, as a matter of fact.

The heated moments in Hawk's arms still flushed her skin, but that was the last thing she wanted River to see. She so did not need him going all big-brother protective on her, especially since she was perfectly able to make her own decisions when it came to who she had sex with.

When, of course, she and Hawk finally got to have sex.

"River." She pulled him close for a quick hug, whispering up a silent prayer of thanks that she'd thought to rearrange her clothes before heading up to her apartment. Although anyone paying attention could likely guess what she and Hawk had been up to, at least her shirt was put to rights and her skirt came to above the knee, just where it belonged. "I'm so glad to see you, but what brings you by?"

"The front door was locked."

"I closed for the afternoon." *An impromptu decision for an impromptu interlude.* "Hawk's helping me package up Maggie's wedding dress for delivery."

The dress worked as far as excuses went and River sauntered over to where it still hung on the frame, giving her the final few moments she needed to fuss with smoothing her hair. "Maggie's going to look gorgeous."

"She's absolutely stunning."

"Thorne's not going to know what hit him."

"Most men don't," Hawk interjected, a bright wink in her direction. "Why don't I give you two a few minutes? I wanted to fiddle with the position on the cameras over the front of the store anyway."

He disappeared out of her studio as quickly as he'd come in earlier and Claudia gave herself a moment to watch him go. The man's backside view was as enticing as the front and she barely suppressed the sigh that crept up her throat.

"And there's the reinforcement I needed to confirm I walked in at the wrong time."

"Nonsense."

"Come on, Claudia."

She waved a hand at him. "No, you come on. You're my brother and I'm glad you're here. That said, I can't believe you're really all that concerned with shopping this fine Thursday afternoon, so what has you out and about?"

Since the subject of her sex life wasn't one either of them was all that keen to discuss, it proved fairly easy to distract him.

"Did you know La Bonne Vie is up for auction?"

"No." She shook her head, the reality of his statement sinking in. La Bonne Vie. Her childhood home. "It's really going up for sale?"

"In a few weeks. Feds have hung on to it long enough, I guess. Apparently new management wants to get out from under it all."

"And we didn't get any notice?"

"My thoughts run along the same lines. If I hadn't had a nosy bank manager helping me with my savings account, I wouldn't have heard, either."

Although she had no interest in going back to the home she grew up in, La Bonne Vie was still rightfully theirs, though it was seized after her mother's arrest. They'd all been allowed to take the basics of their possessions, each of them watched by a different member of law enforcement as they emptied their rooms of personal effects.

Knox, Leonor, River and Thorne had already passed the age of eighteen and were already making their lives. They'd had some sparse, leftover things from childhood, but most everything of theirs had already been collected.

Not her and Jade.

Even now, she still remembered that day—the watchful eyes and the seething hatred that had permeated the house as Livia Colton's children gathered up what was theirs. She'd felt like the criminal as she was watched over, boxing up her things. The town had always had a love-hate relationship with her mother, but by the time Livia's crimes had fully come out, the pendulum had definitely swung toward hate.

Thankfully, they'd had Mac. He'd already ensconced himself on the far edge of the property with his own home and ranch and he'd provided a welcome haven. For her and Jade until they reached eighteen, but for all of them whenever they needed a soft place to land.

"Do you ever wonder about it all?"

"Wonder about what?"

"Mom. Her crimes. What's hidden out at the house."

Whatever earlier embarrassment she might have felt faded in full. River wasn't there on a social call. And his normally still waters were most definitely rockin' with waves.

"You think something's hidden out there?" she asked.

"You don't? She made La Bonne Vie her home base for a long time. I'm hard-pressed to believe she didn't leave a few things behind when she was arrested. I always figured that's why the feds were holding on to it."

"Then why not search it?"

"I'm sure they did. But she knew how to hide things. Hell, she hid a life of horrible crimes from the people she should have been closest to. I think if she were able to do that, she could find a few hiding places in her own home."

His assessment made a frightening amount of sense and as they discussed it, Claudia added one more dimension to the puzzle that was her mother.

For years, she'd assumed that her strange life under the orbit of Livia Colton was all she was meant to have. She and her siblings lived noticeably different lives from the other kids at school. Claudia had chalked it up to the weirdness of her family and did her best to try and fit in.

Then her mother's crimes had come to light. While it was horrible to know all she'd done, it had also given them an amazing sense of freedom. Livia went to jail and they all moved on to their new normal.

To their new lives. She and Jade living with Mac while her older siblings got their adult lives off the ground. Knox had found his way to the Texas Rangers and Leonor to an art gallery in Austin. River had found his solace in the marines and Thorne a place cattle ranching with Mac.

They'd all moved on.

So how frustrating it was to find that all of it had caught up with them. Almost as if they'd simply been marking time in all the years that had followed.

Waiting.

"What do you think Mom hid at the house?"

"Details. Notes. Files."

"On her…businesses?" Claudia swallowed around the euphemism. Prostitution and human trafficking and murder weren't business, but depravity.

"Her interests. Her businesses, both the legal and the illegal," River agreed. "Likely all her perceived slights, too. And I'd say there was no one who filled that list like her husbands."

"Wes certainly paid a price." Mac had nearly paid one, too, Wes's mindless ramblings and desperate need for revenge as misplaced as they were dangerous.

"He wasn't my father. Or at least he doesn't think he was."

"Oh, River." Claudia knew her brother was battling secrets, but she had no idea it was this bad. "How did you find out?"

"When I returned from active duty I went to see him. He's being held until his trial and I wanted to talk to him. See him for myself."

"Was it awful? Having to see him locked up like that?"

"No." His gaze narrowed, the scars he'd returned with seeming to groove deep lines in a face that had seen too much.

Lived too much.

"It was sad. To see how far he'd fallen. How badly Livia's actions had affected him. He told me he loved me. That he'd always loved me, which is something. But then he told me he didn't think I was his son."

More pain. More secrets. More lies.

Their lives were full of them. And until Livia Colton was caught, it seemed none of them would ever really have anything resembling a normal existence.

She didn't want to feel compassion for Wes, but knowing what her mother had done to him, she also couldn't find it in her heart to hate him. He'd been as manipulated and emotionally abused as the rest of them. To think he'd spent much of his life thinking he had a child when River was never really his.

And just like that, she saw River's pain reflected in her own.

A lifetime of thinking of one person as your parent, only to find out that was very likely not true.

Did she dare tell him? About the Krupids and their daughter, Annalise? About Livia's trip to Europe and the sketchy details about her own birth that Hawk had brought to light with his arrival in Shadow Creek?

She wanted to tell him. Wanted a chance to share her theories and get her big brother's in return.

But something held her back. The same reasons she hadn't wanted to upset the others mattered here, too. Why add to River's latest personal trials if it was all for naught?

She'd know soon enough when they got the DNA test results back.

Even as she decided she wouldn't tell River about Hawk's real purpose for visiting, she couldn't stop the question that had haunted her for years.

"Does it make a strange sort of sense to you now?"

"What part?"

Claudia thought about what she wanted to say. About how to ask River if he'd always known he wasn't Wes's son. "Did you ever have a sense Wes wasn't your father?"

"No. I mean, he never treated me differently, but I'd have moments. Flashes where I wondered if he was my father. I had no reason for it and I always chalked it up to the behavior of a dumb kid. If that makes any sense."

It made more sense than she could ever describe. Only her flashes of insight had come when she looked at her siblings and saw no resemblances to the person who stared back from the mirror every day.

"Is there anyone she hasn't used or manipulated?"

Claudia thought about the details Hawk had shared about Annalise Krupid. The way the young woman and so many others had been smuggled out of Russia, supposedly part of a mail-order bride scam to hide what was really happening to them. What they'd really signed up for.

Livia's cohorts had made vague promises to vulnerable young women who gave in before they realized they were signing on to a life of slavery and servitude, all directed toward one outcome. Their conscription as unwilling prostitutes in her mother's vile business.

Even if she wasn't Annalise Krupid's biological daughter, it didn't change what her mother had done. What she'd built and run, from the ground up. Just like River's questionable parentage. Like Livia's betrayal of Mac and her manipulation of Leonor.

The joyous moments with Hawk that had filled her afternoon faded as if they'd never been.

Why did that keep happening?

How did every conversation about her mother somehow sink her toward a depression that she then had to take precious time digging her way out of?

No more.

And certainly not tonight.

She had too much joy still humming in her veins. Between the excitement over the wedding and the beauty of being in Hawk's arms, she was determined not to give in to the dark forces.

"We need to go dancing."

"Go where?" River's clear eye widened even as both eyebrows lifted at her suggestion. "Now?"

"No. Tonight. Let's get a group together and head

down to that dance hall a few towns over. I'm tired of talking about Mom and all the horrible things she's done. I want to have some fun. Some happiness and I want to do it with my family."

Her *family*.

Hawk had stressed to her that they'd be her family no matter what the outcome of the DNA test. She'd initially taken his comments as lip service, but maybe it was time she started believing it. They were the people who'd stood by her no matter what. And they'd be the people who continued to stand by her, no matter what she discovered.

River was no less himself if it turned out his father wasn't Wes Kingston. She'd be no less herself, either, if she was the daughter of Annalise Krupid.

"You want to go tonight? It's short notice."

"So was dinner the other night but we pulled it off. Come on, River. Let's get out of here and go dancing. Even if it's just for a few hours."

She saw the moment she convinced him, the layer of skepticism on his face fading as a small smile spread. "I've heard there are a lot of pretty women that hit ladies' night on Thursdays."

"Then it's settled. Let's start making some calls."

Hawk had to hand it to her, the idea to go dancing was inspired. And this from a man who'd wanted to do nothing more than spend his evening wrapped up in her arms. Even with the needs of his body drumming in a dull throb, he couldn't deny the fun of squiring her around the dance floor, the music creating a different sort of seduction between them.

"You're quite a two-stepper." She clung to his hand

as they wended their way through the dance hall, a string of songs that had kept them busy for the past half hour finally at an end.

"I'm rusty."

"If that's rusty, I'd hate to see you at the top of your form." She lifted her head and planted a quick kiss on his lips. "You're definitely a natural."

"Wait till you see my other moves."

Need sparked low in her eyes, visible even in the dim lighting of the dance hall. "I can't wait."

They headed for the members of their group who had stayed to hold their table and Claudia gripped his hand, squeezing tight when they were a few tables away. "I'm so glad Evelyn came. Look at her and Mac talking. This is going so well."

"You're hopeless."

"No, I'm hopeful. I'm also so very right. It's a dangerous combination."

It was a dangerous combination, but not for the reasons she meant. Hawk let go of her hand and wove behind her toward a few empty seats on the opposite side of where Mac and Evelyn sat quietly talking.

Hopeful and right.

Hadn't she been trying to prove that to him from the start? That his life wasn't over and that it was okay to begin again? Better than okay, actually.

He'd thought about it all afternoon. Once the immediate claws of sexual need had eased their grip, while she was visiting with her brother, Hawk had made a series of mental lists in his mind as he puttered around her shop.

All the reasons he should keep seeing her, pitted

against all the reasons to hightail it home to Houston at first light.

And the reasons to stay always won.

In fact, he'd had trouble coming up with even a handful of reasons to leave.

"Should she be doing that?" Mac pointed toward the dance floor, where Maggie and Thorne danced, their arms thrown in the air.

Since Hawk's experience with pregnant women and babies extended about as far as what he saw on TV, he opted out of an answer. But it was Evelyn who spoke, her smile warm as she stared out over the dance floor. "Why not? She's going to dance on Saturday, too, I hope. It's nothing more than a little exercise. The real issue is that she's going to tire out before the baby's done doing cartwheels tonight."

"Babies do cartwheels?" Mac asked, his voice panicky.

"It feels like cartwheels. It's probably more like very vigorous swimming." Evelyn patted his hand. "And it's all one hundred percent natural and healthy."

Her words seemed to calm Mac, and Hawk had to admit Claudia seemed right about the sparks between Mac and Evelyn. Not that he wanted to encourage her, but it looked like she'd pretty accurately pegged the situation. The pointy-toed kick to his shin was a completely unnecessary reinforcement of the same. "Hey!"

"Hopeful and right," she leaned over and whispered in his ear. "Like I said, an unbeatable combination."

Laughter and conversation ran high throughout the evening, their table forming and reforming as people got up and danced, moved into different conversation groups and ordered beers and burgers. So it seemed perfectly natural when River Colton sat down next to him and laid a casual arm on the back of his chair.

"My little sister's crazy about you."

Hawk saw her gaze flick over toward them from where she talked to Jade on the opposite side of the table before returning fully to her sister.

Looked like he was on his own.

"I'm pretty crazy about her, too."

"Crazy like you're going to stick, or crazy like you want to screw around with her?"

River maintained that easygoing smile, but Hawk felt the big-brother menace washing over him in a steady stream of male territorialism.

"I'm not going to hurt your sister."

"See that you don't."

Since that didn't require a response, Hawk decided to give the man his moment and focused on their small group instead. Leonor and Joshua were talking with their heads bent at the corner of the table, sharing a plate of fries. Maggie and Thorne had gotten up to go dancing and had persuaded Mac and Evelyn to head out, as well. Even now, both couples were whirling their way around the dance floor.

River eased up, his pose casual as he slouched back in his seat. Although Hawk had spent minimal time with any of the other Coltons, he couldn't deny the very real sense that the man sitting beside him was a lost soul. River Colton showed moments of clarity, as if he were awakening from a dream, but those times were counterbalanced with a lost look that lurked deep in his lone eye.

"This meant a lot to her." Hawk didn't have to ask to know that River meant Claudia. "I'm glad she organized this. Things have been entirely too serious lately and it's nice to do something that has no more reason for being other than it's fun."

That dreamy state faded as River leaned closer. His gaze flicked to his sister to make his point. "She's spent enough time dealing with jerks. It's time she got what she deserved. A good man who'll stand beside her and support her."

"I won't argue with you there, but you act like she's got nothing." Hawk gestured to the table, then toward the dance floor. "I'd say her family's done a damn fine job of standing beside her up to now."

River straightened out of the casual slouch, his good eye going sharp with awareness. "You notice things, Huntley."

"I'd like to think I do."

"Then what do you make of these threats against her? That weird menagerie outside her shop and then the issue yesterday morning."

So River Colton did know what was going on. More than he'd initially given him credit for.

Hawk bent his head, his tone lower than the ambient din that surrounded them. "Several of your mother's known associates are still on the loose."

"You think this is Livia's doing?"

"I think we'd be mistaken if we didn't consider it."

"Have you considered the actual threats? They're dangerous, escalating and creepy. Take your pick on which is worse but I'm bothered by the sense of escalation."

Since that element had bothered him, too, Hawk nodded. "It's why I fiddled with the cameras in her shop. Why I'm installing a few more tomorrow."

"Good."

"And it's why I'm not leaving her alone until we get to the bottom of this."

The idea had been swirling through his mind, but now that he'd put it into words Hawk acknowledged to himself he'd just been looking for the proper time to lay down the gauntlet. Whether or not he and Claudia slept together, he wasn't leaving her alone.

And that started tonight.

Happy, rosy, rich, smiling faces.

Dirty, rotten, corrupt smiling faces.

The Forgotten One nursed a beer in the back corner of the dance hall and watched the Colton family enjoy their little evening out. They'd been there all night, laughing and joking, completely unaware she was even watching them. Waiting for them.

Waiting for one of them in particular.

Claudia Colton. The golden girl of the family and the one who'd believed herself too good for Shadow Creek.

Too good for her roots.

Look at her now, throwing herself all over her protector. The man hadn't been here even a week and she'd already whored herself out for him. Had draped herself over him like a common streetwalker.

She deserved what was coming to her.

They all deserved what was coming.

But the golden girl would be first.

Chapter 16

Claudia floated out of the dance hall into the hot Texas night. Stars shined high in the sky and she couldn't stop the crazy, wonderful energy that coursed through her veins.

Nor did she want to.

She was happy. For the first time in longer than she could remember, she felt carefree. Unencumbered.

Content.

She'd felt that way her first few years in New York. The pace and energy of going to school, immersing herself in fashion and earning her degree. Those had been special days and she'd drunk them in, forming friendships for the first time in her life that weren't tainted by the fact that she was a Colton.

Her friends in New York didn't know where she'd come from. The Colton name didn't mean anything to anyone unless they chose to go internet hunting for details and she hadn't given people any reason to go looking. She was just Claudia, a hard worker and a student who loved fashion. A friend who could be trusted. A girl who was trying to make her way.

That girl had graduated to a hardworking, dedicated employee and, once again, she'd managed to avoid sharing details about her past. The studios she worked in appreciated her for her eye and her style and there wasn't any reason to go looking for more or assume she had a past worth digging up.

Growing up in Shadow Creek, she'd lived with the knowledge that everyone knew her family and knew what she'd come from. It had been positively glorious to find that in New York, no one cared.

She was just one of many and she'd reveled in the anonymity.

"You look good." Hawk spoke, his voice mixing with the music that still spilled out of the dance hall, filling the air along with the lightning bugs.

Something in his expression stopped her. The sweet smile? The attraction that spilled off of him, like the music behind them? Or maybe it was just the needy, hungry way he stared at her, as if she were the most essential woman alive.

Was there anything more wonderful than that?

"I feel good, too. Dancing was a good idea."

"Dancing was an inspired idea." Hawk pulled her close, his mouth finding her neck and nuzzling a small kiss there. "Even though I'd initially protested in my mind in favor of staying home and doing something else."

She ran her fingers through his hair, the short strands

soft against her palm. With her lips pressed near his ear, she whispered, "Why do you think I suggested the dancing?"

He lifted his head, his grin flashing in the moonlight. "Vixen. It really is going to be my new word for you."

"Let's go home, Hawk. Let's keep dancing. Please."

Although he'd stopped drinking after a few beers, his movements were slow and easy as he half danced them through the parking lot. She could hear other couples laughing as well, some walking to cars, others pressed against each other in the warm night air.

The simple joys of summer, she thought happily, as she moved with her man in the moonlight.

Although the sexual tension was high, the drive home had an easy quality to it. Need rose and fell in tempo with their conversation, along with the laughter and conversation. From a remembered joke at dinner to a particularly vigorous number the DJ had played, to her quiet comments about just how happy she was for Maggie and Thorne, they discussed it all.

And that simple conversation of their shared experience had carried them home.

Claudia ran a hand over her fluttering stomach, the lights over her apartment door spilling onto the small parking lot behind Honeysuckle Road. Main Street was quiet and the late hour meant both Whiskey Sour and Aldo's had closed for the evening, their patrons already headed for home. The diner still boasted a few patrons in its windows, but otherwise, Shadow Creek had quieted for the night.

That quiet wrapped around her like a cocoon—

wrapped around them both as Hawk came around and helped her out of the car.

His gaze was steady, his question simple—gentle almost—when he spoke. "Are you sure?"

"Yes."

She took his hand, the grip firm, and walked with him up the back stairs to her apartment. A few mosquitoes flitted against the light over her door and she swatted at them easily as her gaze caught on an envelope stuffed in the door. The landlord was forever sticking things in the jamb to communicate and she tugged on the envelope, fumbling when something fluttered to the ground.

"What's that?"

"Likely just more—" She broke off as her gaze alighted on the newspaper letters that covered the small wooden platform in front of her door. "What?"

She dropped into a squat to pick up the letters, Hawk doing the same but careful not to bump heads. "Claudia. Don't touch it."

His voice was sharp—alert—and was enough to break through the dreamy haze that had carried her up the stairs, already making her imagine being in Hawk's arms.

"What is it?"

The letters were like a waterfall, spilling out and fluttering over the small porch. *K*'s, *I*'s and *L*'s filled the space, their edges flittering in the barely there breeze.

The letters made a jumble, but several spelled out one word, repeating, over and over.

KILL.

"I'm calling the police."

* * *

Hawk did his best to leave the scene as they found it. Although the small breeze kept tickling the thin newspaper, he took off his boots and laid the length of them sideways to keep the majority in place, right where they'd fallen. He'd also snapped off several photos and made a quick video in hopes of preserving what he could before he'd laid down the boots.

Although he'd been less than impressed with the Shadow Creek police to date, the blue flash of lights had arrived quick enough and even now he could see the deputy from the other day, along with another one, heading for their stairs. Maybe they'd escape the sheriff's influence this evening.

He could only hope.

Claudia hadn't said much and it was her silence that bothered him even more than the dull look that washed out the pretty gray of her eyes beneath the porch light or the tired set of her shoulders.

She'd been so happy, only a short time before. And now they were right back to where they'd started, danger seething in the shadows around them.

He hadn't wanted to leave her, but he'd done a quick perimeter search in his socks, his gaze shifting between the ground, the surrounding area and the woman who sat as a lone figure on the top step.

"Why is this happening?" She hadn't moved from her seat, her gaze focused outwardly on the surrounding area behind her store. "Who would want to do this? My mother? Her minions? Her enemies? Who?"

Hawk silently vowed to find out before standing to greet the two officers.

"Evening, ma'am. Sir." The guy from the day before tipped his head. "What's happened here?"

Hawk walked them through what they'd discovered upon returning home. The second deputy lifted the edge of one of his boots to look at the letters and let out a low whistle. "There are a lot of them."

"Is that a letter, too?" The other deputy snapped off a few photos before moving off the other boot and lifting the envelope.

The move pulled Claudia forward and she reached for the envelope, ignoring the deputy's protests to leave it alone.

Several more letters fluttered to the ground before she pulled out a folded sheet of white paper and opened it up, a sob catching in the back of her throat.

KILL CLAUDIA COLTON

"Give it to me, please." Hawk took the note from her, refolding it so the letters were hidden from view once again.

She touched his arm, her eyes pleading. "Who is doing this?"

"We're going to find out, ma'am. We are." With Jeffries out of the picture, it was interesting to see the deputy's behavior had changed. His quiet demeanor had faded out of the oversight of his sheriff, his tone conciliatory and committed to helping her.

The officers took down his and Claudia's statements and then their own photos. They also gave him an email address where he could send the pictures and videos he'd captured. Both had insisted on checking the apartment as well, the move going some way toward improving Hawk's image of the Shadow Creek PD. The officers followed procedure and had good form as they entered the apartment and swept it fully.

It was proof just how dangerous Bud Jeffries's assumptions about the Colton family really were. He was more content to throw innuendo and dismissive suggestions than deal with the fact there might actually be a problem.

They'd spent another five minutes wrapping up questions and finalizing statements and then were on their way, the flash of blue fading as they turned off the police lights and drove out of the parking lot.

Hawk stood at the window and watched them go, his gaze drifting to the perimeter of the parking lot. Was someone out there, watching and waiting? He thought about River's words earlier.

Escalation.

While this didn't have the element of death that the rodents and the road incident at Jade's had, the kill reference coupled with the obsessive capture of letters from the newspaper smacked of a growing need to do harm. And while the approach had an amateur feel to it, the desired effect was shocking.

Claudia sat on the corner of the couch, her legs tucked up underneath her. She'd said little other than answering the questions asked of her, but her gaze had followed all that took place.

"Who's doing this?"

"I don't know."

"It's because of Livia. I know it."

He knew it, too, but had no idea how to prove it. Nor could he center on a motive. There was menace and anger, but nothing tangible to lead them toward the reasons for why the faceless person was acting.

Just like Jennifer.

Of all the leads he'd followed—and there had been hundreds—nothing ever panned out. Instead, all roads led to dead ends, nothing ever quite connecting. It had nearly killed him to do it, but he had found a modicum of peace the day he'd decided to accept her death had been random and senseless.

It lacked closure in finding her killer, yet made a strange sort of sense for all its chaotic simplicity.

Some things simply were.

The deputies had taken the note and cleaned up what they could of the newspaper letters, but it was those elements that Hawk focused on as he moved to sit beside Claudia on the couch.

Unlike Jennifer, these things weren't random. Nor were they senseless. They were deliberate actions, designed to deliver a focused goal. Scare. Intimidate. Disarm.

Livia Colton's influence was all over this, whether as the conduit or as the object of the violence.

She finally spoke, her weariness invading her tone beneath each and every word. "I'm sorry our night was ruined by this."

"That's not possible. Not when I'm with you."

She shuddered when he pulled her against his side before sinking into his hold.

"Who wants to do this?" she asked. "It's hateful. No, it's evil. Purposeful and deliberately cruel."

"Someone dangerous. It's also someone with a vendetta."

"What do they have against me?"

He debated what to say, finally settling on the truth. He kept his voice gentle as he ran his fingers over the silky strands of her hair. "They may have nothing against you. They may have everything against you. The motive isn't clear yet, but it will be. We'll find it. *I* will find it."

He spoke the words as he meant them. As a promise, yes, but more as a vow.

"I won't leave you alone, Claudia. And I'm not going back to Houston until this is through."

She lifted her head from where it rested against his chest. "Make love to me."

His body hardened at her suggestion and he struggled to find the right words to reassure. "Shh, now. It's late and it's been a difficult evening. There's time for that. Time for all the things we want to do."

"But what if there isn't?"

He sat up at that, his hold gentle as he gripped her arms. "I will keep you safe. I'm not going anywhere and I will help you find answers."

"But don't you see? This is exactly why I don't want to wait. I want you. I want to be with you. We need to take this, Hawk. For us. To prove that the good can drive out the bad."

Was it weakness that had him considering her words? The primal lure of sex erasing all his better judgment?

Or was it something more?

When she shifted, reaching up to take his hands, he wanted to believe it was something more.

But when she leaned in, capturing his mouth with hers, Hawk knew the truth. Being with Claudia wasn't simply something more.

It was everything.

* * *

Claudia kept a hand in Hawk's as they walked the perimeter of the room. She doused the lights beside the couch and TV and left one small light burning in the kitchen before walking him down the short hallway to her bedroom. The apartment was small, but big by New York standards, and she had all the space she needed. Space that was now filled with the presence of the most amazing man she'd ever met.

She wanted him. With a need that increasingly bordered on madness, she wanted to join their bodies and reclaim—if only for a moment—some of that joy she'd had while dancing.

He followed behind her, his hands everywhere and nowhere as he touched her. The soft strokes against her hair. The light tickle of his fingertips against her back. The warm press of his palms when he laid her gently back onto the bed, then lowered to his knees to remove her heels.

He'd never put his boots back on and he made quick work of his socks and T-shirt, tossing both toward the corner so he was left only in his faded jeans. The flesh she'd only touched earlier was now bare to her gaze, moonlight flooding in through the windows highlighting every rounded muscle.

The man was truly magnificent, the strength she'd felt in him both physical and emotional. Here was a man who'd seen things. Had lived with things. Yet he still rose every morning. Still worked to build a life.

Did he realize that? Did he truly understand what he'd managed to overcome? The thought humbled her and she vowed to tell him how she felt. What she believed.

Not now and not tonight, but soon. The pain of his wife's death didn't belong in this moment—but she would tell him. Would tell him how it drew her in and warmed her. Let her know she was safe.

But now. This moment. This moment was only for the two of them.

With seeking hands, she reached out and trailed a finger over those ridges of muscle. Her touch had his skin contracting slightly, the reaction teasing forth a slow smile. "Ticklish?"

"Needy," he growled as he came down over her on the bed. "There's a difference."

"Perhaps you could show me?"

His hands roamed over her sides, teasing the edges of her blouse before drifting to the hem and pulling the loose tank up her body. Cool air flowed over her stomach before he warmed her with his mouth, the soft strands of his hair ticklish where they met her flesh. That delectable mouth continued on its journey, exploring over the path from her belly button to the rim of her bra.

He pulled her against him, tilting them to their sides while his hand plucked deftly at the hook of her bra. Claudia felt the material slide free from her back before he used their positions to his advantage. He made quick work of the tank as well, lifting it off along with her bra in one smooth motion over her head.

And then she was bare to him, his gaze warm and appreciative as he stared at her breasts, before he reached out his index finger to trace their shape. "You're so beautiful."

The normal urge to cover herself—to hide the generosity of her flesh and the slight bit of extra courtesy of the biscuits and gravy she'd joked about earlier—simply evaporated in the warmth of his gaze.

"You are so, so beautiful."

And then he showed her, the appreciation in his gaze translating to an appreciation of her flesh. He kissed her while his hands roamed over her body. A lightly trailing fingertip over her clavicle.

The press of his lips to the sloping mound of her breast.

And the glorious sensation when his mouth closed over her nipple, his tongue teasing the tip to a turgid point.

In every move, in every way, he showed her she was beautiful.

And she believed him.

Hawk filled himself on the lushness of the woman beside him. She was responsive and generous, her moans of delight matched only to the determined seeking of her hands as she touched his body.

He was on fire.

Great, galloping waves of heat consumed him everywhere she touched. Her palms flowed over his chest, and the kisses that followed had him falling under her spell. His breath caught, the simple joy of being with her—of feeling her pressed against him—was nearly his undoing. Until—

Her temptress's fingers slipped beneath the waistband of his jeans and briefs to wrap around the throbbing length of him and Hawk was lost.

His control, already ragged from their teasing touches earlier that day, had reached a fevered state and he wanted to make it last. Wanted to prolong the exploration and the pleasure that arced between them.

And while he knew he waged a lost battle, he reluctantly gripped her wrist, stilling her movements. "You're killing me."

"Isn't that the whole idea?" Her smile was witchy and so full of promise in the moonlight.

He waged an inner battle with himself. Knew it was a losing one, but fought to hang in as long as he could. "Soon, baby. Soon. But until then—" He gently slipped her hand from his jeans, moaning in spite of himself as she drew a finger along the underside of his shaft.

"Vixen."

Her voice was husky. "Don't forget it."

As if he could.

Determined to give all he could for as long as he could, Hawk continued his deft exploration of her body, his fingers gliding down to the edge of her skirt. With quick movements, he dipped beneath the hem, following the line of her inner thigh. His body throbbed against his jeans as he felt the heat of her. Grew even more urgent when her thighs parted to give him better access, the moment full of promise.

He took full advantage of that promise, his finger slipping beneath the edge of her panties. Then slipped farther to sink into her body. Her chest contracted against his, her breathing growing tortured, as he found a rhythm.

The promised pleasure of earlier in her studio returned, more urgent now. More needy. Desire was a living entity between them, the knowledge of all they could make together.

Her head fell back, exposing the long column of

her throat. It was simple—passionate—but it was the response that let him know she was close to the edge.

He dragged pleasure from her with his fingers. Demanded it. Wrung it from every pore as he drew a response forth, stroke by stroke. And when a hard moan rose up in her throat, he swallowed the cry with a kiss.

He knew she was nearly there by the way her body clenched around his fingers. Deliberate now, he changed the game, determined to drag her to the most ragged edge. His own movements equally ragged, he hooked her panties with his thumbs and dragged the silk along with the heavier material of her skirt.

And then simply stopped to look his fill.

She was exquisite, open before him. Ready for him.

He wanted to make it last. Wanted the moment to go on and on, forever perfect. But his own needs betrayed him.

Hawk felt her hands slip into his back pocket. Felt her free the foil packet he'd stuffed in there earlier. He rolled to the side, removing his jeans and briefs as she worked the foil.

They were both feverish, their movements jerky in their haste to join. His jeans fell off the bed and he'd already returned to her side before they hit the floor.

Her hands flowed over him, unrolling the condom over straining flesh.

And then they were joined, bodies pressed together as they sought only what the other could give.

Claudia glided him into her body, pulling him home as he eased past her entrance. The subtle rhythm that had driven them up to now rose up, growing stronger.

It was a steady, driving heartbeat linking them both as one.

Hawk wanted that heartbeat to go on forever. Wanted to wrap her up in his arms and never let her go. Wanted to tell her all that was in his heart.

But the crashing needs of his body won the moment and he began to move inside of her. Exquisite pleasure swamped him as her body sheathed him. Drew him in.

Welcomed him home.

Chapter 17

Hawk held her close, his arms tight around her. Abstractly, Claudia wondered why she didn't feel claustrophobic, only to realize she felt the opposite.

She felt free.

Was it possible?

With all she and her family had dealt with, was it possible to lift beyond that? To not only believe in her future, but to have hope for it, as well?

A resounding yes filled her, buoying her up.

The desire for freedom and escape—something that had dogged her for her entire life—had simply vanished. Instead, she'd gladly stay here forever.

So long as she could share it with Hawk, of course.

The events of the night before had been everything she'd hoped, and more. Whatever reticence he'd initially had to pursue a relationship seemed to have faded. Even the pain of losing his wife—and the life he'd had before—didn't feel quite as sharp, either.

They would need to address it. If she hoped to have a strong and lasting relationship with the man, they'd absolutely need to address his pain and the guilt he carried as a survivor. Jennifer Huntley wasn't a part of his past to be shoved away and forgotten. Nor would Claudia want her to be.

It was something she'd always hated about her mother and had vowed never to do.

People weren't disposable. And while not every couple got fifty years and happily-ever-after, it didn't diminish the love they shared when they were together.

"That's an awfully fierce look on your face. You always wake up loaded for bear?"

Hawk's voice was sleepy as he grinned down at her. His beard had grown overnight and it gave him an edgy look—rather as fierce as he'd just teased her for being.

"I'm not mad."

"You sure about that? I could have sworn I saw your lips move."

"I was thinking about my mother." She quieted, not entirely sure if she should press on, then decided better of it. If they had any hope for a relationship, then it needed to be one steeped in honesty.

She wasn't Livia Colton and that wasn't simply a statement about maternal biology. It was a statement about how she wanted to live her life. How all she'd observed growing up had helped shape her and the decisions she wanted to make as an adult.

"I was also thinking about Jennifer."

He went from sleepy to awake in a matter of moments, his body seeming to brace for an attack. "That's a lot to think about. Mind if I ask how you connected the two?"

"I was thinking about my mother and how she went through relationships like they were last season's fashions. She used and discarded men. She obviously did it with the poor souls involved in the various businesses she ran, enterprises that were fronts for the worst sorts of crimes. And she did it to her children."

"Yes, she did."

Wariness still lurked in his eyes, but she'd sensed the slightest easing. As if he wasn't bracing for pain.

"I was also thinking about Jennifer because I don't know where things are going with us. I know where I'd like them to go, but there are two of us in this bed. In this relationship." She stopped, scrambled to sit up, the words filling her chest. "But I don't ever want her to be a subject that's off-limits. She was your wife. You loved each other and made vows to each other. I don't expect that to go away. More, I don't want it to go away."

He lay in that same position, unmoving, for several moments. His gaze remained steady on her, but he didn't say anything. Worse, she had the horrible, sinking feeling that she'd overstepped.

Claudia pulled the sheet up, draping it over her breasts, then tucking it beneath her arms. Her stomach did a slow, slinking slide, through her body and on toward the floor. At least she'd tried. At least she'd tried to say all she felt. She'd take solace in that.

Well, it was fun while it lasted, Colton.

"I love you."

His eyes remained inscrutable but the words were unmistakable.

"You what?" She scrambled to make sense of it. Of him.

"I love you, Claudia. All of you. Everything about you."

Acceptance. And love, without any strings. "I love you, too." She reached for his hand, the beauty of the moment not fully able to erase the lump in her throat. "I thought I just upset you."

"You couldn't be farther from the truth." He pushed himself into a seated position, uncaring of the sheet as he pulled her close, pressing his forehead to hers. "Wherever I've been. Whatever pit I've lived in for the past four years, nothing I could have imagined could compare to you. You're generous and warm. You're loving. And you've embraced me along with the woman I loved."

Hope filled her. Even with all they faced, she couldn't deny the bright, blooming streams of hope that burst in her chest. "She died, Hawk. That doesn't erase her existence. I wouldn't want to do that and I don't expect you to do it, either."

"That's what I've been doing. For the past four years, I've been trying to erase her. To pretend she didn't exist." A hard sob caught in his throat and Claudia felt the tears that rolled hot down his face, where they splashed against her cheeks. "I don't want to forget her anymore."

"I don't want you to, either." She placed her hands on his cheeks, wiping the tears away with her thumbs, only to stop the futile effort.

It was time to let the tears fall.

Time to let him grieve death so he could move on to life.

* * *

Saturday morning dawned bright and pretty, a perfect June day. She and Hawk had spent all their time together since heading to the dance hall on Thursday night. Their idyllic day and a half had been full of laughter and exploration and even a few more tears.

But they'd spent it together.

As they turned into Mac's driveway, there to help with the final preparations for the wedding and for her to assist Maggie with the dress, Claudia looked forward to her future. Quiet hope for all that was to come had been her steady companion and with the sun shining high in the sky, everything seemed possible.

Even the lurking danger seemed less severe. She fought thinking too hard about it, because she didn't want to obsess over it or, on the opposite end, become complacent. But she refused to look over her shoulder. She'd done that for far too long with Ben and it needed to stop.

Hawk had even helped allay her fears on that front. He'd reached out to a few contacts and also used some of the resources at his disposal to confirm Ben Witherspoon hadn't traveled out of New York over the past month. Additionally, the history of his credit card transactions matched much of what she knew of him— expenses at his club, a few visits to bars he favored, and a rather pricey purchase at Tiffany's.

But no trips or expenses linking him to Shadow Creek or to Texas.

She'd like to warn off whatever woman would be the recipient of the jewelry, but had no way of knowing. So instead, she said a small prayer the woman would wise up far faster than she had.

All there was to do now was enjoy the wedding. And they'd figure their way around all the rest.

She was sure of it.

She glanced around the bedroom that used to be hers and Jade's. Maggie's dress hung from the closet door, the beautiful folds capturing the light. She'd set that up first, then her prep stations for makeup, hair and nails. Claudia had even convinced Jade to get in on the fun when they were together Thursday night and took that as a major victory.

So when everyone tumbled in a half hour later, it was to the feminine oasis she'd created in the only home she'd ever loved.

"This is awesome!" Maggie couldn't stop exclaiming over everything, her bright smile lighting up her face. "I even did as you asked. I did nothing to my hair. My face is bare. And my nails are, well—" She broke off, giggling. "Embarrassing."

"Welcome to my lair." Claudia winked at her and seated her before a small table and a bowl of warm soapy water. "Nails first."

The chatter was high and no topic was off-limits. From honeymoon destinations to Allison's advice on a good flooring subcontractor to Jade's recommendation of a new farrier she'd tried.

All in all, the Colton women had diverse interests and it showed in their discussion.

And if the men in their lives all made it a point to amble their way past the door, only to be shooed off, well, that was family, too.

"They're convinced we're having pillow fights in our panties in here." Allison stood by the door and said the words as loud as she could.

Knox's resounding "I'm coming!" winged back down the hallway from the kitchen.

Allison then made a fuss about slamming the door, her smile satisfied as she leaned against it. "Men."

"Speaking of which, I've been patient. I really have. But when do we get details on the delectable Hawk Huntley?"

Although Maggie asked the question, Leonor, Allison and Jade were all quick to line up behind where the bride sat on a stool having her makeup applied, their expressions equally eager.

"He's a great guy, Claudia—"

"Tell us more—"

"Spill. Come on with the details—"

"Why do I feel like I've suddenly fallen into a Broadway production of *Grease*?" Claudia asked, unable to work up any sense of anger at the four eager faces that stared back at her.

She wanted to share. It felt good and right. And it was fun.

And who could argue with that?

Hawk finished hanging about a hundred yards of bunting, ordered about with laser-sharp precision by Cody. Although the majority of the wedding would take place in a large tent about a hundred yards from the house, Maggie had wanted to celebrate her marriage ceremony under the big Texas sky.

Hawk had already heard the arguments—Thorne had wanted everything hung the day before—but the concerns over a summer thunderstorm had marred that final bit of preparation. It had been an easy chore to take on and seemed to set everyone's mind at ease that they could worry about one less thing with respect to the preparations and he'd taken on transforming the seating area with his little helper in tow.

"It looks good, Hawk." The boy nodded. "I think we've earned pancakes."

"We?" Hawk eyed the small boy, his gaze already distracted by the horses visible across the property.

Dragging his gaze off the horses, Cody pointed toward the sky. "Sure. I mean, I helped you and all. Told you where everything needed to go."

"You sure did, kiddo." He ruffled the boy's hair and stood with him, assessing their work. "It does look good."

"Uncle Thorne and Aunt Maggie are going to have a baby."

"Yes, they are."

Thoughts of Cody's pony discussion earlier in the week had him wary, so the boy's next question wasn't entirely unexpected, even as his specific angle was a shock. "Are you and Aunt Claudia going to have one, too?"

The question was spoken with all the innocence of a child, yet freighted with the weight of a lifetime.

"Oh. Well. I don't know, buddy. We haven't talked about that yet."

"You should, you know. Kids have to have other kids to play with. We don't want the baby to get bored. I keep telling my mom and dad they need to have another one."

"I suppose that is something."

As reasons went, creating playmates wasn't quite enough rationale to sign up for a lifetime of parenthood, but it made a lot of sense in the realm of kid logic.

It was the bigger question, though, that dogged Hawk as he followed Cody into the house to the promised pancakes.

Did he want a lifetime of parenthood with Claudia at his side?

He thought about the large manila envelope tucked away even now in his car. He'd had the results of her DNA test sent over to the B&B and he'd swung by and picked them up yesterday, along with the rest of his things.

Those unopened results detailed her parentage, but they were no predictor of the sort of mother she'd be. Not that he needed a piece of paper for that.

She'd be an amazing mother.

What he hadn't given much thought to was the sort of father he'd be.

Children had always been an in-the-future conversation for him and Jennifer. They were agreed on having children, but had wanted to build their life together first.

How bitterly he'd regretted that after losing her. Then, when that grief had passed, he'd come to think of it as a gift. One less motherless child in the world was a good thing. And since he was barely able to care for himself, he had no idea how he'd have cared for a small child totally dependent on him.

All of it meant that he'd spent the last several years convinced fatherhood wasn't in the cards for him.

So how had that turned completely on its ear with the questions of one small boy?

He hovered at the entry to the kitchen and took in

the scene before him. Mac sat beside Thorne, the two of them talking quietly with their heads bent.

Father and son.

Knox stood behind Cody and helped him flip pancakes with a large spatula.

Father and son.

His own relationship with his parents had always been good, albeit strained over the past several years as he'd checked out of life. But he did have a good, solid relationship with Tom Huntley.

Father and son.

Was it really so simple to believe the same joy and satisfaction could belong to him?

The thought kept him company all the way through his pancakes, and on into the house's other spare bedroom to get ready. He'd been willing to leave the men to their prewedding ritual, but Thorne had been insistent on having him share the space as he got ready with his groomsmen.

"The odds really are sort of wild when you think about it. Mom goes on the lam and we all end up hitched. Allison and I reconnect and end up together. Joshua and Leonor. Now you and Maggie." Knox slapped Thorne on the back before turning his attention toward Hawk, his finger cocked in a shooting motion. "Don't think we're going to let you play fast and loose for long, Huntley."

"I think your sister has something to say about that."

"I suppose she does," Knox agreed.

The photographer picked that moment to interrupt, taking a few candids before waving them out of the room and toward the area set up for pictures in the living room. The men began to file out, the conversation about weddings already forgotten when River came up beside him. "Knox can rib all he wants. It's not like hitching up to this family is easy."

The somber tone stopped him, but it was the bleak emptiness in River's eye that had Hawk reassessing his initial impressions of the man.

River Colton was suffering. Yes, he'd had outward pain in the loss of his eye, but best Hawk could tell it had nothing on what the man was dealing with inside.

"No, your family's not easy. But your sister's worth it."

"That she is."

Hawk clapped the man on the back as they headed for the festivities in the living room. "Best I can tell, all of you are."

Although his outward emotions remained as hidden as ever, River did brighten as the men began posing for pictures.

Hawk watched from the periphery, amused by everyone's antics. Ritual, he thought to himself as he opened a fresh beer from a small cooler. Today they celebrated one, together as a family, all looking forward toward the future.

The future.

As he looked at all the Coltons, he had to admit that was something Livia hadn't been able to taint, no matter how hard she'd tried.

Her life's work had been about maximizing her own personal situation at the expense of everyone she came into contact with. Despite that—or perhaps in spite of it—she'd managed to give birth to six children who all saw the world as a place to make better instead of as a toy to use and break at their whim.

Once again, the emotional weight behind that manila envelope struck him.

Regardless of what the results said, Claudia would always be a part of this. Would always share her life with these men and women she'd spent a lifetime calling brother and sister.

The day carried them all along with its series of rituals and rites and after mugging for a few pictures with Thorne, he'd drifted outside to the altar and the rows of seats set up for the wedding. Guests had already begun to assemble and he smiled at them all, leading some to seats, others to the gift table to drop off items, still others to a registry to sign their good wishes to the happy couple.

The waitstaff helping with catering buzzed in and around like bees, setting everything up. He gave everyone room to work and almost made it to the ceremony without a hiccup before nearly railroading a petite server in his attempt to back up to take a photo.

A light "oof" filled his ears as he tripped backward over a small, but solid, form. Hawk twisted, but not before he made sure to keep a firm grip on his cell phone, to catch the woman in his arms. Clicking echoed from the camera app open in his hand as he fumbled phone and woman, focused on not dropping either.

"I'm so sorry."

"You need to watch yoursel—" She reined in the sharpness, her tone turning immediately conciliatory. "I'm sorry."

The sharp tone surprised him but it was the hatred darkening her gaze that had him dropping his hands. "No, it's all on me. I'm truly sorry."

The woman seemed to catch herself once more, her

tone moving from conciliatory to groveling. "No, no. It's all me. I'll be on my way. I am so sorry."

He watched her go, curious about the absolute darkness he'd seen cover her features before shrugging it off. Stressful day. Stressful job. Some handled it better than others.

And speaking of jobs, he had one of his own. The last of the guests had been escorted to their seats and Allison had asked him if he'd help Cody get ready to walk down the aisle. The two of them had bonded and her trust in his ability to get the little boy to do his part was humbling.

And, if he were honest, a bit scary.

The pretty strains of classical music drifted from speakers as the wedding party moved from the house to the lawn. Cody had already run over to take his place next to Hawk and he had a hand on the boy's shoulder when Claudia came through the door.

His breath caught as he watched her step over the porch steps and down onto the white runner that had been set for the procession. All that gorgeous blond hair was pulled up on her head, a series of curls spilling down over the crown like a curly halo. Her always-present heels were a perfect match to the pale lavender dress that highlighted her breasts before dropping down to hug her gorgeous curves.

She was beautiful.

And without benefit of any further probing from the imp by his side, their earlier conversation came back to him.

Did he want a baby with Claudia? A life with her? Marriage?

For the first time in four endless years, questions about his future filled him with hope. With excitement.

And with the shimmering promise of life.

Claudia fought the urge to throw her flowers, kick off her heels and race toward Hawk. He stood at the back of the chairs, waiting with Cody to help her nephew down the aisle.

And he was perfect.

His suit was expertly cut, the material showcasing his broad shoulders and narrow waist. He'd had a haircut the day before and it left him with an extra sharp look that was fresh and crisp. Professional.

And wildly sexy.

Since their beloved town preacher stood a few feet away from her, Claudia opted to rein in her more adventuresome thoughts and focus on the intangibles instead. Yes, the man was sexy, but he was so much more.

The strong, firm lines of his body showcased his strength, but it was his kind blue eyes and the way he gently encouraged Cody down the aisle that showed the real strength. Strength of conviction.

And, as she'd seen firsthand, strength of heart.

It was the same quiet grace Mac displayed each and every day. It was what she saw in her brothers and was what her sister had found in her husband.

For all the evilness her mother had brought into their lives, there had been good, too.

More than that, there had been love. The bone-deep kind that made a person stick around. The lifetime kind they were about to celebrate today.

With that in mind, she turned with the rest of Maggie's bridesmaids and faced the back of the aisle. And sighed in contentment as her soon-to-be sister-in-law came down the aisle. Each step was a careful march toward her future, and Thorne's smile as he gazed at Maggie was a promise that this was only the beginning.

The two of them joined hands and turned to face each other. Words of love and commitment were exchanged, followed by symbols of that love.

Happiness for Thorne and Maggie burst inside of her. For the new life Maggie carried that would bring more love and happiness into their family. And for the commitment they both made to building a life together.

When she'd left New York, she'd been convinced that love—especially romantic love—was an illusion. The pain of her relationship with Ben and all the ways he'd betrayed her had left her constantly looking over her shoulder, afraid he'd find her. More, afraid that what they'd shared was her one and only failed shot at love.

Hawk had brought it all full circle, helping her to fully heal, but it was her love for her family—and the examples they set—that had started her on the journey to putting her past behind her. They had shown her that what she was looking for in her life wasn't an illusion or simply a mirage found only in dreams.

More, they'd shown her in every way that love was not only real, but it was the only thing in life that brought true and lasting happiness.

"What was that sigh for?" Hawk held her close, his hand on her lower back as they danced. The wedding had moved from the aisle and seats outside to the large tent that dominated the back of Mac's property. Twinkle lights streamed from the top of the tent, the lighting soft and dreamy as they transitioned from the seriousness of vow-taking to the fun and laughter that came with celebration.

"I was just thinking about their dreamy kiss there at the end of the ceremony." She stared over Hawk's shoulder to where Thorne and Maggie danced, their gazes nowhere but on each other. "And how happy they are. And how that will multiply when the baby gets here."

Hawk's hand tightened briefly on her back before he spoke, the move bringing her attention back to his face and the humor that lit his eyes. "About the baby."

"Oh?"

"I got a stern talking-to from Cody earlier."

"Did you get the pony question, too?"

"Better."

Visions of what her nephew had possibly asked danced through her mind. "Better than where ponies came from?"

"In all his nine-year-old wisdom, he informed me that babies needed playmates. That it was no fun to be a kid all by yourself, and that you and I needed to make sure his uncle Thorne and aunt Maggie's baby had a new playmate. So you and I need to get on that."

An image of that very thing—holding Hawk's baby in her arms—had her pulse thumping hard in her chest. "A baby?"

"As soon as possible, if your nephew has anything to say about it."

Hawk spun her around, the lights whirling in a dizzying arc before her eyes, before he pulled her tight against his chest. Thoughts whirled even faster in her mind. Did she dare tell him all that was in her heart?

And then it didn't matter because he beat her to it. "Would you want that? A baby?"

"I'd love a baby." No, that wasn't the whole story. She shifted the hand she had positioned over his shoulder, pressed it to his chest. "I'd love to have a baby with you."

"I wonder if Cody's onto something, then, because I'd like to have a baby with you. More than that, Claudia Colton, I'd like to have a life with you."

The joy and happiness she'd sought for so long—that had remained elusive for what had felt like forever—settled around her, gentle as a warm breeze. And it all centered on the amazing man who held her close.

"I'd like that, too."

He bent his head and captured her lips with his. Love beat strong and true between them, layered in every moment of the kiss. Promise twined with passion, laying the path to their shared future.

Long moments later, after Joshua and Leonor had deliberately bumped into them, teasing them out of their kiss, Claudia ran the tip of her finger over his jaw.

"We should keep this to ourselves for a few days. Let Thorne and Maggie have this time."

"It'll be our secret."

Our secret.

She smiled, tamping down on the small shot of anxiety that accompanied his words. They had another secret—one that wasn't quite as joyous—in the DNA test results.

Would they show that she was a Colton? Or reveal something else.

The implications of that secret still haunted her a half hour later as she ran toward the house for her small sewing kit. Maggie's heel had caught in the edge of her dress when she tossed her bouquet and Claudia wanted to fix it so Maggie didn't accidentally trip over the small tear.

It was the work of a few minutes and would ensure nothing marred their fun. Even if she was doing a damn fine job of that all on her own.

Secrets. DNA tests. She'd been so determined to enjoy the day free of those thoughts, it was humbling to realize just how quickly they could gnaw at her if given free rein.

"Worry about it tomorrow," she muttered to herself as she rummaged through the small kit.

The talk of a baby and a life with Hawk had filled her with joy. Why couldn't she hang on to that, even if only for the night? The DNA test results would tell the truth soon enough.

Her hand closed over the small kit and she ran back through the house, oblivious to the threat that hovered behind her.

The path to the tent had been laid with a sturdy runner for the guests and catering staff and Claudia skipped over it, light on her feet in her rush to get back to Hawk. When she was with him, it was easier to forget all that was still to come.

So she'd go to him and take that solace. Would use the time to regain her equilibrium.

A small noise had her slowing, almost stumbling, as the heavy tread of feet suddenly felt as if it was on top of her. Claudia whirled, intending to move away if the catering team was laden down with trays, when she saw the gun.

And the small woman dressed in a catering uniform who had it pointed directly at her chest.

Chapter 18

"Where's Claudia?"

Hawk wondered the same thing as Mac and Evelyn waltzed past him where he stood at the edge of the dance floor, their smiles bright.

"She went to get some thread to repair Maggie's dress. A small tear in the hem she doesn't want her tripping over."

"Well, what's taking her so long?" Evelyn demanded. "I saw her duck out of here at least ten minutes ago."

"I'm sure she just got stopped talking to someone."

It was rational and reasonable. The sort of thing that happened at weddings, especially when it was a family member who got married. Claudia knew many of the guests. Heck, she'd smiled and chatted with people all evening.

So why couldn't he see her?

Mac held Evelyn close but slowed their movements,

pulling them to the side of the dance floor. "What is it, son?"

"Nothing. It's nothing."

"Why don't we go look for her, then?"

Evelyn slipped from Mac's arms, her smile warm as she patted Hawk's sleeve. "Let her know I'm happy to help with the dress repair. In the meantime, I'll stay near the bride and make sure she doesn't trip on that hem."

Evelyn disappeared into the crowd and Hawk turned toward Mac, feeling as silly as he was uneasy. "I'm sorry to pull you away."

"It's a few minutes." Mac's eyes were overbright. "We'll find her and then we can both go back to dancing with beautiful women."

They both had a height advantage and used it to quickly scan opposite sides of the tent. When that search proved as futile as the others he'd done, Hawk followed Mac from the tent toward the house.

He was being stupid. If he couldn't let the woman out of his sight for five minutes, then he was farther around the bend than he thought. She wasn't Jennifer. He didn't need to assume the worst because she stopped to talk to someone or had to make a stop at the ladies' room.

She was coming back.

"It's okay. We'll find her." Mac's quiet voice echoed next to him as they hotfooted it to the house.

The thick runner the catering staff laid down was soft beneath their feet and Hawk flew over it, barely paying any attention to the ground when his gaze caught on something. He slowed, curious as something small glinted in the combined glow of moonlight and the corral lights that had been left on for the evening.

"What is it?"

"There. Look." Hawk took a few steps off the runner and reached down for the small white object glinting in the light.

Only to wrap his hand around a small spool of white thread, a needle sticking from the top.

"What do you want from me?" The words slurred against her tongue and Claudia had no idea if she'd even formed a coherent question, her voice was so thick and heavy in her ears. She sat in the back of a car, bumping over an old dirt path behind Mac's property toward La Bonne Vie.

The woman's arrival on the path to the tent had startled her, but she'd assumed the staff needed to get into the tent for something.

And then the woman had pulled a gun.

She might have tried making a run for it, but a snap decision at the last minute not to draw possible fire into the party, putting everyone at risk, had her following along. And then the decision to run the other way was taken away from her as a swift prick stuck the back of her arm.

A warm, hazy feeling spread instantly, like she hovered somewhere outside herself. She'd wanted to fight it, but knew she was fast losing the battle so she'd dropped the spool of thread when the woman wasn't looking and hoped it would be enough.

Hawk would understand her clue, wouldn't he?

Would he find it at all?

Her body was heavy and her feet felt like lead, but

she'd followed along in the woman's wake as she was half dragged, half pushed toward the small dirt parking lot on the far side of the corral. Claudia had stumbled a few times, but hadn't had the energy to protest when she was shoved into the back of a car.

Her head bobbed against the seat, lolling to the side as her gaze drifted to the car's ceiling. The sedan was old, but it was the thin drape that hovered in a thick fall from the ceiling that caught her attention.

A drape?

Focus, now. Focus!

Claudia ordered her mind to pay attention, trying to make sense of what she was looking at. The dark material that made up the ceiling of the sedan had pulled apart and hung loose over the front passenger seat, separated from the seam. The material was gauzy and long, its width the same as the car.

It would be easy enough to pull it down and lower it over your face…

An image of the driver that nearly ran her off the road filled her mind, the hazy image growing clear as she made the connection on the draped material.

"You!"

"Shut up."

"You were the one who ran me off the road."

The car sped up, bumping harder over the dirt path. The frame rattled from being pushed and the driver muttered to herself.

"I must do this. The Forgotten One will be remembered."

Forgotten one?

Claudia took several deep breaths, and fought for equilibrium from the confusion that swirled in her mind.

Who was this woman?

If she was one of her mother's minions, she hadn't been quick to announce the connection.

Mother? Was Livia even her mother? Wasn't that what she and Hawk had been talking about for the past few days? Wasn't that why he'd come to Shadow Creek at all?

Because Livia Colton wasn't her mother.

Why wasn't that thought more upsetting? And why was there a strange lightness in her chest at the idea she might not have been conceived and carried by Livia Colton?

The car uttered another quaking moan as the woman made a sharp turn off the dirt path. The dirt path out of Mac's?

"Where are you taking me?"

Again, more silence.

But as the car flew over the taller grasses that lined the dirt road, Claudia knew she was headed back home.

Back to La Bonne Vie.

"You found it here?" Knox paced the small area beside the path between the tent and the house, his gaze focused on the ground where Hawk had recovered the spool of thread. Mac had quickly rounded up Knox and Joshua and the four of them were even now trying to understand what was going on without causing too much alarm inside the wedding.

"Thorne'll want to know," Joshua said.

"Not yet." Hawk shook his head. "Not now. It's his wedding."

"And this is his sister," Knox pointed out.

Hawk knew it was a fair point, but he didn't want

to panic anyone. Didn't want to put into words what was rapidly becoming very real.

"Who was even here to do this?" Joshua scanned the area, his gaze doing a slow roll from the house to the parking lot to the horse corral. "There are people everywhere."

"Not since we moved into the tent." Hawk's gaze followed Joshua's, his mind racing through the same information he'd already assembled.

There was actually little foot traffic other than the waitstaff. And it would be easy enough, if one bided their time, to lure someone away.

The damn question, to his mind, was why Claudia was lured. Why hadn't she run?

Images of Jennifer haunted him, racing through his mind as if they'd only just happened. He'd asked the same questions then. Why had she been lured away?

What had possibly made her think going with her killer was a better choice than trying to run for it?

Forcing his focus back to the moment, Hawk tried desperately to shake off the ghosts. This wasn't Jennifer. The situation wasn't the same.

So why the hell did it feel like his life was on repeat?

"Is it Livia? Is it possible she's here?" Mac asked the question, his agitation only growing by the moment. "Hasn't that damn woman made enough trouble? Why is she so intent on ruining this family?"

"I might know."

The small voice trembled behind them, coming from the direction of the paddock.

Cody?

Knox moved first, racing toward his son where

the boy stood in the shadows thrown off by the corral lights.

"Cody! What are you doing over here?"

"I'm sorry, Dad." Tears glinted in the boy's eyes, spilling over as his bottom lip trembled. "Mom told me to stay in the tent."

Knox pulled Cody close, lifting him in his arms. "It's okay. I'm not mad."

Hawk had seen the boy's horse mania earlier and his longing glances toward the corral as they set up the bunting and put the two ideas together. "Were you out here looking at the horses?"

"Uh-huh." His eyes still glistened, but he seemed to come to some resolution in his mind, straightening in his father's arms. "I know Mom didn't want me out here but I wanted to make a quick visit to see Bunny and make sure she didn't need any grooming or anything. I took some sugar cubes off the table and wanted to give them to her."

Whatever fear the boy had about his eventual punishment, it didn't stop him from telling his story. And in his mind, Hawk praised the stubborn will of nine-year-old boys.

"I'm not mad, Cody." Knox's voice was gentle. "But you need to tell us what you saw."

"A lady. She was dressed like the servers but she ran after Aunt Claudia. Got up in her face." Cody swallowed. "I think she had a gun. I'm sorry, Dad. I'm sorry I didn't do anything."

Hawk's heart clenched, a crazy beating fist that slammed against the wall of his chest.

Why had she gone with the woman? Why not make some sort of noise or try to get away?

Knox kept his hand on Cody's shoulder, but his hand shook at the mention of a gun. Joshua stepped in, his focus on the boy. "You did the right thing, Cody. You never run at someone with a gun. But you paid attention and you got us the important details we need to find Aunt Claudia."

"What did the lady look like?" With the time to gather himself, Knox kept his voice calm, the urgency banked as he sought information from the boy. "Did the lady look like your grandmother?"

"That blonde lady from the TV pictures?"

"Yes, that's who I mean."

"No. It wasn't her."

"Are you sure?" Joshua probed.

"Positive. That lady was blonde and tall. This lady was short. She had dark hair."

So not Livia.

Hawk wasn't sure why that thought comforted, but for some reason it did.

"Cody," Hawk asked, "can you remember what she looked like? Any detail you can tell us would be good."

The boy nodded and began to describe what he remembered.

"What do you want from me?" Claudia sat in a chair, her hands bound against a wooden captain's chair that had seen better days. Whatever light sedative had been used on her was fading, and Claudia had reclaimed her mind and her voice. She wasn't exactly sure where she was, but thought it was a small caretaker's cabin on the edge of the La Bonne Vie property.

While her mother had employed relatively few employees to avoid too many people prying into her affairs, she'd built La Bonne Vie to look lavish to out-siders. The caretaker's cottage was one more outward example of that, the dwelling more for show than any-thing useful.

A distant memory rose up of another use for it. She'd been too young to fully understand the connotation, but Knox had bragged to a friend that it was a great place to take a girl to make out.

Simpler days. Easier times.

Claudia hadn't believed it then, but things *had* been simple. Back before they knew what their mother was capable of. Long before she'd been carted away in handcuffs.

Was Livia part of this?

The silence in the bumpy car ride over had nothing on the weird muttering the woman kept doing now that she had Claudia in the cabin. She'd stomped around, lost somewhere in her mind, and Claudia desperately hunted for some key to unlock whatever hatred and anger seethed beneath the surface.

"What's your name?"

"I'm the Forgotten One."

There it was again. The same things she'd muttered in the car. *Forgotten.*

She didn't want to feel sympathy. This woman had held a gun on her and kidnapped her from Thorne's wedding and it would be a mistake to let her guard down.

But there was something buried in that sad state-ment. Something dark and deeply damaged.

"Why do you think that?"

"You don't speak to me!"

The scream echoed off the walls, the fearful agony

of an animal in pain. Claudia's stomach clenched at the pain—an animal was never more dangerous than when it was wounded—yet she knew she needed to probe harder.

The answers were there, buried deep inside that pain.

"What's your real name?"

Cody's description of the woman who took his Aunt Claudia had proven more helpful than he ever could have realized. As the boy described the small woman in the waitstaff uniform, Hawk's mind reeled through why the description nagged at him.

The woman. The one from catering he'd tripped into.

Her hateful gaze, so jarring at the time, had been forgotten in the rush of the wedding festivities, but Hawk pulled it back now. And dug into his back pocket for his phone.

The camera had clicked over and over as he'd accidentally pressed the shutter button. It was a long shot that he got anything useful, but he had to try. He flipped through the shaky images before catching one. He kneeled down by the boy. "Is this the woman you saw?"

"That's her! That's the lady."

Knox pulled his son close for a tight hug. "Good job."

Allison had slipped out of the tent, looking for her son, and Mac had brought her up to speed during Cody's story. The moment he finished recounting what he knew, Allison had leaped forward, dragging him close as she kissed his head.

"Mom." He hugged her back before squirming. "I'm sorry about going to see Bunny."

"Shh. Just hush, sweetie. It's okay."

It was more than okay, Hawk thought. The boy was the reason they had any idea of what happened. But it was Mac who made the connection.

He pointed toward a small road just visible through the trees. "Cody. What way did the car go?"

"Over there, Grandpa Mac. Through the trees."

"That's the way to La Bonne Vie." Knox made the connection first.

Mac nodded his agreement. "That's where she has her."

"I don't have a name."

"Of course you do." Claudia kept her voice gentle. "What is it? I'm Claudia."

"I know who you are."

"Then you have me at a disadvantage."

"About damn time." The woman's eyes were narrow, but she seemed to make a decision as she stood there. "Maria. My name is Maria."

"Hello, Maria." Claudia had no idea if it was true, but she'd read long ago that using someone's name created a connection. She'd read it in a sales manual but figured it couldn't hurt.

"Why are you doing this?"

"It's her. It's all her."

Those edges of madness blotted out the moment of lucidity and Claudia tried again. "It's all who, Maria?"

"Your mother. Livia."

"Did you know her?"

"She made me work for her. She told me I'd have a better life here. She took me from my home."

The haunting quiet vanished as Maria began to speak, a flood of emotion embedded in a torrent of words. Claudia let it flow, Maria's description forming a picture in her mind.

"You worked for her?"

"I was her slave! She smuggled me out of Mexico like a criminal, then told me I had to work for her."

"Livia was the criminal. You must understand that."

The madness broke for a moment. "Livia? You call her that?"

The question opened the door Claudia needed. "She's not my mother."

"Yes, she is."

Claudia held her chin high. "My mother was Annalise Krupid. Another woman like you. Another woman Livia betrayed."

"Annalise?"

Claudia's intention was to remove Maria's focus off of using her as a conduit to Livia. She had no idea Maria might be a conduit to her mother.

Her real mother.

"You knew Annalise?"

"She was one of the mail-orders. That's what they were called. Tall and pretty, Annalise had hair just like yours." Maria's eyes narrowed, her gaze steady. For the first time, Claudia felt like the woman saw her.

"I'm sorry for this. For all the pain Livia caused."

"I remember Annalise. She was so scared. Kept talking about her parents and how sorry she was. How much she just wanted to go home."

The picture Maria painted—of a sad, lonely young

woman aching for home—had tears pricking the backs of Claudia's eyes.

"Why do you call yourself forgotten?"

Maria stilled, the gun she'd held since they walked into the cottage shaking. "I was forgotten. By my family. By everyone who knew me. I was spirited away in the night and they never knew where I went."

"Couldn't you go home? After Livia was arrested? Your family would have wanted you back. They'd be overjoyed to know you were okay."

"Home?" Maria barked the question, the gun shaking once more. "Would you go home a whore?"

"But you're not—" Claudia stopped as the gun steadied once more, Maria's eyes blazing with a white-hot hatred.

With startling clarity, Claudia understood the situation. Whatever she believed didn't matter. All that *did* matter was the pain that had haunted Maria.

Pain that had twisted her mind beyond comprehension.

Mac's SUV flew over the property as the boundary of his ranch morphed at the border into La Bonne Vie. He'd driven the roads his entire life and Hawk saw that surety as Mac navigated the land.

"It's one of two places. It has to be."

Mac had already told them of his suspicions where Claudia may have been taken—an old grain elevator or a small caretaker's cottage—and he'd chosen the cottage.

They'd quickly told Thorne what was happening, mobilizing him back at the ranch and instructing him to call for police backup, while Hawk, Mac, Joshua and

Knox fanned out over the property. Joshua and Knox headed for the grain elevator while he and Mac raced toward the cottage.

Over and over, Hawk fought the pernicious thoughts that threatened to pull him under. The whispers he'd be too late. The nasty taunts that she'd already been killed. Pushing them back by sheer force of will, he focused on the goal.

This wasn't Jennifer.

It wasn't the same.

God, how he wanted to believe that.

A lone light burned in the cottage window in the distance as Mac bumped over the property. He'd turned off some ways back, heading toward the small structure from the grounds instead of the dirt path that lead to the property to avoid detection.

The phone in his lap rang and Hawk took point.

"She's not in the grain elevator. Place is empty." Knox barked out the details.

"Come to the cottage." Hawk said the words, his focus already toward the small building that beckoned him and Mac. "Lights are on inside."

Mac had already slowed and crept forward as far as he dared. He'd cut his lights before turning off the dirt path and finally came to a stop. "This is open ground. I can't risk having her hear the engine."

Hawk nodded, already climbing out of the car. Both men were careful to avoid the noise of door closures and that went double for the trunk. Mac lifted out the shotguns they'd carefully packed earlier, then handed Hawk one of the four handguns he'd retrieved from his case.

One for each of them.

The weight was familiar in Hawk's hand, his days on the force rushing back with the sense memory. He'd been on ops before. He'd been trained to handle a hostage situation.

But he'd never faced off with a killer, holding someone he loved.

"You ready, son?" Mac had his own gun held firmly in his grip. When Hawk only nodded, Mac pointed toward the softly glowing light. "I'll follow your lead."

From Mac's earlier description of the location of the grain elevator, Knox and Joshua weren't that far away, but they couldn't risk waiting any longer.

The rain that had threatened the night before had never come, but the storm appeared ready to make its presence now. Clouds covered the sky, obscuring the stars and, as they drifted, the moon. That worked in their favor and Hawk and Mac gestured to each other on their approach.

They came at the house from the back, their focus the darkened windows on the opposite end of the one that was lit. Hawk's mind whirled as they skirted the edge of the dwelling, their footfalls gentle as they worked to cover the ground quickly.

Conversation filtered from the window, a screaming voice heartrending for its brokenness. "Would you go home a whore?"

He knew every step counted—knew with the deepest certainty he had one shot—but the agony in that voice was one he knew.

He'd lived the life of the hopeless. Had believed there was no light left in the world and it had colored every choice he made. But he'd never taken that last step. Whether it was the memories of Jennifer's love or his own stubborn will, Hawk had never taken the last step into despair.

But the voice who screamed inside the cottage had long since passed that barrier.

He couldn't wait and risk Claudia's survival for another moment.

With the sharp skills he'd honed in his years with the Houston PD, Hawk moved. He had the gun firmly in hand, the safety off, ready to fire. He stood, assessed the scene through the window and lined up his shot.

The small woman who he'd nearly run over at the house stood there, an avenging angel hovering over the woman he loved.

Hawk didn't wait.

Didn't consider or check himself.

He lined up the shot and fired.

One moment she sat there, the recipient of Maria's agony and pain, and the next the woman was falling in front of her eyes on a hard scream.

Mac slammed through the door, Hawk on his heels, their heavy shouts echoing off the walls of the sparse room.

They were here? Mac? Hawk?

They'd come?

Mac ran to Maria, kicking her gun that still hung from her hand across the room before kneeling down beside the woman. He gently lifted her head into his lap, his movements tender.

Hawk raced to her side, dragging at the ropes that bound her to the seat.

"Claudia." He whispered her name over and over, his movements frantic as he worked to free her.

"I'm okay. We're okay." She said the words, the adrenaline mixing with the drugs that were still residual in her system. "It's okay, Hawk."

But it wasn't until he pulled her up out of the chair, his arms wrapping around her, that she gave in to the fear that had been her steady companion since being dragged from Mac's.

Would they find her? If they did, would they be in time? And worst of all, would she die without seeing all of them one last time?

Gratitude filled her and spilled over in a hard sob. They were okay. And the sight of Hawk and Mac, and then Knox and Joshua as they barreled into the cabin, were the solid proof that she'd survived.

She had her family. And she had the man she loved.

"You're okay? She didn't hurt you?" Hawk whispered against her head before stepping back to look at her for himself.

His gaze drifted to Mac and Claudia saw how Joshua helped him disengage from where he sat cradling the woman. "Is she gone?"

"Yes," Mac said.

"I'm sorry." Hawk pulled her close once more. "She had you and she was screaming."

Claudia was sorry, too. Sorrier than she could say, even as she knew with absolute certainty Maria's pain had driven her mad. "She was going to kill me. It was there. In her eyes."

"Hawk did the right thing." Joshua's training took over and he stood, doing his best to block the body from view. "Once an officer, always an officer, eh?"

Claudia felt the import of Joshua's words in the easing of Hawk's tense frame and she was grateful for his assessment. They'd deal with this for a very long time, but the acceptance of a fellow law officer went a long way toward reassuring Hawk of a split-second decision.

When she could swallow around the lump in her throat, she asked, "How did you find me?"

"Cody. He snuck a visit to Bunny and saw you being taken."

Knox wrapped his arms around both of them in a hard hug. "Hard to reprimand my little sneak for being the hero of the day."

"He's getting a whole stableful of horses," Mac said with absolutely finality.

As Claudia stood there in the arms of the man she loved, surrounded by the family she loved, she couldn't argue with Mac's fatherly wisdom.

"Put me down for stable duty."

Epilogue

The manila envelope lay faceup on Mac's dining room table, unopened. Until she took that final step, she was still in the dark, making assumptions about who she was. But once opened, she'd have answers. Everyone gave her the space she needed, but it was hard to miss the furtive looks that kept stealing toward the center of the table.

Especially now that everyone had departed, both police and guests, and it was just the family.

The Shadow Creek police had arrived at the cottage on the La Bonne Vie property and claimed the area as a crime scene. She and Hawk had given initial statements along with Mac, Knox and Joshua. It had only been Joshua's subtle threat of calling his contacts at the FBI that had gotten them all a stay until the following day for more formal questioning.

It was that same FBI weight and influence that went a long way toward identifying the events of the evening as self-defense. A process Joshua had already begun with the feds since everything had taken place on seized property. Bud Jeffries might hate the interference, but there wasn't much he could do about it.

So here they were.

Claudia reached for the envelope, the subtle conversation around the table quieting. Hawk had kept an arm draped over the back of her chair, his fingers floating lightly over her skin. His touch was warm. Reassuring. And, she well knew, as much for him as for her.

It gave her the strength she needed. And Mac, sitting sentinel on her right, gave her the courage to push forward.

Mac stilled her hand. "You're one of us, Claudia. You know that, don't you?"

"I do."

"I've loved you since the first day I saw you. You're my daughter in every way that counts and nothing will change that."

The weepy tears she'd fought all evening filled her eyes, but broke on a hard sob of laughter when she heard a matched response from Maggie and Leonor.

She'd waited long enough. It was time to find out.

Claudia slipped her finger under the seal and broke it quickly, pulling out the paper inside. It was the work of a moment, the impact of a lifetime when she read the words.

"My DNA is a match with Annalise Krupid's. There is a one hundred percent certainty she is my mother."

Mac spoke first, his voice deep and resonate when he spoke. "Well, then. It looks like our family just got a whole lot bigger. We've got some new family members to welcome very soon. You make sure they know that, Hawk. That's a personal invitation."

"Yes, sir."

Emotions burst around the table after that, everyone echoing Mac's sentiments. As she felt their support and received each and every embrace, Claudia knew two truths.

Her family loved her. And they *were* her family and nothing could change that. Nothing would.

Livia Colton had done her level best to ruin the name of Colton. But the men and women around the table were the ones who'd restored it. They'd renewed all their family name had always stood for. Honor. Grace. And love.

Always love.

The round of hugs nearly finished, Claudia was surprised by the small tug on her hand. Cody had fallen asleep on the couch, but the noise had obviously woken him up. "You're okay, Aunt Claudia?"

"I'm fine, sweetie." She bent to hug him. "And you're our hero for keeping such a watchful eye and telling everyone how to find me."

"I know I shouldn't have snuck out to see Bunny."

"Sometimes the things we're not supposed to do work out just fine."

"Can I tell you something else?"

"What is it, honey?"

He lifted up on tiptoe, his lips pressed to her ear. "I took a piece of cake, too."

Mac was close enough to hear the confession and he threw back his head and laughed. "We can't forget the cake!"

As Allison and Leonor went into high gear retrieving the cake from the kitchen, Hawk pulled her to her feet and into the living room. "I just need a minute."

"You can have all the minutes you'd like."

He pulled her close, nuzzling her neck and breathing deep before he stepped back. "We went through something big tonight. Something that will have repercussions for both of us."

"I know."

"I know, too. And we will get through it together. But it's important to me to say that so you understand the other thing I'm about to say."

She stared deep into his vivid blue eyes, awed to see all the strength and love and support she'd ever need shining back. "What's that?"

"I want a future with you. I want to court you and laugh with you and make love with you."

"I'd like a future with you, too."

"I'm very glad to hear that since I want to marry you and spend the rest of my life with you."

"Then there's only one more thing we need to do."

"What's that?"

"Let's go get some cake."

She pulled him close, pressing her lips to his. Cake might be sweet, but it would never be sweeter than a life with this man.

But that wouldn't stop either of them from having a very large piece.

* * * * *

If you loved this novel,
don't miss the next thrilling romance in
the COLTONS OF SHADOW CREEK *miniseries:*
THE COLTON MARINE by Lisa Childs,
available in July 2017
from Harlequin Romantic Suspense!

And check out other suspenseful titles
by Addison Fox, available now from
Harlequin Romantic Suspense!

SPECIAL EXCERPT FROM

(H) **HARLEQUIN**®

ROMANTIC suspense

*Edith Beaulieu is supposed to be getting the Coltons'
former estate ready for its mysterious new owners
when a series of accidents puts her in harm's way—and
pushes her into ex-marine River Colton's arms!*

Read on for a sneak preview of
THE COLTON MARINE *by* Lisa Childs,
the next thrilling installment of
THE COLTONS OF SHADOW CREEK.

"You overheard enough to realize that he'd make me fire
you."

"Oh, I know that," he heartily agreed. "What I don't know
is why you wouldn't want to fire me." Was it possible—
Could she be as attracted to him as he was to her? He'd
caught her glances whenever he went without a shirt. Had
he just imagined her interest?

"So do you want me to fire you?" she asked.

"No." And it wasn't just because he still wanted to search
for those rooms. It was because of her—because he wanted
to keep spending his days with her. "I told you that I need
this job."

"You don't need this job," she said, as her dark eyes
narrowed slightly with suspicion. "With your skills, you can
do anything you want to do."

"Really?" he asked.

"Yes," she said. "Your injury is not holding you back
at all."

It was, though. If he didn't have the scars and the missing eye, he might have done what he wanted to do sooner. "So you really think I can do anything I want?"

She sighed slightly, as if she was getting annoyed with him. "Yes, I do."

So he reached up and slid one arm around her waist to draw her tightly against him. Then he cupped the back of her head in his free hand and lowered her face to his.

And he kissed her.

Her lips were as silky as her skin and her hair. He brushed his softly across them.

She gasped, and her breath whispered across his skin. With her palms against his chest, she pushed him back but not completely away. His arm was still looped around her waist. "What are you doing?" she asked.

"You told me I can do anything I want," he reminded her, and his voice was gruff with the desire overwhelming him. "This is what I want to do—what I've wanted to do for a long time." Ever since that first night he'd heard her scream and found her in the basement with her pepper spray and indomitable spirit.

Her lips curved into a slight smile. "I didn't mean this…"

But she didn't protest when he tugged her back against him and kissed her again. Instead she kissed him, too, her lips moving against his, parting as her tongue slipped out and into his mouth.

Don't miss
THE COLTON MARINE by Lisa Childs,
available July 2017 wherever
Harlequin® Romantic Suspense books
and ebooks are sold.

www.Harlequin.com

JUST CAN'T GET ENOUGH?

Join our social communities
and talk to us online.

You will have access to the latest
news on upcoming titles and special
promotions, but most importantly,
you can talk to other fans about your
favorite Harlequin reads.

Harlequin.com/Community

 Facebook.com/HarlequinBooks

 Twitter.com/HarlequinBooks

 Pinterest.com/HarlequinBooks

THE WORLD IS BETTER WITH *Romance*

Harlequin has everything from contemporary, passionate and heartwarming to suspenseful and inspirational stories.

Whatever your mood, we have a romance just for you!

Connect with us to find your next great read, special offers and more.

"I've only been here a few days, but it's been long enough to know that anything Colton-related is hot gossip around town."

Claudia sighed. "Sad truth. But still true all the same."

"Hey." He brushed several strands of hair behind her ear. "I'm sorry. I didn't mean to be insensitive."

"It's not insensitive when it's the truth."

"I'll take that under advisement." Hawk traced the shell of her ear before trailing a path down the column of her throat. "But right now I'd really like to kiss you."

"I'd really like that, too."

The last vestiges of fear that lingered at the afternoon's events faded as Hawk lowered his lips to hers. With his body pressed to hers and the door at her back she should have felt claustrophobic.

Trapped.

She felt anything but as she wrapped her arms around his neck and clung.

Simply clung as the touch of his hands, the warmth of his body and the sheer power of his kiss carried her away from all the pain, trouble and confusion that was life in Shadow Creek.

The Coltons of Shadow Creek: Only family can keep you safe...

* * *

Dear Reader,

Have you ever wondered what life might be like if you'd been born into a different family? As a daughter of notorious criminal Livia Colton, Claudia Colton wondered it plenty of times. She never felt like she fit into her family, despite a deep and abiding love for her brothers and sisters, but it is a genuine surprise when Hawk Huntley shows up in Shadow Creek and suggests she really isn't a Colton after all.

While Claudia may be willing to accept the suspicions of this new stranger to Shadow Creek, she can't hide her increasing fears as she discovers she's been targeted by a new threat. Is her mother, recently escaped from prison, back in Shadow Creek making trouble? Or is it more personal than that?

Welcome back to the world of the Coltons. I'm so excited to bring you the fourth book in this year's Coltons of Shadow Creek miniseries. The Coltons have a long history in the Harlequin Romantic Suspense line and it's always great fun to revisit different branches of the family, each loaded with new secrets to reveal.

I hope you enjoy *Cold Case Colton*, and be sure to watch for the fifth and sixth books to close out the series, coming in July and August.

Best,

Addison Fox